THE CATALYST

A Novel

BY
Gordon Brown

Published by Gallus Press

Gallus Press is an Imprint of Olida Publishing established January 2013

www.olidapublishing.com

First printing: May 2013

Copyright (c) 2013 by Gordon Brown

All rights reserved.

This is a work of fiction. Names, characters, places, and incidents are products of the author's imagination or are used fictitiously and should not be construed as real. Any resemblance to actual events, locales, organizations or persons, living or dead, is entirely coincidental.

No part of this book may be used or reproduced in any manner whatsoever with- out written permission, except in the case of brief quotations embodied in critical articles and reviews. For more information e-mail all enquires - olidapublishing@gmail.com

Printed in the United Kingdom and the U.S.A.

ISBN: 978-1-907354-53-3

Thanks to the two Allans (Guthrie and Sneddon) - one for inspiration and one for believing in this novel.

Also to Lesley, Scott and Nicky for being there for me.

Prologue

I'm next to a bloodstained wall. Somewhere in Iraq. Cut off from my unit. It's dark. I'm scared. Someone is after me. I don't know who. I'm cold. Noises come from the other side of the wall. I sit still. I want the voices to vanish but they don't. My name is being whispered. Over and over. *'Craig'. 'Craig'. 'Craig'.* The accent is American. That should make me feel better but it doesn't.

'Craig'. The voice is close. This side of the wall now. But there's nobody there. *'Craig'.* In my ear. The voice inches away. I can feel breath. I reach for my gun.

'Craig'. The other ear. *'Craig'.* Both ears. I lift the barrel and point it to my left, then to my right. I can't speak or won't speak. A second voice joins in. *'Craig'.* In stereo. Then three voices. Four. More. The hubbub grows. Hot air and words buzz around my head. The air is alive with people whispering my name.

Then one of the voices shouts. *'CRAIG'.* I wrap my finger around the trigger. *'CRAIG'.* A second shout. They all join in.

Still there's no one there. I try to stand up but the voices force me back to the ground.

Something touches my hair. A gentle brush. My head won't move. It's stuck with crazy glue to the wall. Another touch. Touching and shouting. The touches become strikes. Flicks and hits. I put some pressure on the trigger. Not enough to fire but just short of what's needed.

Somebody or something bites me. A vampire bite to the neck. Not a nip. A full chunk of flesh between teeth. Ripped from my body the flesh falls to the ground. I pull the trigger and spray bullets around my head. Keeping the pressure on until the clip runs dry.

Blood floods down my body. More bites. Harder. Faster.

Tearing my face apart. A tooth touches my eyeball.

* * *

Light floods my world.

'Time to get to work Mr McIntyre.'

The dream is gone and I'm back in the room. Sweat thick on me. A feeling of disconnect clouding my thoughts. The voice from the speakers is the man in the white linen suit. Lendl. 'Rise and shine.'

The door opens and Buzz 1 enters. His hair cut as sharp as a box-cutter blade.

'Mr Mather will show you the washroom. I'm sure you would like to freshen up.'

Behind Buzz 1 there are two more suits. They're taking no chances with me.

The washroom is heavy on showers. Six in a row. I'm guessing all-night stints are not unusual in this place. I strip off and take the full force of the water. I finish and towel down. A cupboard reveals some deodorant, toothbrushes in sealed bags and toothpaste. I scrub and spray and Buzz 1 times his re-entry to perfection.

A new room. An examination bed against one wall. A table and chair against another. A computer sitting in sleep mode squats on the table. Cupboards line the third wall and an oversized TV sits on the space next to the door. Light shines through Plexiglas sheets above.

On the wall next to the examination bed there's a metal panel the length of the bed - about four feet high. It looks like a screen.

The speaker fires up. Lendl's voice fills the room. 'On the bed.'

I obey and sit with my legs dangling. Buzz 1 moves to the corner of the room and the door opens to bring a tall, skeletal man in a white coat into my life. He pays me no attention. Sitting at the table he fires up the computer and begins to tap away. A second man comes in pushing a cart loaded with electronic equipment. Monitors, wires, keyboard, small blue boxes – none of which make any sense to me.

'Wire him up,' says the skeleton without looking up.

The second man wheels the cart next to me. He's heavy-set, thick around the gut and sweating freely in the cool air. 'Could you please lie down?'

I wonder what will happen if I say no but even my slight hesitation brings Buzz 1 out of his corner. I lie down.

The sweating man rubs some gel from a tube onto my forehead and opens up my shirt. He smiles as he pulls out a small razor. 'Sorry I've no shaving foam.' With practised ease he shaves four patches of hair from my chest before attaching wires to my head and chest.

'Is he ready?' asks the skeleton. He doesn't look my way as he speaks.

'Just waiting for the signals to come online.' The sweating man hits a power button and the monitor jumps into life.

'Straps,' orders the skeleton.

Straps? Suddenly Buzz 1 is at my shoulder with another suit in tow. They reach under the bed and too late I realize what they are going to do. I try to sit up but Buzz 1 whips out his gun and pushes it into my leg. 'A bullet in the thigh won't affect the tests.'

I freeze. Buzz 1 pulls up leather straps and coils them around my wrists and ankles, pulling hard on the buckles to secure them. When they're fastened he puts the gun away and helps the other suit finish the job. Buzz 1 reappears above my head. He holds a head restraint in his hand and slides the top of my skull into it. With a pull, he tightens the fastening and I'm all but immobile.

'Ready?' asks the skeleton. I can no longer turn my head to tell if he's still looking at the computer.

'Good to go,' says Buzz 1.

'OK. You two can leave.'

I hear Buzz 1 and the suit exit.

'Open the screen,' orders the skeleton.

There is click and the sound of movement.

'OK.' he continues. 'Do the subjects in the next room have any idea what they're here for?'

Lendl's voice rings out from the speakers in reply. 'No. As requested they were picked up from the streets on the promise of drugs and booze.'

'Have they been given any?'

'Enough to keep them calm.'

'Good.'

'What are you expecting?'

'I don't know. I've a few ideas but we'll see. I have to say I don't hold out much hope. It all seems a little thin.'

'We've seen more from less.'

I'm beginning to lose my grip on the reality of all this. How the hell did I end up strapped to a bed and wired up to the moon? What is it they want?

'Mr McIntyre, please relax,' says Lendl. 'Before we start I want to ask you a few questions.'

'Before you start what?'

'A few little tests. Nothing to worry about.'

'If I shouldn't be worrying why am I trussed up like a turkey?'

'For your own safety.'

'Bullshit.'

'Have it your own way. Now think back to Iraq. To the street outside the brothel. Did anything strike you as unusual?'

'Apart from getting mugged?'

'Have it your way. Start the tests.'

'What the fuck is going on?' It's the only question I want an answer to.

Lendl spits a few words. 'Shut him up.'

The sweating man's dripping face appears above me and he pulls a mouthpiece over the lower half of my face. I'm silenced.

'First scenario.' Skeleton talking. 'Both times the subject claims to have been asleep. On each occasion two people died and on both occasions they killed each other. Would the subject need to know the victims?'

'He did but let's try it without any knowledge,' says Lendl.

I'm lost. No idea what they're doing.

'OK.' The Skeleton sounds like he's dictating a memo. 'The subject is now aware we have two test subjects in the next room. Let's put him to sleep and see what happens.'

Put me to sleep. How?

The prick in my arm is a giveaway.

Chapter 1
(3 Days Earlier)

The murder weapon lies a few inches from my feet, hidden beneath a rusting Pepsi can and a blue plastic bag. The broken handle from an axe – thrown from a car three days ago.

The heat forces sweat from my armpits, and my blue shirt - a poor color choice - is stained. A stream flows down my back, soaking my boxers.

The dust is a constant companion. A storm blew through yesterday and left a coating on the world. My sunglasses help a little.

Four a.m. Lifeless. Stained cinder-block canyons. This is no place to be caught unawares. Footsteps and my antennae pops. I size up the approaching man, who's dressed in a traditional Dish-dash-ou. His Shumagg, the white headscarf worn in the summer months, shadows his face. He shuffles in ill-fitting sandals.

I touch the bulge under my lightweight jacket and feel the weight of the gun.

The grip is cool and too small. A P99 Rad – a Polish copy of a Walther. At one time it had interchangeable grips but this one came from the back shop of a local merchant who was apologetic that he didn't have the original packaging and the optional extras.

The old man pads along the road, head down and I eyeball the handle-less, sheet metal door my employer walked through an hour ago. It's sealed tight.

My fingers curl around the top of the gun's slide. I pull it back until the click tells me the weapon is cocked.

I hope it works. I didn't have time to check it over.

The old man stops. Ten yards away. The smell of baking

drifts over. Iraqi flat bread – I've grown used to the smell over the last few days. I take a quarter step sideways to give me a bead on the target.

He lifts his head and stares at me through cheap Foster Grant sunglasses. I can't see his eyes and he can't see mine. Not good. Alarm bells are going off in my head. I focus on his hands, which are thrust inside the Dish-dash-ou. He walks towards me and stops a few feet away.

'Masa il Khee,' he says – not the usual formal greeting I have come to expect.

I hesitate while I try to remember the appropriate reply. 'Masa il Noor.'

'Kayf Halak?'

How am I?

I root around again for an answer and come up with 'Qwayysa.'

He tilts his head to one side as if I've said something wrong and laughs. 'You mean Qwayyis?' His English is clipped.

'Do I?'

'But of course. Qwayysa is the response had I been a woman.'

'Sorry.'

I take a step back. The old man has closed in on me during the exchange. The smell of bread is joined by a sour tang and it's either him or me but I don't recognize the scent.

He coughs. 'You are new to Basra?'

I have a job to do and any distraction is one too many. 'I'm waiting for someone.'

'What? In this place? My friend, this is not somewhere that you wish to be meeting people.'

He smiles, teeth pure Billy Bob. 'I am only here myself because this is the quickest way to get home. I worked late tonight and am looking forward to some food and half an hour of CNN. Do you like CNN?'

Say nothing. Usually a good way to lay a hint on someone but it doesn't work on this occasion.

'I like CNN,' he keeps talking. 'My wife does not. She prefers *Extreme Makeover*. That makes me smile. I think she wants the man in the program to come to our house. She likes the houses she sees in MTV's 'Cribs'. I like them too but I am not a pop star - although I can sing a little. Would you like to hear?'

I scan the road and the buildings. He takes this as a no. 'That is probably a good thing. You are American are you not?'

'Look…'

'Ahmed. My name is Ahmed.'

'I'm busy. Could we take a rain check?'

'We get a lot of rain here in the winter. Very little in the summer. It has not rained in two months but the waterway keeps the crops supplied. Have you seen our waterway? Impressive isn't it?'

I back away from him. Trying to keep the smell at a manageable distance. He follows. Behind him the metal door opens.

'McIntyre.' My employer appears. A small man and small-minded with it. I have instructions to guard him but he told me to stay put while he went inside.

'McIntyre, get the car.' He throws a bunch of keys onto the road and vanishes. I walk over to pick them from the dirt.

'Mr Taylor is demanding?'

I spin round as the local speaks.

The old man is picking his nose. 'A member of your government is he not?'

I'm standing half way between the door and the old man, the keys warm and sticky in my hand.

He takes a step forward. 'Is he your employer?'

I pocket the keys, check the alley once more and walk up to him. 'Will you just fuck off?'

His hands whip out from under his clothes and I see the dull glint of metal as he leaps towards me. I jump to the side but he twists in mid-air and metal connects with my skull.

Chapter 2

The world returns and I need a box of Tylenol. I try to lift my head and gag at the pain. I can't focus.

My left hand is pinned under my body and, trying not to move my head, I shift a little to extract it. Pins and needles roll in and I bite my tongue. I reach for my head and my hand finds a sticky mess. Not wet, just sticky. If it's blood then it's congealed and that means I have been lying here for a while. I close my eyes and force my head off the ground. Flashes of light replace the dark. Jesus, how hard did the old man hit me?

I open my eyes. The road is empty. The Pepsi can I saw earlier is lying a few feet away. No longer near the storm drain. I pat down my jacket. No gun. To be expected. I pat my hip and can't feel the familiar bulge of my money clip.

I prop myself up on an elbow.

'There.'

The voice is faint. Maybe at the other end of the street. Help or more grief? I turn to look. A freight train crosses my temple and the Diet Coke and kebab I had a few hours before makes a return journey.

I throw my head to one side to avoid my own puke but some of it splatters on my jacket. I want to collapse back to the ground. I take another breath and hold a sitting position.

'See, I told you.'

The voice is closer.

I wipe my mouth, licking the back of my teeth as I do so. I turn to the sound, closing my eyes, waiting for the dizziness to pass.

When I open them again four figures are approaching. Three IPs and a civilian. I've had a couple of run-ins with the Iraqi Police since I got here and I'm grateful it's not the National Police. IPs means this is a local problem.

The metal door is ajar and two heads are sticking out. Both locals.

I'm glad the old man took the gun. Iraq might still be all but a war zone but the IP don't take kindly to freelancers.

'Stay still!' The largest of the police officers is shouting. His sandy-colored uniform is straining to hold in his stomach. He's carrying forty pounds of excess fat above his belt and sweat stains have turned most of his shirt into a dark smudge. 'Lie down. On your front, hands behind your back.'

What the fuck? I don't want to lie down. On your front, hands behind – that's the perp's position. I've done zip – other than getting mugged by a senior citizen.

The fat IP's two colleagues back him up. All three have their guns trained on me. The civilian stands back. He's ripping into his fingernails with his teeth.

The fat IP steps forward. 'Get down now.'

I want to stand up not lie down.

'I *will* shoot.'

Shoot? What the hell for? I'm no threat.

'I will not ask again. Lie down *right* now.'

He raises his gun a few inches and points the barrel to the ground – indicating I should follow.

Maybe they have me mixed up with someone else.

'I'm…'

The discharge of the weapon is a thunderclap. Whatever is going on it's not worth getting killed over.

Instantly my face is back in the dirt. I hear a shuffle of feet and a knee lands in the small of my back. Someone pulls up my hands. My shoulders protest big time. Plastic cuffs are tied off and a foot kicks me in the side. The restraints cut into my wrists. Fuck. My arms are on fire.

'Up.'

I try to gain my feet but with my hands tied it's difficult. I stumble and fall. Road fills my face. I try again. A hand pulls at the cuffs and I scream as I'm hauled to within a finger's width of the fat officer's face. His breath is sweet - mixing with expensive deodorant.

My head spins and I vomit again. The fat officer jumps back, cursing. I stagger to the wall for support. I stop retching and look back. Taylor and a young girl lying in the middle of the road.

The dust around them is thick with blood.

Chapter 3

I stare at the bodies. Taylor is face up with the hilt of a pick axe rising from his stomach. The girl is topless. Her tongue lolls from the side of her mouth and her small breasts are lathered in blood. Some of my vomit has puddled in one of her shoes.

The fat officer is back in my face. 'Why did you kill them?'

Two locals are watching the scene from the door.

I shake my head. 'I didn't.'

'They're dead and you're here'

'He,' I point at the dead body, 'was my employer. I'm his security guard.'

'Easy to kill him then. He would trust you.'

He's interrupted by the roar of a supercharged engine and the scream of tires digging through dirt. The noise echoing along the walls. A black SUV races into the road and kicks up a dust storm as it brakes hard. The fat officer spins to the noise, gun at the ready. His fellow officers are on the move. Spreading out. Eyes on the new arrival. Trained well.

The passenger door at the back right of the SUV opens and a man emerges, dressed in a suit too dark and heavy for the environment. From the front passenger door a human tombstone steps out. He cradles a semi-automatic machine gun. The man in the suit walks towards the fat officer. The officer lowers the gun. They meet near the bumper of the SUV and go into a lengthy conversation. At one point one of the locals standing at the door is ordered over.

The man in the suit pulls out a laptop and places it on the hood. All three look at the screen for five minutes. The suit closes the computer and the man from the door is sent packing. A bit more chat and the fat officer steps to one side as the suit walks towards me. 'Free him!' says the suit. The officer next to me looks to his boss for instruction and receives a nod. He reaches behind me and frees my wrists.

'Come with me.' The man in the suit's accent is west coast. Californian but with a hint of something more southern.

'Why?' I ask.

'Have you seen 'Midnight Express'? Trust me it's got nothing on what they will do to you.'

'Who are you?'

'Later.'

I weigh up my choices and walk with my savior.

We approach the SUV - pumping cold air into the night. The AC is on full blast. The driver ignores me. Next to him the tombstone has slid into the passenger seat. In the back a small man with a white linen suit looks out of place in the black interior.

I slide into the middle seat next to him. My savior gets in beside me and closes the door. 'Get us out of here.'

The driver selects 'reverse' and swings the SUV around. He flicks to 'drive', and guns the engine as three more identical SUVs rush past us heading for the crime scene.

'Close,' the man in the white linen suit says and sighs.

I chirp up. 'Who are you?'

'Your friendly neighborhood safety squad.'

'What in the hell went down?'

'I've no idea.'

'Taylor and the girl are dead.'

'Yup.'

'And that's OK?'

He shakes his head. 'Far from it. Now shut up and give us a little quiet. You can talk all you want when we get back to the ranch.'

His voice is a tone too high for comfort. Makes him sound like he's squeezing the words out through a straw. I sit back, the aromatic mix of vomit, sweat and road dirt emanating from me.

I rub at my head.

I wish I had some morphine on me.

The ride is smooth and the car's suspension evens out all but the deepest potholes in the road. The blackened windows show little save a succession of lights flicking by. I close my eyes and try to put some perspective on what's going on. I've seen dead bodies before. I've even woken up next to them. But I'm surprised I'm in the car. Given the IP had just found the bodies my first port of call should be the local station. My rescuers hold some sway. 'Anyone have any Tylenol?'

No answer.

The car hits a set of speed bumps and slows. The driver's window slides down and a soldier appears with a flashlight. The driver shows a card and the soldier checks us out. His eyes rest on me and then on the blood. He backs out and signals the gate to open. We move forward and stop a couple of car lengths later. The gate behind us slams shuts and another gate opens in front. Twenty yards more and stop. The driver opens the window and another soldier asks for ID.

A garage door opens and we glide in. No one moves until the door closes behind us and, as if choreographed, all four passengers open their doors at the same time and exit.

'Out.' My savior stands clear and I follow orders.

We are in a gray cube of concrete. Two more black SUVs are parked to the back of the lot. I'm beginning to think that the dealer with the franchise for these things is on a bonus. The man with the white linen leads off and we cross to a small door. My savior steps forward and places his hand on a gray box. A small whirr. A click. And the door swings open.

We walk into a whitewashed corridor, me the sandwich between the tombstone and the driver. The space is barely large enough to hold us. A second door is guarded by another gray box and my savior places his hand on it. Same procedure and we're through.

The room beyond is dark but, as we walk, the ceiling lights spring to life. The place is full of empty tables and plastic chairs. Dust lies everywhere, the walls are unpainted and there's a heavy smell of old sweat.

My savior pushes me towards a chair. 'Take a seat and we'll see about a doctor.'

White Linen and my savior do the box thing on another door and vanish. The driver and Tombstone pull up a couple of chairs and sit down to stare at me.

I settle back to wait. Tombstone occupies himself by mining his nose and the driver closes his eyes. I touch my head. It's messy. Head wounds can be tricky - I've had experience. Years ago I was training in northern Canada. An army exercise to accustom new recruits to the cold. I was buddied up with a fellow grunt and told to find a spot to bed down for the night. It was dark by the time we found somewhere suitable and we decided to pitch the tent beneath an old cedar tree. In the middle of the night I got up for a piss and walked straight into a branch – knocking myself out. The next morning I woke up feeling fine. An hour later I collapsed as I packed up the tent. Head wounds can do that.

Tombstone stops mining for a second and I smile at him. He rams his finger back in his nose.

The door opens and a man in a white lab coat walks in carrying a large brown case. He sports a heavyweight beard to make up for the lack of hair up top.

'Is that him?' he says pointing at me.

Tombstone nods and the lab coat walks over.

'My name's Kelly - Medical Corp on assignment. Head wound I hear.'

He grabs my head and twists it around.

'I feel a bit faint,' I say.

'Not surprised. Don't pass out on me. I've been told to fix you up. Take these.'

Warm pills, their coating melting from the heat of his hand are shoved at me.

'Get him some water,' he says to Tombstone without turning.

Tombstone heads for the water cooler and returns with a plastic cup.

I pop the two pills. 'What are they?'

'Painkiller and anti-nausea.'

He finishes the examination and stands back. 'You should be in hospital. You might have a fractured skull.'

The door opens again and my savior walks in. 'And?' he asks.

'Hospital,' says the lab coat.

'Not going to happen,' replies my savior. 'We need him here. Just fix him up.' He turns and exits.

The doctor flips open the case. 'Clean it first. Then a bandage.'

The painkiller is good. The headache is fading and I no longer feel like I'm going to keel over. The doctor cleans the wound and wraps my head in cloth. He hands me a small pile of pills. 'One an hour. Any more and you'll lose the power of speech.'

He leaves and Tombstone stands up, indicating I should do likewise. We walk through the door and into another gray corridor. At the far end he plays with the ubiquitous gray box and we enter a new world.

At one time the room had been a large single entity. Now it's divided into a sea of glass walls. The place is alive with activity. White coats dominate. Computer equipment fills each room and there could be a hundred or more people working.

Tombstone walks through the room, ignoring it all while I

snap my head left and right to take in what's going on. Tombstone stops at a door. 'In here.'

He opens the door and pushes me into a room with two chairs and a small table. The door closes behind me.

As interrogation rooms go it's old school. A large panel of mirrored glass indicates the presence of a viewing room. Two CCTV cameras, one facing each chair, sit at the junction of ceiling and wall. The table is bolted to the concrete floor and has metal rings welded to the underside for feeding prisoners' chains through. The chairs are fixed to the stained floor by heavy-duty bolts. The door to the room has no handle and the tabletop is dotted with cigarette burns. A smell of bleach adds to the sense of menace. I'd been taught to spray it around for just that reason

My adrenalin is souring and, combined with the painkiller, I'm starting to feel sleepy.

The door opens and my savior enters. 'Coffee?'

'I'd love one.'

He nods at Tombstone who wrestles himself from his chair, feet dragging. He is making it clear he's not happy.

My savior sits opposite me. 'So let's start with the basics. Your name is Craig McIntyre. Ex US military. 1st Infantry Division, 4th Brigade, 2nd Battalion, 16th Infantry regiment. Spent three months in Iraq in 2003 in Ramdi before being sent home on the Permanent Disability Retirement List. Mental problems. Suspected of being a mercenary in the attempted coup in Equatorial Guinea. The same nonsense that put the British Prime Minister's son in the spotlight.

Hometown is Los Angeles. Mother's a Brit and father's from New York. Married with no kids and now working for Steel Trap Security. Entered Iraq six days ago. Given the job of babysitting Tom Taylor – now dead, along with an as yet unidentified female. Did I miss anything?'

I shake my head.

'Good.'
Then he punches me.

Chapter 4

The blow knocks me off the chair. Tombstone chooses that moment to return, places the coffees on the table and helps me back onto my perch. My savior rubs his knuckles. 'Tom was a friend of mine,' he explains.

I'm still stunned from the punch but I give him my best 'fuck off and die' look. He blanks it. 'So what went down?'

'I was mugged. Woke up to find two dead bodies next to me. That's it. I had nothing to do with their deaths.'

'We know.'

I let my mouth hang loose for a moment. 'And the IP?'

'They know you didn't have anything to do with the killings.'

'How do they know that?'

He turns to Tombstone. 'Get me the laptop.'

Tombstone vanishes again and comes back with a laptop, flipped open.

My savior spins the screen towards me. 'Watch.'

A black and white movie fires up. Only this is no early Charlie Chaplain but a view of the road I was mugged on from up high. I'm standing against the wall, the old man approaching. Tom Taylor appears from the door, the keys fly out, I walk forward, the old man approaches and bang, I'm on the ground. The old man rifles around me, lifts my gun and the money clip before vanishing.

I lie on the ground for a few minutes and the door opens again. Taylor walks out with the young girl on his arm. He looks up and down the road and spots me sprawled out. The young girl hangs back as he approaches. A new face appears at the door and I recognize him as one of the local gawkers.

Taylor bends down to touch me and the young girl walks over to the edge of the road. She reaches down, picks up the broken pickaxe, wanders over to Taylor and taps him on the shoulder. He spins round and she shoves the wood into his stomach.

He staggers forward and latches onto her dress, pulling it down over her breasts. She doesn't seem to notice. He works his hands up and around her neck. They both go down. His hands stay on her throat until she stops moving. He flips on his back, shudders and all is still.

I stare at the blank screen as the video finishes. My savior plays with the laptop. 'Look closer.' The scene rewinds and the man in the suit fiddles with the controls and zooms in on her face. 'Do you know her?'

'No.'

'Are you sure?'

'Damn sure. Anyway why would anyone have CCTV in the back end of nowhere?'

My savior stands up and digs out a packet of Marlboro. 'Smoke?'

I shake my head and he lights up.

'I'll level with you.' The first plume rises from his lungs. 'Tom was using a brothel and wasn't being too discreet about it. That CCTV has caught a few naughty boys – not just Tom. Our Iraqi friends are not too wild about us lifting you but the CCTV footage convinced them to let us talk to you first. But they'll be back. Not least because the cars you saw pass us on the way here were out to limit the damage and that means the locals won't be happy.'

'So who are you? CIA? Military? Freelance?'

'I work for the government.'

'So does my aunt but she can't remove a suspect from a crime scene, interrogate him and slug him on the chin.'

He smiles. 'So you don't know the girl?'

'No idea who she is.'

Another lungful of smoke drifts to the ceiling. 'Doesn't it strike you a bit crazy that she would ram a pick axe into his stomach?'

I shake my head. 'Look, figure it for yourself. Your boy Tom gets a bit frisky. Forgive me speaking ill of the dead but he wasn't the friendly type. She has a bit too much of the illegal hooch. He pushes it too far in the club. She hits fresh air and decides she doesn't want to go wherever it was they were going.'

'Don't buy it.'

'OK. What do you think?'

'I'll have a better idea when my colleagues get through. I'm just the vanguard on this one. If I were you I'd settle in for the wait.'

He takes one more draw and leaves me to breathe in the second hand smoke. I pull out a pill and pop it. It's been no time at all since the last one but I need it.

I know the routine and try to get comfortable. I try lying on the floor, lying on the table, lying against the wall and finally lying across the table again – this time with one leg on the floor and one knee on a chair. It takes another pill to make this comfortable.

Somehow three hours crawl by.

The door opens and Tombstone blocks the view. 'Up.'

I follow him back through the glass maze, into an elevator and we rise. In the rarefied atmosphere of the higher floors the world has carpet and soft furnishings. Tombstone escorts me to a set of over-polished oak double doors. He knocks – surprisingly gently - and a voice tells us to enter.

White Linen sits behind an oversized desk. 'Take a seat Mr McIntyre.' Then to Tombstone. 'That'll be all.'

I drop into a leather couch.

He settles back in his chair. 'Coffee?'

'Please.'

White Linen pours from a glass jug sitting behind him.
'Milk?'
'Black.'

He pushes the china cup across his desk and I stand up and retrieve it. The closed blind behind him can't hide the fact that we're enjoying the first rays of a new Iraqi day.

He throws a manila folder towards me. I catch it and open it to find a single typed sheet inside. A brief summary of the events of the last few hours.

'We've arranged for you to take your leave.'

'Not before time. I've a job to get back to – not to mention a hospital visit.'

'You'll be doing neither. When I say you're leaving, I mean you're leaving Iraq.'

'Am I hell!'

He reaches into a drawer in the desk and takes out an envelope. Tosses it to me. I rip it open. Inside is my passport, a few hundred dollars and a letter. The letter is my dismissal, a simple statement of termination with no references, from Steel Trap Security.

'Your bag's downstairs and there's a car waiting to take you to the airport. Unfortunately we've had to send you the long way home but it was prudent to put you on the first flight out of here.'

I sit forward in my seat.

'Who the hell do you think you are?'

'Your friends, Mr McIntyre. The IP are looking for someone to hang, and you're the perfect candidate. I'm convinced there's more to last night than you're letting on and giving you to our hosts won't help me unravel this. So you need to go home and we'll pick up on this somewhere more congenial.'

I lean forward. 'You have it all. On tape. I did nothing'

He leans back in his high backed chair. 'We'll provide an escort to see you safely back to US soil.'

I sip the coffee and work through the options. With no job in Iraq and the IP on my tail I think I'm in for Hobson's Choice, but I'm damned if I'm just going to roll over. 'And what do I do when I get back? This is the first legit job I've had in years and it took a lot of persuading and a crap salary to get me here.'

'Not my problem. You're the one who screwed up. If you'd been on the ball you wouldn't have been mugged by a geriatric and Tom might still be here. You're lucky we're giving you a way out.'

He hits a buzzer and Tombstone appears.

White Linen points to me. 'Mr McIntyre is leaving. Take him to the car pool. Mr Cameron will join you. I want you to drive and take no shit at the airport. If need be call in our boys but get Mr McIntyre safely on his plane.'

He turns back to look at me. 'Nice to meet you.'

He lifts a file from the corner of his desk, opens it and begins to scribble some notes.

* * *

'What's your name?'

I'm trying to engage Tombstone in a conversation as he escorts me through the building. 'Just your name. Come on – how can that hurt?'

'Bo Peep.'

Funny guy.

The car pool turns out to be a high-walled compound with a half dozen of the black SUVs parked, nose out, against one wall. Tombstone walks to the furthest away, hits the remote and the lights flash. 'Inside.'

I throw my bag over the back seat into the trunk and jump

in. It can't be much past seven but the heat is already a killer. I'm an open faucet of sweat. 'Can you switch on the AC?'

He ignores me and slams the door. My sweat is already pooling in the seat. There's a clunk and the central locking kicks in. I flip the manual switch but the doors are deadlocked. I try the electric windows but these are dead. I'm a fucking US citizen in a US building and I'm being treated like the lead from 'Most Wanted.' Who in the hell are these guys? CIA but not CIA – something doesn't add up.

The leather on the seats burns to the touch and my headache is back. I reach for a pill. I should have asked for more. There are five left. I pop one but I don't have the spit to swallow it dry and it sticks in my throat.

I scrabble into the front seat and rifle the glove box and the central console for water but the car is a clean as the day it was delivered. I cough and the pill lodges somewhere near the top of my gullet. I gag and cough again. It won't shift. It feels like it's taking up my whole throat. I grunt to try and help. I inhale hard and the pill slips down a little to wedge further in. It feels like the size of a baseball. I gag and begin to cough.

The door opens. 'What the hell are you doing?'

A new dark suit is looking down on me. Tall, six feet plus, and well muscled- up, my new friend is gym-hardened. His nose has taken a beating at some point and his face holds the pits of long -dead acne. 'Move over.'

'I need a drink. Got any?'

He gets in and tilts his head to one side and slaps Tombstone over the back of the head. Tombstone spins round. 'What the...?'

I'm surprised at the action. Tombstone doesn't seem like the playful type. The new suit takes a bottle of water from his pocket. He hands it to me.

'What did you hit me for?' spits Tombstone. The most

consecutive words I've heard from the walking wall. I unscrew the cap of the bottle and am delighted to find its cool. I start drinking.

'What?' says the new suit.

''Why did you hit me?'

'What are you talking about?'

'When I got in the car you hit me over the head.'

'Did I hell. Fire up the car. We've a plane to catch.'

Tombstone turns away with a growl. I'm not sure what game my new friend is playing and I don't care. I turn to him. 'Mr Cameron?'

'What do you care?'

'You're my buddy. If I have to fly with you I can't keep calling you Mr Cameron. Have you got a first name?'

He circles his head, cracking some bones in his neck. 'You don't need to know.'

The gates unfold in front of us and we exit onto a busy intersection. Cruising past the Indian Market we swing west way from the crime scene. My eyes close.

When I awaken there's a gun in my face.

Chapter 5

The car window is wound down and a blast of heat fights the AC. The gun belongs to an Iraqi National Police Sergeant. The blue and white camouflage clothes a copy of our boy's kit. The man is rabbiting on in Arabic and Cameron is right back at him.

Suddenly the gun vanishes and the window rises as Tombstone hits the button.

'What was that about?' I ask Cameron.

'You.' Cameron leans forward towards Tombstone. 'Keep driving.'

We negotiate some concrete blocks and stop a couple of car lengths further along. Tombstone's window goes down and he flashes his ID. The guard hands him a piece of paper, we drive another fifty yards, we stop, the window goes down and Tombstone hands over the paper. It's inspected and we are waved through.

'Fussy about their security,' I say.

Cameron smiles. 'Wait till you see how many X-ray machines we still have to go through.'

I look out the window and trace the perimeter fence running into the distance. We're still a couple of miles from the terminal but there's good reason for setting the fence so far away. The Brits used the airport from the get-go and the perimeter was set up to keep the nutters at bay, and the best way to do that was to keep them at a distance.

Tombstone drops us outside the airport entrance and Cameron isn't joking about the X-ray machines. I count four before we get on the plane. Add in a few more security checks and it takes us ninety minutes to cover less than three hundred yards.

We are in the air twenty minutes later.

Our first destination is Amman - a small airport with basic

facilities. We touch down to find the plane to Cyprus is ready to roll and, as I pop the last of the pills, we take off and I fall asleep.

In Larnaca we have a four hour stop-over. I'm all for going to the bar. My minder is all for avoiding the place.

'Did they really send you just to escort me home?' We're sitting in the airport café and I'm sipping strong coffee.

'I'm being transferred.'

'Promotion?'

'Kind of.'

'Look, I'm not your enemy. We have twenty-four hours of travel left. All I want is a little company. If you don't – fine.'

He drains the cup. 'Another?'

I nod. He has to wait in the queue as two women argue over who'll pay. He returns with two large mugs and sits down. 'I screwed up.'

I try not to smile. 'That makes two of us.'

'Yeah well at least no one got killed on my watch.'

My smile fades. 'What happened with you?'

'I fucked up.'

'Well lighten up and let's have a drink. Nothing you can do about it until you get stateside.'

'I'm a bad drunk.'

'So am I.'

Five minutes later we're in the bar. I'm on a JD and Coke and he's on his second Ballantines and telling me who it is that's forcing me to go back home. 'We take on some of the more unusual issues that our government faces. My boss always says *If it don't fit - we'll get it*. He makes it sound like a rhyme.'

'Unusual. What is the agency called?'

'I'm not going to go into it any more. I can't.'

'So what's your name?'

'Mike.'

'Where's home?'
'Anchorage, Alaska.'
'Cold.'
'Sometimes.'
'Do you get back often?'
'Not for over a year.'
'Are you married?'
'What do you think?'
'No but I'll guess you were.'

'We lasted two years and by then she was a stranger. She's moved in with an old friend of mine.'

'Nice.'

'And you?'

'Married and live in LA. My wife and I went to school together and lost contact. I met her in a bar a few years back and we got married last year.'

'And she's happy you're doing security work in Iraq?'

'It's my first real job in years. We had no choice. It doesn't even pay that well but it was a six month contract and keeps the roof over our heads for another year. She teaches.'

'You're ex-army?'

'It was a short affair. Can we drop it?'

'You avoid the department and I'll avoid the army.'

'Deal.'

He drains the whisky and orders another. I'm not halfway through mine. When the waiter returns he swallows most of it in one go. 'What'll you do when you get home?' he asks.

'I'm not sure. It'll be a surprise to Lorraine. My wife. I haven't been able to contact her. Your lot didn't let me take a piss on my own – never mind a phone call.'

'You had them rattled.'

'I did?'

'Tom wasn't just a grunt. He was number two to Lendl.'

'Lendl?'

'The man in the white linen suit.'

'So why didn't you supply Taylor with his own security?'

'This is the twenty-first century. Freelance contracting is all the rage. It means we don't have to put our people in the line of fire. People like you are the new cannon fodder?'

'No shit.'

'Private firms are plastered all over Iraq. It's cheaper than employing your own people, less risky and more flexible. The downside is you don't always get the most competent of operatives.'

I wince. I'm saved from any further embarrassment by the departure board announcing our gate.

Cameron glances at the board. 'Time for one more?'

Chapter 6

Thirty minutes later and we're sitting near the back of the Cyprus Airways Airbus 320. There are three seats either side of the walkway. The flight is quiet and we have a spare seat between us. Mike orders another two whiskeys as the trolley rolls past and I'm beginning to regret suggesting we had a drink. I decline the stewardess's offer and lean back in the chair. My headache is growing. I have stocked up on over-the-counter painkillers at the airport but I'm not sure they are heavy-duty enough. I pop two.

I must have dozed off because I'm awoken by the sound of Mike's raised voice. 'Two more whiskeys.'

The stewardess is standing above him. Her arms folded and standing a little further away than would seem polite.

'I'm sorry Mr Cameron but I've been told not to serve you any more at the moment.'

'Fuck off. I want a drink.'

I reach over and put a hand on his shoulder.

'Calm down Mike. She's....'

I don't get to finish my sentence.

'And you can fuck off as well.' His eyes are wide and the whites have hair streaks of red snaking through them. I've no idea how long I've been asleep but Mike is a good few drinks to the bad side of things. He turns back to the stewardess. 'Get me two drinks now.'

'Sorry sir I can't do that,' she replies.

He moves to stand up. I place my hand on his shoulder. Again he spins round. 'I told you to fuck off.'

'This isn't going to get you anywhere.'

'It's got nothing to do with you.'

'Keep this up and they'll restrain you.'

He stands up and the stewardess backs off. He turns to face

the rear of the plane. 'I'll get one myself. Where's the fucking bar on this thing?'

Mike has the full attention of the people around us. A young couple on the row opposite are leaning away from the incident – as if the plane walls are rubber and will let them gain a little more distance. She's pretty but her face shows fear and this diminishes her looks. He's a little geeky and has his head stuck in a book trying to ignore what's going on. In the row in front of them a head sticks out from behind the back of the chair, level with the stewardess's rear. The owner is in her seventies or has aged badly. Her hair is a tight crop of curls with a heavy rinse of black that makes it look like she is wearing a wig. She shows no fear – just morbid curiosity. The smile on her lips has a little evil twist to it - she probably reads the details of real-life crime for kicks.

Mike has set off to find some drink. We are only four rows from the rear and he's back double-quick. 'Where are the drinks? It's only fucking toilets back there.'

The stewardess has been joined by a colleague. I can't read the name badge but the new arrival stands with an 'I'm in charge' hands on hips pose. 'Mr Cameron, will you please return to your seat.'

'Will I hell. I want another drink.'

'I'm sorry but I can't do that. Now can you please sit down.'

'Or what?'

This is going nowhere good. I try one more time. 'Look Mike. Sit down and we can get you a drink later.'

He takes a step towards the stewardess. She holds his gaze.

'Or what?' he repeats.

I like the stewardess. She's not panicking but she is scared. I'd be scared. She's been trained well and I'd guess this isn't her first drunk passenger. Mike's shoulders are tense and he is leaning forward. When I was young I did a little work on the doors of the local nightclub and I know the pose. Mike is spoiling for a fight. The stewardess opens her mouth to say something but her colleague steps in. 'Sir, if you don't return to your seat I'll have no choice but to inform the captain and arrange for the police to be waiting at Heathrow.'

The stewardess flicks her head round and gives her colleague a look that would wither a concrete flower. Her boss is only doing her job but her tone is setting Mike on edge and the stewardess can sense it.

'Fuck off.' Mike takes another unsteady step. An inch or so. Closer to something more violent. He's a southpaw. His left hand is loosely balled up. The old woman with the bad rinse ducks out of sight. The couple have stopped leaning away now the danger has moved down the plane. The geek has his head out of the book and is stretching his neck to get a better view over the headrest of the chair in front.

'Look sir, I'm sure we can resolve this.' The stewardess's voice seems to lessen the tension a little.

Mike eases down a quarter of a gear. 'Just get me a drink.'

'If you could just sit down.'

'Drink.'

'Look sir,' the boss intervenes again and the tension is back. The stewardess's shoulders slump. She doesn't need help. She's doing OK. I can see it in her face. *Shut up bitch – you're making it worse.*

A grunt comes from behind me and I spin my head. Four people behind me are half standing - trying to get a better view. The grunt is from a man with a triple chin. Rubberneckers.

'Sir,' says the boss.

I need to stop this now. I size up Mike and stand up. He's focused on the two woman and I hope he stays that way. I need distance between him and the aircrew. Distance is good.

I take a step and he senses something and does the one thing

I'm not prepared for. He lashes out with his left foot – kicking straight back. He catches me in the stomach and I go down.

He backs up and stamps down on my leg. I try to roll away but in the confined space I can do little more than scrabble around. He tries for three in a row and I snatch at his foot. I catch him off balance and he starts to fall but he grabs the nearest armrest and kicks out again clipping the top of my shoulder.

The stewardess stops looking at us and turns away to face her boss, pulling her head back as she twists. Her head snaps forward and her forehead impacts on her boss's nose. A dull click as bone gives way. The noise bounces off the walls of the plane. The boss reels back and an arc of blood sprays into the air. A ribbon of crimson against the white fuselage.

The boss staggers back, and falls to the floor. The streamer of blood reaches its apex and sprays across the chairs on either side. Shouts go up from the passengers.

The stewardess drops down to land on her boss. Her hand starts to pump up and down and I hear screaming.

Mike steps back. Struggling to comprehend what he's witnessing. The stewardess gets up, her uniform sprayed with blood. She rotates her head as if she has just finished a difficult set of exercises, reaches down and brushes her skirt – removing the wrinkles and creases. She swipes at her hair and swings back towards Mike. Her pupils are dilated. Her face white. Mike puts his hand out to steady himself and works himself back along three headrests and shuffles away. I stand up - wary that Mike still has a kick left in him. We both slump into our seats as a woman starts screaming and two more aircrew rush into the cabin.

'Jesus,' one of them shouts. He is looking down at where the stewardess's boss is lying. The other gags and bends over.

'Did you see that?' I realise that Mike is talking to me.

I nod. 'What in the hell...'

The captain appears and pushes the new aircrew to one side. He bends down to attend to the stewardess's boss. He orders one of the aircrew to help and they lift her up and carry her out of the cabin. The stewardess is shepherded by the remaining aircrew to the front of the plane. Minutes tick by before the captain returns. 'Ladies and gentlemen, can I firstly apologise for the incident that some of you have experienced.'

He closes the curtains behind him. 'We are expecting to land in Heathrow in thirty minutes. The police have been informed of the incident and have requested that everyone in this area of the plane remain seated until they can take some statements.'

There is some murmuring and the captain walks up the aisle, stopping to answer the occasional question. When he reaches us he stops and looks at Mike.' 'Mr Cameron. I believe you had an issue with one of my cabin crew.'

Mike keeps his eyes focused on his lap.

'The police want to talk to you. I hope I can count on you to remain in your seat for the remainder of the flight.'

Mike nods.

Chapter 7

'Let's start from the top.'

The accent is thick with London. There are two of them – one in uniform and one plain-clothed. I'm in an interview room inside Heathrow airport. It looks much like the one in Iraq but with fewer stains on the floor.

The plain-clothed officer leans forward. His breath could stun a horse. He's two days from the last shave and wrinkles crowd his face, white wisps of hair falling onto gray eyebrows. 'Tell me once more what happened on the flight.'

I rattle off the same story I have been through three times already. I don't vary from the core events and when I finish the cop stares at me. 'Why would the stewardess attack her boss?'

I shake my head.

'Nothing else you'd like to say? No detail you might have missed?'

I shake my head again. 'Can I go now? My flight leaves in just over an hour.'

'I need to check with my colleague first.'

'But my flight.'

'Mr McIntyre, the cabin director is in hospital with multiple facial wounds. Until I'm satisfied you are not involved then you're going nowhere.'

'I want to see someone from the embassy.'

'That I can do – once they have finished with Mr Cameron.'

'Someone from the embassy's already here?'

'They were here in a flash – for your friend. You obviously fall somewhat down the food chain. I'll pass on the message that you want to see someone. The constable here will keep you company.'

I try to strike up a conversation with my new guard but I would get more out of the wall. So we sit in silence.

The door opens and in walks another man in a dark suit. Not embassy. Agency. Squat, with a bodybuilder's physique, he adjusts his tie. A dark mole dominates a solid face. Definitely agency. I'm beginning to be able to smell them.

'Good afternoon Mr McIntyre. Please don't get up.'

I have no intention of getting up.

'Trouble just follows you around.'

'Who are you?'

'A friend.'

'I don't need friends. I need answers. I've done nothing wrong.'

'So you say and so you said in Iraq but there are two dead people, a mutilated cabin director and a stewardess who seems to have no memory of her workout on her boss. The only common link in all this is you.'

'And? I was out for the count in Iraq when the lovebirds killed each other and I was trying to calm your boy down when the airline staff decided to settle a dispute.'

'Still doesn't look good. So here's how it's going to go down. We'll see you safely home. Mr Cameron won't be joining you. He is in need of a little, eh, love and attention.'

'Rehab would be more appropriate.'

'As you say. I think our British cousins are happy to release you into my custody and your plane leaves in forty minutes.'

'Custody? I've done nothing WRONG.'

'For your own safety Mr McIntyre. We only have your best interests at heart.'

Ten minutes later and I am being trailed through the back end of the airport to be deposited at my gate with none of the nastiness that comes with passport control.

My bodybuilder friend hands me an envelope. 'Your tickets.'

'You wouldn't have anything for a headache?'

He smiles and points to the plane. 'Try sleep.'

As I collapse into my seat I have acquired two more minders. Both have standard-issue dark suits. Both are about five feet ten with identical haircuts – buzz with a hint of a fringe. Buzz 1 is on my left and Buzz 2 on my right. We are coach class again. I down a couple of JD and Cokes with three Tylenols acquired from Buzz 1. A minor Mickey Finn.

New York is still deep in night when we land and the transfer to the LA flight is simple enough. Buzz 1 and 2 keep a respectful distance behind me before placing me as the meat between their sandwich for the last leg.

The JD and Coke/Tylenol mix doesn't work this time and the pounding in my head grows as the plane crawls across the Mid-West. A slow dull pounding that eclipses everything else. Rooted at the back of my skull. Buried. A series of explosions going off releasing a stream of hot poison that is spreading through my head. Building in waves. Peaks and troughs. Each peak slightly higher. Each trough deeper.

Nausea wells up and I try to focus on the small graphic on the seat screen that indicates where we are. It's frozen over Kansas. As far to go as we have come. I place my head between my knees and gag as the movement pumps up the pain.

My vision begins to tunnel. The drone from the engines, the people chatting and the clink of the drinks trolley are sore noises. Hard noises. Penetrating noises. I'm going to be sick.

I grab for the vomit bag.

Then a cool wave washes down the metal tube. Cold – filling the space around me. Crashing over me. Menthol fresh. I breathe deeply and my lungs shiver as the ice-tinged gas expands into my tissue. I open my eyes and the air is blue. A cobalt haze fills the cabin.

The spitting fire in my head is extinguished. Snuffed out at the source. Forced into a tiny, tight ball. A neutron star forming at the top of my backbone. Wrapped in a blanket of ice. Still there but trapped.

I lift my head and the light-headedness that accompanies the movement momentarily blurs this new, surreal new world. I press my eyelids down and wait. Floating in the lack of pain.

I reopen my eyes and smile. The blue is pulsing – a soft, gentle action – between light and dark . Morphing from one to the other.

I turn to look at Buzz 1 but he's iPod bound, and if he can see the color or sense the chill he's giving no indication. Buzz 2 is reading and turns to catch my eye. I smile and his forehead creases in confusion. The wrinkles in his skin are the color of a sunny Caribbean bay – the peaks a mountain-high sky blue. He shakes his head as I keep up the smile. I'm on my own in my new blue world.

'Drink sir?' The stewardess's voice has a light tinkle attached to it. Then she seems to jump forward and her words tumble out with the speed of a DVD on 'skip'. 'Drink sir?'

I catch the words – but only just. 'Jack Daniels and Coke.' I reply.

She pours the drink on fast-forward and hands me a midnight-blue version of my favorite fix of alcohol. Then she's all slo-mo as she asks my minders if they want a drink. Buzz 1 and 2 decline. I take a sip and the blue wave washes clear of me and the blue world vanishes. My headache has gone but I can still feel the kernel rooted to my brain stem. Waiting.

I contemplate the moment. Trying to figure out what the hell has just happened. There's still the faintest tinge of blue to the world. A hangover from the full effect. It's not unpleasant but it's also something that feels wrong. In the way that a snort of cocaine is both good and bad at the same time. A feeling of elation earned through a substance that will destroy you.

I view the plane's progress on the small screen. We are

nearly out of Colorado. An immense leap in distance in a few minutes. I wonder if the system is broken and tap it with my forefinger. Nothing. I watch as the plane leaves Colorado and, crossing at the corner of Utah and New Mexico, we enter Arizona. No great leap forward, just a slow progression. How long had the blue world gone on? Minutes? An hour? It felt like seconds.

The JD is spreading through my system and I have an irrational fear that the warm alcohol will somehow melt the coating around the headache ball that is squatting in my skull. I clench my teeth waiting for it to explode. An ice cube dropped in a hot-fat fryer. Spitting. But the headache stays buried.

I lean back in the seat and glance at Buzz 1 and 2. Both are still in music or word land.

My thoughts turn to home and the conversation with Lorraine that lies ahead. I dump the thought and slug some more JD. I'll deal with it when the time comes.

I close my eyes and bathe in what's left of the blue world.

Chapter 8

I should be shattered. It's been over a day since I wasn't on a flight or waiting for one. LAX was the usual. Too busy. Too noisy. Too everything. I'm sitting in my apartment. The theme is white with more white and the only thing that isn't white is Lorraine in a red gingham dress. A little under six feet tall she could have cut it as a model. Dark, shoulder-length hair, a round face, green eyes and she can stop a bus with her smile. She is showing it off now but it's not warm. She's already ahead of the curve, knowing my early return is not good news. When she saw the bandages on my head the smile had faded. She has brewed up some industrial-strength coffee and is sitting, hands between her legs, waiting. The pose she takes when bad news is on the horizon.

She leans forward. 'Well?'

I take a breath and offload. I start with the brothel and work my way through the events. Some of the story isn't for telling today. The blue. My suspicions that the agency wasn't finished with me. The feeling that I'm not as innocent in all this as I'd like to believe. I love Lorraine and I should trust her. That's the way it should be. But it isn't. And that hurts.

My lack of trust is my own insecurity. I'm scared of losing her. When we met I never thought she would show any interest in me. It's not that I'm bad looking and I can turn on the charm if need be, but I was frazzled from my experience in the army. I was mentally in a bad place and Lorraine was too good a thing to be happening to me. I was scared to open up to her. Still am. Scared I'll chase her off. That she will see me for what I am. A burnt-out shell that is struggling to keep things going. So things that should be shared between husband and wife are quietly buried by me. Not a recipe that has much future.

She sits in silence and when I finish she starts to take it all to pieces – bit by bit. She has a disarming way of asking the most awkward questions. Working with kids has given her an insight into interrogation. Ask the easy questions first. Work up to the hard ones. Keep a few easy ones up your sleeve in case things get bogged down. Open questions. 'How did that make you feel?' 'Why do you think that happened?' Or in this case. 'So what do you want to do now?'

It is the question I've been avoiding.

'I don't know. Something will come along. Won't it? I'll contact Steel Trap. This is their problem to sort out.'

'Craig....'

I let my head fall. We've been here so often. She met me as a wreck. An ex mental-ward case who had frittered away the last of his parents' inheritance. She reaches out and touches my hair. 'Craig this is insane. Murder. Secret agencies. What the...'

'You knew that the job wasn't great,' I say. 'Iraq. Bodyguard. And I did fuck up. Two dead bodies and I was the point man. I got mugged by a man twice my age. It all happened on my watch.'

Her face is close. She's stunningly pretty. I'm still amazed that she chose me. Amazed and grateful. She once told me that there was something special about me. An energy that she found intoxicating. When we're together she brushes my hair and whispers 'I love you' so often that I wonder who she's trying to convince. Me or her.

'We need to fix this,' she says.

'How?'

'Phone Steel Trap. See what they say first.'

'Now?'

'Now!'

I pick up the phone and dial the number.

'Dan, it's Craig.'

'Hi Craig.' Cold.

'I take it you've heard about Iraq.'

'No. I never hear when employees fuck up.'

'Funny. What's going on?'

'You screwed up. Your boy is dead and our name is being trashed. Lot of money to be made in Iraq. You're history.'

'And that's it.'

'That's it.'

'Come on. I got kicked out by some black ops agency. Don't you care?'

'Craig you fucked up with the wrong people. They pay well and they don't want you around. What can I say? Most of our work is through them at the moment. They want you out – you're out.'

'That's bull. I'm an employee.'

'Were an employee. We'll pay you a month's salary.'

'I want to meet.'

'What for?'

'To discuss this.'

'We've been doing that.'

I could see him. Sitting in the tiny office that Steel Trap called their head office. His back to a window that looks on to a back alley. Cheap rent area.

'Come on Dan. It wasn't my fault.'

'Taylor's dead. The client's pissed off and I'm probably not going to see any work from them in the near future. What's not your fault?'

'A coffee.'

'Craig it's done. You're out.'

Silence.

'Just a coffee.'

Silence.

'Fuck you.' I throw the handset onto the sofa.

Lorraine shakes her head. 'That went well.'

'He's a tosser.'

'Can't you sue?'

'Maybe but it'll cost money and we aren't exactly floating in cash. I'll ask Gerry in the morning. I need a drink.'

Gerry is an old lawyer friend but I know I'm not going to ask him anything. It's over.

Lorraine leans closer. 'Craig we need to talk.'

'And I need out of here.

'Craig…'

'Michael's.'

'A bar? You want to go to a bar?

'I need to think and Michael's is a good place.'

'No it's not. It's a dump with a leech for an owner.'

'Well I'm going. You can come if you want, and I need a shower.'

'What's stopping you?'

I tap the bandage.

She shakes her head and walks into the bedroom to reappear with a shower cap.

'Try this.' She throws it at me.

* * *

We walk down North Cahuenga. Lorraine has changed into fitted jeans, a tight white T-shirt and a pair of wedges to show off her legs. She's topped it off with a lightweight jacket, and I sigh. I'm going to watch guys watch my girl for the next few hours.

We leave the residential stretch and enter low-rise commercial territory. Around us sits the edge of Hollywood. Production companies, agents, marketing companies. We pass the art deco front of the studio that Lorraine pulls extra bucks from. We hit the corner of Melrose where a small shopping mall, a car dealer, a loan shop and a shuttered strip of stores sit. We turn right.

Lorraine keeps her distance. Her hands are rammed into her jean pockets and her head is down. A sure sign that I'm not Mr Popular at the moment.

To our left trees hide apartment blocks and we keep to the sidewalk that bounds the shops. We cross Stewart Street, pass the Latin restaurant that sits on the corner and enter Michael's.

It claims to be an Irish pub but it's really a typical downtown, randomly decorated bar with paraphernalia that might claim some tangential connection to the Emerald Isle. The bar stretches the length of the premises. A platform made of fifty per cent alcohol and fifty per cent wood. The AC is wound up and the cool air is welcome. Booths sit opposite the bar and the place is dotted with a few customers.

Charlie, the owner, is pouring a Bass Ale and smiles when he sees us. Or rather when he sees Lorraine. Weighing in at two-fifty pounds he's a bodybuilder when not juicing people up. Clean-shaven, bald, always on the edge of bursting out of one of his many T-shirts. This one says 'I'm Free.' Charlie is cheer personified.

'One thousand dollars?' he shouts over.

'One thousand and one,' replies Lorraine with little humour.

'Too expensive,' he replies.

I shake my head. Charlie has been offering Lorraine a thousand dollars to sleep with him since the first night we found his place. He refuses to pay more so Lorraine always insists on a dollar extra.

'Are our chairs free?' I ask.

'A little late for the alley.'

'Won't be dark for another hour.'

'Give me five minutes to set it up but don't let me forget you're out there.'

'We won't,' says Lorraine.

'What can I get you?' he says, already pouring our drinks. Me a JD and Coke, Lorraine a white wine spritzer. He places the drinks on the bar and makes for the back door to set up our spot. I sip at my drink and Lorraine plays with hers. She's not a drinker and one spritzer can last all night if she has a mind. 'I need to pick up something from the library.'

'What. Now?'

The John Freemont library is just across the road.

'You dragged me out.'

'We need to talk.'

'We will but Mary's doing the Civil War with her kids and wants a book our regular supplier doesn't stock.'

'What's wrong with her legs?'

'Funny.'

'Is she being a nuisance?'

Charlie comes back and stops her from replying. 'Your thrones await.'

We follow the signs for the washrooms and push out the emergency exit into the alley behind. Charlie has placed two folding chairs and a small plastic table against one wall. The alley is deserted and since it wraps round the block you can't be seen from the street. On a Sunday there can be ten or twelve people out here but this late on a Saturday there is no one else.

'Mary?' I say as I sit down.

Lorraine sits down. 'A real pain. She thinks we owe her big time for letting us stay in Carl's place. Now it's got worse.'

'In what way?'

'The school principal is looking for a new number two. Mary should be a shoo- in but the PTA are against it.'

'So what?'

'They hold sway. We're short on funds and the PTA dug us out last year.'

'Ah, the old Hollywood 'C listers'.'

'Don't knock it. Some of the parents take home in a month what we take home in a year.'

'So who do they like for the job?'

'Me.'

'You're kidding?'

'Nope.'

'Fantastic – what's the salary?'

'I haven't got the job yet.'

'But if you did?'

'Another twenty thousand a year.'

'Touchdown.'

'What?'

'I knew coming here was a good idea. We haven't even finished our first drink and we're already sorted for cash.'

'I haven't got the job yet and Mary won't take it lying down.'

'Does she know about the PTA?'

'I think so.'

'Forget her. What can she do?'

'Throw us out of our home. Do you know what we would get for a thousand a month around here?'

'Carl won't do that.'

Carl was Mary's husband and a developer. We had the apartment on the cheap while he tried to fill it

'He will if Mary turns it on. He was round yesterday.'

'What for?'

'Nothing but he talked about upping our rent.'

'We have an agreement.'

'Not in writing.'

'So you're her skivvy?'

'No choice. The meeting about the position is on Tuesday – they're drawing up the shortlist. I need to keep her sweet till then.'

She drains a little spritzer. 'It'll take me five minutes to get the book. Then we talk.'

* * *

I suck in the alley atmosphere and the door opens. Charlie appears with another drink for me. 'I thought if I got you drunk you might forget you came with Lorraine and I'd have to walk her home.'

'You can try.'

'What's with the bandage?'

'I forgot to duck.'

He places the black liquid on the table. 'You out of a job already?'

Charlie knew my history – it's what happens when you have a year to sit on the wrong side of a bar.

'Yeah.'

'Careful you don't lose her. She deserves better.'

From anyone else I would have taken issue but Charlie had become more than the bartender. I'm into him for a good thousand in back tab and he really doesn't expect me to pay. I think I'm his charity case. 'I know. Got a job going?'

'You behind a bar? My profits would vanish.'

'I can be teetotal.'

'And I can run the hundred in less than ten.'

'I'm not that bad.'

'You can be.'

'Could you keep your ear to the ground? I need a job – just to prove I can hold a one down for a while.'

'I'll keep a lookout.' He looks up at the sky. 'Thirty minutes and then inside. The sun will be gone by then.'

He is right. It's turning to dusk. I nod.

He pauses before he re-enters the bar. 'There was some trouble last week just up the street. So in before dark.'

He vanishes.

Chapter 9

'Sorry.' Lorraine rolls up as the sun vanishes.
'Charlie wants us in. He's having a quiet fit.'
'Tell him to take a chill pill. It's lovely out here.'
Lorraine sits down, a book in her hand.
Silence.
I finish my drink.
More silence.
Suddenly the door to the pub slams against the wall. Two men crash to the alley floor. I leap from the chair, grab Lorraine and pull her to one side as the men roll around on the ground. They're dressed head to toe in leather. One has long hair and the other is a skinhead. The skinhead lands a punch and their world has no words – just grunts. There is more noise from the bar. Shouts, glass breaking – chaos. I need to get Lorraine away but not through the pub. 'Along the alley. We'll go round the front,' I shout. I thrust out my hand and Lorraine takes it and we leave the two leather boys rolling in the dirt.

The alley is short and, as we swing round the corner, we find the exit that leads to the street beyond is full of bikes and bikers. Three bikers are laying into one guy on the ground. He is taking a serious kicking. One of the bikers is doing nothing other than aiming his boot at the victim's head.

I want to step in and Lorraine knows it. She looks at me, talking to me in silent movie language. Mouth moving – no sound. *Don't go. Leave it. It's not your business.* All with a flick of an eyebrow.

My heart is racing in anticipation. Two people have died in the last forty-eight hours. I won't stand by and watch another. But I can't put Lorraine in danger.

Lorraine grabs my shoulder as I step forward. Her fear finds voice. 'No, Craig.'

I hesitate. A police siren howls in the distance. The three stop the attack and run for their bikes. Footsteps echo behind us. I turn round and the two fighters from the pub door, shaking themselves down, are sprinting in our direction.

I step in front of Lorraine. But they split like water around a rock and vanish into the night.

The siren is joined by others.

'Back along the alley,' says Lorraine.

I agree.

We jog back to the bar.

'Inside,' she orders,

The bar is a disaster zone. Tables and chairs are wrecked and split. Glass litters the floor. The back bar a wasteland of spilt drink and broken bottles. As we enter, the last of the leather clad invaders hobbles out of the front door. The front window is gone

'Charlie?' Lorraine is shouting in the direction of the bar.

Charlie's head pops up. 'Are they gone?'

She nods.

'Get behind the bar with me,' he says. 'Tell the police you ducked down as soon as the first biker came through the door. Otherwise they'll want to know where you were.'

'Charlie, they ain't going to care,' I say.

'And if they do?'

I don't answer and we join him behind the bar. 'What happened?'

The police sirens are close.

'A biker came in through the window and four others followed him through the door.'

'Do you know them?'

'No.'

'Lorraine?' The new voice is out of place. 'Lorraine are you here?'

Lorraine sticks her head above the bar. 'Mary? What on earth…'

I pop up. Mary is standing at the door to the washrooms. 'I was looking for you and when the fighting started I hid in the washroom.'

Lorraine stands up. 'How did you know where I was?'

'I decided to pick up the book myself and the library told me you were here.'

The door to the men's washroom slams open and a biker steps out. His eyes are glazed. He takes in the scene, looks at us and throws his arm around Mary's throat. She screams and he pulls her close.

Mary is small. Four feet ten in her stockings soles. Her hair adds a few inches and is always lacquered with a full can of hairspray. She wears three inch heels as standard and five inch of an evening. She's a touch old for the skinny jeans but they help with the illusion that she's taller. The biker is six feet plus, heavy with stubble and with a small skull tattooed on to his left cheek. His dress is top-to-toe leather.

'Let her go.' My voice is loud but the biker ignores me.

'What's going on?' A young officer has arrived through the door, looking confused. Baby-smooth skin that probably sees a razor once a week.

The biker staggers forward with Mary. He reaches the bar and rests his free arm amongst the debris.

The officer watches and then pipes up, 'Ma'am do you know this man?'

Mary shakes her head.

'Sir, can you please release the lady?'

The biker looks at the officer. Eyes swimming. High on something. 'No way, man.' His voice is gravel and glass.

A second, older officer walks through the door. Where his colleague is a fresher, this one is time-served. Grey hair drops below his cap. Wrinkles map his face. A red, blood-burst nose suggests he enjoys a drink. The young officer turns his head to the new policeman, looking for help.

There is a click of steel releasing from steel. A crack as metal hits metal and a blade catches the light of the neon Miller Lite sign at the end of the bar. The biker lifts a flick knife into sight and places it against Mary's throat. She stiffens at the touch of the blade.

'Get backup,' says the older officer to the younger one. 'Tell them it's a possible 207.' He turns to Mary and the biker. 'What's your name ma'am?'

Mary says nothing.

'Ma'am?'

Mary is too scared to answer.

'She's called Mary,' says Lorraine, trying to help.

'What do you do for a living, Mary?'

Odd question.

'A teacher.' A small voice.

'Local?'

Silence.

'King Street Elementary,' says Lorraine.

'Do you hear that sir?' He's directing his question at the biker. 'Mary here is a teacher. Now you wouldn't want to be hurting a teacher would you?' He has an Irish lilt to his voice. 'Good people, teachers. We need them. Too few in the world.' He takes a small step forward. 'Mary are you married?'

She nods.

'Kids?'

Mary shakes her head.

'Enough kids to deal with at school?'

Another step closer.

The biker collapses a little and Mary shrieks as the flick knife nicks her skin.

The officer stops. 'Careful sir. No one has been hurt so far and you wouldn't be looking to change that. Put the knife down. Nobody here wants to harm you. Knife down and step away from Mary.'

'No way, man.' The biker turns and rests the small of his back on the bar. Mary is shivering and a trickle of blood dots her pink blouse.

'A knife,' Lorraine gasps. 'In his back.' She's pointing and I follow her finger. A wooden-handled knife is embedded between the biker's shoulder blades. The jacket is black and the light is poor but a large stain is visible. It spreads from the blade and forms a ragged triangle that finishes at the jacket's hem.

That's a lot of blood. No wonder he's leaning against the bar.

The policeman nods at me. He's seen it too. The biker isn't out of his head on drugs or booze. He's losing blood. 'Sir, put down the knife and we can get you to the hospital.'

'No way, man.' He slides along the bar. His blood coating the woodwork. He's only a few feet from Lorraine, Charlie and me and we're all pressed up hard against the wall. Mary is sidestepping with him, trying to keep the blade away from her throat. With my back against the wall I move behind the biker. Lorraine's eyes widen and I try to pass a silent message to her. *Stay still.*

The biker is focused on the police officer. He stumbles again and Mary yelps. The movement takes him another few feet down the bar. I'm now directly behind him. My heart is tripping at triple sixty but my training tells me not to give in to the adrenalin. Use it. Channel it. Suppress the desire for action. Kill any panic.

I take a breath and move, grabbing the biker's knife arm from behind, forcing it forward, away from Mary. He swings round and I pull him hard to the side and away from Lorraine and Charlie. Mary falls forward and the officer starts to move.

The biker wrestles his arm free and I follow up with a blow to the back of his head. He staggers away from me and, without the support of the bar, he's too weak to stay upright. His chin bounces off the edge of the bar as he goes down and vanishes out of sight.

Two more officers run in and the older police officer reaches Mary and pulls her away. He gestures to the two new cops. 'Make sure he doesn't get up. He's armed.'

The officers drop to the ground to secure the biker.

My breath is coming in lumps, and somewhere inside my skull the kernel cracks and my brain explodes. I collapse to the ground.

Lorraine is beside me in an instant. 'What's wrong?'

'My head. Jesus my head.'

I see a blur above me and Lorraine vanishes as a body lands on her. The biker? I turn to see Lorraine lying on her back, Mary sitting astride her with an empty beer bottle in her hand. She brings it down with a sickening crunch and I shout out.

She brings the bottle down again.

Then the police pile over the bar and Mary is dragged away. I crawl over to Lorraine. Her hands are wrapped around her face. I try to pull them away but I have all the power of an arthritic kitten. 'Lorraine?'

She doesn't respond.

Charlie drops to the ground next to me. We are wallowing around in a sea of glass and booze. He takes her hand. Even in the half light I can see that her cheek is crushed. Swelling already starting to show.

My head goes supernova and I scream. Then it's gone. The world drops blue. Then light blue. Then we are back to normality.

A hand drops on my shoulder and I turn to see a paramedic.

I pull away and let him in.
    What the hell is going on?

Chapter 10

The hospital is trying its best to be a place of calm but this is a Saturday night and St Vincent Medical Centre is one of the few local hospitals with a 'walk- in' emergency treatment department. We're only a short ambulance ride from the bar and Lorraine has been taken for emergency treatment. I, on the other hand, have had my bandage renewed, been give a couple of full-strength painkillers and dismissed.

I'm sitting in a waiting room with Charlie, reading the plaque that tells me St Vincent's won the 2010 Emergency Medicine Excellence Award, when the doctor walks in. 'Mr McIntyre?'

I nod and he sits next to me. 'Your wife has suffered a blow-out fracture to the orbit. That's the bone that her eye sits in. We may have to put a plate in if the eye starts to sink but at the moment we are going to wait and see.'

'What do you mean by her eye sinking?' I ask.

'It can happen when the orbit is smashed. The eye can sink backwards. It may not but we'll need to keep her in for a few days to be sure.'

'Can I see her?'

'Not tonight. She's out for the count. We had to give her some high-strength pain killers.'

'I'll wait for her to wake up.'

'Up to you but I'd say you'd be better getting a night's sleep and coming back in the morning. She isn't going anywhere. There's also a police officer who wants to see you. Can I send him in?'

'What for?'

He shrugs his shoulders and I nod. He leaves to be replaced by a heavy-set man in a crumpled suit. Two-day growth on his chin sits above a dirty shirt collar. He hands me a business card that has been living in the bottom of a drawer. It reads: Detective Christopher Jones. 'A few questions and I'm gone.'

The accent is Midwestern.

He trails me through the events and scribbles a few things down.

'Who were the bikers?' I ask.

The detective stops writing. 'Out of town. As far as we can tell. Unusual as well. Bikers are not given to nonsense like that. The boy with the knife in is back didn't make it and the others vanished.'

'So it's a murder investigation?' says Charlie. 'Great. That'll bring the clientele flooding in.'

The detective ignores him and keeps his focus on me. 'What gives with the attack on your wife?'

I shrug. 'One minute I'm lying on the floor, head pounding. Next Mary is ramming a bottle of beer into my wife's face.'

'Any idea why?'

'Not a clue. Are you going to arrest her?'

'Already done. She's up for aggravated assault. We'll need statements from your wife, from you and from you.' The last you is aimed at Charlie.

'Now?' I ask.

'Tomorrow morning. Down at the station. We'll come up here for your wife's statement.'

'Can I be here with my wife? We can both give you a statement at the same time.'

'No. I want separate statements. Anyway you're not under suspicion so just be down at the station for ten.' He turns to leave.

'Detective,' I say to his back. 'What did Mary say about the attack?'

He pauses. 'She claims she can't remember anything. Insists it must be a mistake. I left her pleading her innocence.'

As the door closes behind him I sit back in the chair and let out a long breath. 'Charlie this is a mess.'

'You're on the pony there my friend.'

I turn to look at the window. "You go sort out your bar. I'm spending the night with Lorraine.'

'I don't think they'll let you sleep in her room?'

'I'll sleep here then. Now please go.' My words are hard. No argument wanted and the room drops quiet as Charlie leaves.

Creeping through the heavy blinds comes the sound of horns, squealing of tyres, revving engines - all softened by the double glazing. Voices come and go as people walk along the corridor outside. Whispers and low chatter.

I need a coffee. I find a machine a little way down the corridor and order up a black, extra strong. The machine whirs and coughs until a cup drops and fills with scalding hot liquid. I sip at it and my face creases. Not good.

I wonder where Lorraine is and set off to find someone to ask but I've not gone five paces when I hear voices approaching. I recognise them. Buzz 1 and Buzz 2. I look around for an exit. I'm in no mood to meet them. The waiting room is to my left and there is another door to my right. I try the handle and the door is unlocked. Diving in, spilling the coffee on the floor, I close the door and listen as the voices stop. What the hell are they doing here anyway? As if I didn't know. Another murder and I'm on the scene. The room is for storage - small and shelved on three sides. Mostly cleaning products. I slide to the floor and wait.

I need to be straight with myself. This is not normal. None of this. Iraq, the plane, the bar, Mary. It's all...

There is a bang and the door caves in. Buzz 1 and Buzz 2 rip me from the floor.

Chapter 11

I'm out of the hospital and into the back of an unmarked Regal in less than five minutes. No guns. No arm up the back. Simply Buzz 1 saying, 'Come with us or your wife will suffer.'

I'm not stupid so I obey.

We wheel north on I 10. Dodger Stadium appears and a few minutes later we exit the highway. A sign for the Ernest E. Debs Regional Park flicks by and we run through the gates and into wilderness.

I've been up here a few times with Lorraine. There's not much to it. Mostly trees, scrub and lakes but it's a nice place to chill and pop a picnic. The car starts to bump along a dirt track and we turn onto a smaller track that leads into a wood.

At this time of night this would be a good place to beat up on someone and dump them.

The headlights pick out branches and bushes. The driver takes the speed down to a crawl. Another turn and we're off the road. The car stops and the engine dies.

'Out,' says Buzz 1.

'What?'

The punch is low. In the gut.

'I didn't say talk. I said out.'

I get out.

'In front. Walk.'

A torch flicks on and picks out a worn footpath. It rises into the trees ahead before bending out of sight. I walk with the two Buzzes behind me. I hear the Regal engine fire up before it reverses back onto the track and away. Buzz 1 gives me a push in the back. 'Keep walking.'

The path meanders but, even in the light of the torch, it is clear that it's well used. I need to lean forward as the hill kicks in, and my stomach is still growling at the punch. A set of wood and earth steps appear. Buzz 1 gives me another push. 'Up.'

I start climbing. I count to fifty before the steps stop and we reach a small clearing. A breeze block building squats in the corner. It has the hallmark signature of the power company. It doesn't explain why the path is so well defined.

'Stop.' Buzz 1 walks forward and I wait for a punch or a kick but he keeps going. He reaches the metal door and I notice the little grey box to the side. I've seen one of those before. He flicks his hand at it and there is a whirr and a click. The door snaps open. No light from inside. Just a dark inkwell.

Buzz 2 gives me a push. 'Inside.'

I hesitate. I don't think they're planning to kill me. Not yet. But they're not preparing my birthday party either. A hand shoves me in.

The inside of the building doesn't hold much promise. Damp, cold and with dripping water. I'm pushed into the cramped space and the three of us stand shoulder to shoulder as Buzz 2 pulls the door closed.

Dark. Complete dark. The rods in my eyes fire at random and my own personal firework display rages and dissipates.

Buzz 1 is to my left. Buzz 2 to my right. Buzz 1 has stale breath. Smoker's breath. Buzz 2 is the Aquafresh kid. I can hear them breathing. The floor jerks and I can't help but let out a small shout. I hear Buzz 1 laugh. I'm glad somebody's finding this funny. The floor jerks again and I have the sensation of movement. Down. Another jerk and we stop. The wall in front parts to reveal itself as a pair of elevator doors.

A dim red light shines in and the interior of the elevator is a cleverly crafted illusion. Walls in fake stone, floor in fake concrete and a small speaker somewhere adding to the effect with a dripping sound. No doubt the damp smell is artificially generated as well.

We step into the space beyond and the doors slide shut

behind us. Another gray box and we are into a very different world.

A long corridor stretches out before us. It's as wide as an athletics track and as long. On either side the walls are lined with doors. Each with a number and a letter stenciled into the wood. The carpet is functional but not low quality. The ceiling is a suspended, and hidden lighting gives illumination to the vista. Every wall is plain vanilla and there is the gentle hum of air-conditioning. There's something vaguely nineteen-eighties about the place. As if the interior designer had reached back to the age of no lunches and power suits and brought forward an environment to suit.

I'm encouraged to walk down the wide passageway. None of the doors are open and, if there are people beyond them, the doors are either sound proof or - and this would make sense – empty, unless there's a night shift.

The corridor ends in a T-junction. We go right and hit another junction. We take a left. All the way down, the walls are spaced with stenciled doors. I wonder how the hell you keep something like this secret. If all these rooms hold even two people each that is a lot of traffic for a tiny elevator – not to mention the number of cars that would need to access the place via the wood.

We stop at a set of double doors. Buzz 1 steps forward and pushes them open. A corporate conference room lies beyond. A large polished steel table hosts twenty leather-backed chairs. The walls are bare and the carpet is a continuation of the one in the corridor. I'm pushed into a seat as the two Buzzes sit down opposite me.

Time breathes.

A small clock sitting on the desk ticks. Buzz 1 fires up his cell. Buzz 2 cracks his knuckles.

We sit.

I lean back. Close my eyes. Wait.

The doors swing open and small bald man wearing a white lab coat comes in. He ignores me and makes for the far end of the table. He fiddles around with something underneath and an electric motor kicks in. A large flat-screen TV rises from the table. He waits until it stops rising and swivels it slightly to face me. Flicking the switch on the front snow appears, the grey and white dancing dots lighting up the room.

Sitting on top of the TV is a camera. He plays around with it for a minute and then leaves.

We all sit in the static disco.

'Mr McIntrye. How disappointing to see you so soon. Guys, can you see me?' White Linen appears on the TV. The picture is grainy and flickers a little.

'Yes,' says Buzz 1.

'Good. Can you get Mr McIntyre a coffee.'

The video link is not brilliant. White Linen's lips are out of synch with the image and it has the making of a badly-dubbed movie. I try and dig his name out. A tennis player. It's the same as an old tennis player. Lendl. As in Ivan. 'Mr Lendl what am I doing here?'

'Coffee first.'

Buzz is mucking around with a hidden cupboard. With a hiss and a spit coffee starts to brew. A phone rings and Lendl reaches forward and he is gone. A few seconds later he's back. 'Things are a bit wild over here.'

Coffee arrives and I ignore it.

'Mr McIntyre I promise we haven't put anything in the coffee. So old school.'

He wants me to ask what he means by the old school. I don't.

'I hear your wife will be OK. Maybe a little less the beauty but OK all the same.'

I don't rise to the bait.

'So what do we do with you Mr McIntyre?'

'You could let me go.'

'I don't think so. Not yet. Not before we have a little chat'

I decide the coffee is a good idea after all. I sip at it. Top-notch stuff. I take a larger slug. Buzz 1 and Buzz 2 watch me. I wonder if I should offer them popcorn and a large Coke.

The phone goes off. Another blank screen. Then he's back. 'Sorry.'

'Not as much as I am,' I say. 'Why the cloak and dagger nonsense? Where the hell am I and who are you?'

Lendl pushes back in his chair. 'Let's discuss you, Mr McIntyre. I read the London and LA police reports with interest.'

'Already?'

'But a little backtracking first – indulge me. In Iraq we lose Tom and his friend and you're there. On the plane a stewardess takes out her frustration on her boss and again you're there. A biker dies and your wife's best friend tries to rearrange her face – and there you are again. All in a couple of days.'

'So I've had a crap time lately.'

'Nineteen eighty-three, Ramdi, two men hack each other up and the only witness is you?'

'And?'

'Coincidence?'

'Look at your notes Mr Lendl. I was out of the army on the back of that last incident. I didn't spend nearly five years in the happy farm for fun. I was heading for a breakdown weeks before Clegg and Johnston chose to remove each other's limbs. They found me in the corner of the room sitting in my own pee.'

'You seem to attract trouble. Or maybe there's more. Maybe you cause it.'

'Crap.'

Lendl leans forward. 'Mr McIntyre, in my job I don't talk crap. I may deal in it but I don't talk it.'

I wonder who the hell could get the report from the London police and the LA police so quickly. 'So I was in the wrong place at the wrong time. Sue me. Give me a break. I've lost my job, seen my wife beaten up, been kidnapped and you think it was down to me?'

'I said it could be. I think we'll take this a little further.'

With that the screen returns to snow. Buzz 1 stands up. The door opens and two more suits walk in. Plastic cuffs are dangling from one of the suit's hands. I move to back away but Buzz 2 is behind me. He takes my arm and pushes it up my back. I don't bother to resist. I just want this over.

Cuffs cutting my wrists, I'm frog-marched down the corridor to one of the nondescript doors. With a shove I'm catapulted into the room. I fall to the floor and the door slams shut. I sit up. There's a single chair, bolted to the center of the room and a mattress on the floor.

'Lie down Mr McIntyre. We'll talk in the morning.' Lendl's voice is a disembodied sound with an echo built in. It must be coming from speakers hidden in the walls. The lights go off and I shout out. Then I crawl to the mattress and curl up. I want out. I want my wife. I want food. I want a drink. I want a pee. I want...

Chapter 12

'Wakey, wakey.'

I'm back. Sluggish but back. Whatever they injected me with has drained my mouth of liquid.

'Nothing,' says the skeleton.

I'm still strapped to the bed. Unable to move. The mouth gag hard across my lips.

'Scenario two. Let's inform him on the subjects.' Lendl's voice.

I try to get my head round what is going on.

'Mr McIntyre,' he continues. 'We have two male subjects next door. Both are in their forties. We have David and we have Martin. They don't know each other and are homeless. Bums. David used to be a career banker and Martin has been an alcoholic since college. They live rough. David on Sunset Boulevard and Martin near Santa Monica pier. David is five-ten, gray hair and used to be married to a doctor called Sanya. Martin has never been married and we suspect he might be gay. He's six feet tall with black hair.'

The tall man talks as he injects me again.

* * *

'Nothing.' Lendl sounds disappointed as I waken again. 'Scenario three. Stress. The last two incidents on the plane and in the bar were stressful. We'll try stress.'

Hands grab the waistband of my pants and they're yanked down. My boxers are whipped south and my cock is grabbed. I struggle against the restraints but they're solid. My heart is racing as something cold is placed around the end of my penis.

'Low level stimulus,' is the last thing I hear the skeleton say before I'm hit with an electric shock. I bite down hard. The pain is a living hot wire. I arch my back. I want to scream. I think I'm going to vomit. Gag to death. The pain subsides and I piss myself.

'Heart rate up to one forty. Signs are high but no reaction from the two test subjects.'

'Hit him again.'

Jesus no.

This time I bite so hard blood floods my mouth.

'Heart rate one sixty.' The skeleton sounds like this is something he does every day. 'Signs are very high but no reaction from the two test subjects.'

Lendl clears his throat. An ugly sound through the speakers. 'OK. Let's take it up a little.'

I wait for the next shock but it isn't electric.

'Craig?' The voice is soft. Lorraine's voice. In my ear. 'Craig?' Her voice is distant. A cell phone is pushed to my ear. 'Craig?'

'Mr McIntyre we have lifted your wife from the hospital. She's in this complex. You're being unco-operative and we need you to work with us. We have wired her up to the mains. I'm going to have to give her the bad news.'

I want to shout. To scream. To tell them I don't know what it is they want. Please don't hurt Lorraine. Please. Take this fucking thing from my mouth and let me tell them. What the hell can I tell them gagged?

'Heart rate one seventy. Signs are still very high but no reaction from test subjects.'

'Hit her.'

The howl from the phone is terrible. Lorraine. God what are they doing. Lorraine!

'Heart rate one eighty. Signs are maxing out. Still no reaction.'

'One more time.'

I throw everything I have into getting free but my muscles collapse at the sound of Lorraine screaming again.

'Heart rate still one eighty. Signs still maxed out. Still no reaction from test subjects.'

'Shit. Wheel him next door.'

Buzz 1 and Buzz 2 grab the dolly and the ceiling moves as I'm transferred to the room I spent the night in. None of the restraints are loosened.

This needs to stop. What do they want? Why do that to Lorraine? She could die. She can't take it. Not in her state. What do they want? What in the hell do they want?

The pain around my groin is deep and feels serious. There is the smell of burning flesh. A smell you don't forget once you have been exposed to it. I wasn't in Iraq long the first time round but you didn't need to be around that smell too often to pick up the scent.

I have to take control of this. I need to figure what it is they want.

'How are you feeling Mr McIntyre?'

I want to rip the speakers from their roots and ram them down his throat.

Click, footsteps, fumbling and my head restraint is removed. 'You fucking bastard. When I get out of here I'll kill you. I swear to fuck on everything that I can fucking think off. I WILL kill you.'

Silence.

'Do you hear me?' I shout. 'I'll rip your heart out through the end of your dick. Do you understand?'

Silence.

'Are you there?'

'Are you finished?'

'No. What do you want? Just tell me what you want?'

'I will.'

'What?'

'Nothing.'

'Fuck off.'

'True. Nothing. I'm not sure there's anything we want. I may have been wrong about you.'

'About what?'

I'm straining at the leather. Still trying to tear them from their mounts.

'About you.'

I quit the struggle. 'Please just speak plain English.'

'I am Mr McIntyre. I thought you could be of some use to us. I thought you might have some ability that could have proved a useful aid to our agency but I'm probably wrong. It would seem that you are just one unlucky son-of-a-bitch.'

'Then let Lorraine go.'

'Lorraine? Mr McIntyre we don't have Lorraine. She's still in St Vincent's.'

'Then that wasn't Lorraine on the phone?'

The relief is unbelievable. I'm almost pleased. These people have just wired my privates to the power company and I'm almost pleased.

'Yes it was,' says Lendl.

My heart skips.

'We just recorded it all in the hospital.'

'Fuck you.'

The background hiss that accompanies his voice falls away and I'm back on my own. I lie churning events over in my mind. What do they want? Or do I know what they want?

Do I?

Iraq in 2003, Iraq a few days ago, the plane and the bar. Violence and me in the background – or is it me in the foreground? Five dead, two badly injured and I was there. Coincidence? It has to be. I knew the first four casualties but I was asleep when it all went down. I didn't know the aircrew and the biker was a stranger. OK I know Mary. Know some – don't know others. Would it have all happened if I had been elsewhere? Probably. Tom and the prostitute. He was beating up on her in the club. She was out for revenge. The plane? Clearly the aircrew had some history. You don't try and rip someone's face off without good reason.

The biker? I don't get that one. I wasn't even in the building when he was stabbed. Mary? Well she has history with Lorraine and the sort that was getting worse.

Clegg and Johnston in Ramdi? They had bad history. Everyone knew that. Clegg had been back to the US on leave and decided that Johnston's girlfriend was a better bet than his own wife. All because Johnston had shown Clegg some fairly explicit picture of his new girlfriend. It had been a mistake. Clegg was a nasty person at best. Rape or consensual – it didn't matter. What mattered was that he happily told Johnston all about it on his return. Oh they had history all right.

But I didn't know them. It was my first patrol with them and I only found out the back story after they killed each other.

So where does that leave me?

Nowhere. None of this makes sense.

Buzz 1 and 2 return.

They circle me a few times and slip my bonds. I sit up and take stock. My groin is on fire but I'm not looking at it while Dumb and Dumber are at home. I get off the dolly and drop to the bed. Buzz 1 and 2 move and stand either side of the door. They are going nowhere.

I curl up, facing away from them and check for damage. My foreskin is burnt and it hurts like a bitch. I cover myself up and roll over. Buzz 1 and Buzz 2 are staring at me. I stand up and they tense. I sit and they ease off. I could probably take one of them. Maybe even both if I get lucky but then what? 'Any

chance of a drink?'
 I might as well be talking to the wall.

Chapter 13

There's a vibrating sound and Buzz 1 stares at his cell phone. He nods to Buzz 2 and they leave. I get up and try the door. Surprise, surprise – locked. I walk round the room. Four walls a door and all solid. I'm sure there'll be a camera to back up the speakers. I walk back to the door and slam my fist on the metal.

I feel something go in my head. The breaking of the kernel. A flash of light. I want out and I want out now.

I drop to my knees as my head rips open. Hell's teeth.

Crack.

I slam my head into the wall. Somebody is cutting into my skull with a hacksaw. Head to the floor. Head to the wall. Scream. Scream.

The door burst opens and the Buzzes barrel in.

Scream. Scream.

'Tie him down again.' Lendl's voice echoes around the room.

Buzz 1 reaches down to grab me and stops, surprise written into his face as Buzz 2's arm appears around his neck launches him backwards. Buzz 2 takes Buzz 1's weight on his chest and throws him into the air. As Buzz 1 smacks back to earth Buzz 2 is on him. Fists pounding at face and chest. Buzz 1 does a poor job of defending himself and Buzz 2 goes into overdrive.

Then the world drops blue.

Headache gone I stand up and walk towards the open door.

'Stop him' shouts Lendl.

The Buzz twins have no interest in me. Buzz 2 is head-butting his colleague.

The blue is pulsing again. Slow and sure. Serene. Calm. An alarm begins to howl. But in the blue world it's a far away thing. I turn into the corridor and try to remember the way to the elevator. A door next to me opens and three men exit. No jackets and no ties but still the same white shirts and black pants. They size me up and one of them smiles. One of his front teeth is gold. He steps in front of me and pulls his arm back to throw a punch. Slow motion kicks in and then vanishes. Kicks in and disappears again. A strobe effect that throws him forward in fits and starts.

His smile widens as he winds up for a punch. The gold tooth is obscured as a colleague rushes him and takes him in a football tackle around the waist. The couple bounce off the corridor wall and go down. The third man looks on, bemused. He scratches at a dark mole that dominates his face. I keep walking. Another door opens and two more men fly out. They take in the fighting on the floor and look at each other. One is a redhead. His colleague is six feet six with broad shoulders.

'Get him! Lendl's voice screams from hidden speakers.

The ginger drops his shoulder to charge me but his friend sticks out a foot and trips him up. I watch him go down and sidestep his outstretched hand. His friend uses his height to great effect and drops on the redhead, driving his knee into the small of his colleague's back.

I keep walking.

Two more doors open and bodies tumble out. A man's head swivels in my direction with the handle of a letter opener where an eye should be. A woman with short blonde hair is locked to his ear – trying to bite it off.

There's a howl from behind me and, in the stop/start world of blue, I turn. One of the suits – the man with the mole - is hammering towards me.

The speaker bursts into life again. 'Someone get him and get him *right fucking now!*'

The man with the mole has his eyes fixed on me. He has a couple of yards before I'm going to act as his personal airbag.

'Jim!'

The man with the mole flick his eyes towards the sound. A young woman has just emerged from a door to my left. She's holding something in her hand and with the wind-up of a major league player she heaves it at mole man. We hit slow motion and I can pick out the shape of the missile. A paperweight, swirling patterns in glass, tumbling in the air. The paperweight catches the man high on the forehead. He stumbles, hands flying to his head. I step to my right, he crashes past me, lands on the man with the letter opener for an eye and I hop over the two bodies.

The speakers burst into life again. 'What the hell is going on? Stop him. Stop him right fucking now.'

I turn into the next corridor. Maybe thirty people are crammed into the space in front of me. They are fighting. A mass brawl. No one has any interest in me. I try to walk through the chaos. Two men, one squat and fat, the other thin as sin, catch me on the arm as they fight. The thin man is driving an industrial staple gun into the fat man's gut, pumping the trigger in wild excitement.

I keep going and a woman stands up in front of me. She is a looker. Long dark hair. Deep purple lipstick. I try to sidestep her. Blood spurts from her mouth, spraying my face. She falls forward and reveals a man standing behind her holding a smashed and bloodied laptop.

The alarm continues to blare and Lendl's voice is lost in the chaos around me. I dodge the bodies and reach the next corridor. There are only two men ahead. One has his head buried in the other's lap. He is shaking his head like a dog drying itself. Blood spraying in the air around him. He lifts his head clear, revealing flabby cheeks and a double chin. I don't need to know what he has in his mouth.

I keep on moving and reach the closed doors of the elevator. I look at the gray box and wave my hand in front of it but nothing is going to happen soon. Behind me the castrated man is gurgling, hugging his legs, blood pouring onto the carpet. The double chinned man is running away.

I breathe in a lungful and grab the castrated man by the shoulders, hauling him to the door. He leaves a trail like a snail.

A howl and Buzz 2 rounds the corner. 'McIntyre.'

I pull the castrated man another foot and lift his hand to the grey box. Buzz 2 closes in. I look at the doors that line the corridor. Why the hell doesn't one open?

A click from behind and the elevator doors start to part. I drop the castrated man's hand. He looks up at me. Silently pleading for help. I shake my head as the man goes back to hugging his groin and I jump into the elevator.

Buzz 2 is closing fast.

There are three buttons on the elevator wall. None has markings. One for this level, one for the top and one for emergency? Maybe. I hit the top one and the door starts to close. Buzz's hand reaches into the gap and the doors stop and begin to open again. I charge at him, shoulder first and we fly out of the elevator. I grab the edge of the elevator door to stop me arriving back into the corridor. Buzz 2 trips over the castrated man and I scrabble back into the elevator and hit the button again. Buzz 2 tries to get up but the castrated man grabs his wrist. 'Help me.'

The doors close and the elevator heads up.

The smell of damp and the sound of dripping take over and I lie against the wall. The blue world provides all the light I need. Instant night vision. I spot a small camera in the corner.

'Mr McIntyre. Stay where you are.' Lendl's voice springs from the hidden speakers.

'Fuck off Lendl.'

The elevator stops and I press myself against the side as the door opens. Morning air rushes in but it is unaccompanied. No one standing outside waiting for me. I sprint out into the sunlight. My eyes blinking.

I start to jog down the trail. If my captors are going to be anywhere they'll be on the road at the end of the path. I change direction and push into the bushes on my right, fighting my way through the foliage. The blue is fading. Still there but thinner. Less obvious.

I pop out of the undergrowth to find myself standing at the top of a small rise. Dodgers Stadium and the freeway are maybe a half mile away. Beneath me is scrub and more bushes. I start down the small hill, keeping my eyes open for the suits.

A couple are out walking their dog. They see me and turn round and head in the opposite direction.

I've been up here a couple of times with Lorraine, visiting a sick friend in a nursing home that sits on the edge of the park. I know if I can reach the perimeter I can try and lose myself among the buildings that surround the far end of the park.

I hear a roar of an engine and spin round. A motorbike is bearing down on me. I start to run but the bike changes direction and cuts me off. The rider pulls it to a halt and sits revving the engine. He's wearing a black, full-face helmet but his T-shirt doesn't look like something the suits would wear.

The biker pulls his helmet off. Long blonde hair falls to his shoulders. 'Hey man. What ya running for? You wouldn't have a stick would you?'

He can't be more than eighteen-years-old and the bike he's sitting on is a battered trail model of some vintage.

'A stick?' I say.

'Cigarette, man.'

A second engine growls in the distance and a black SUV bounces into view.

'A cigarette for a shot of your bike?' I say.

'Eh.'

'You heard.'

'Not sure, man.'

'I've eighteen left in a packet. You can have them all for a go on your bike.'

'Nah. I just want one. Don't need that many.'

I move forward. The SUV is putting on speed.

'OK. Here.' I reach into my jacket and he involuntarily leans forward in the seat. I pull my hand from my jacket and reach out to offer him a cigarette I don't have. As he puts his hand out I grab it and yank him towards me.

'Hey.'

He falls and the bike throws him clear. His helmet lands at my feet. I snatch it up and ram it on my head. It's a snug fit but it goes on. The young man is trying to get up and the SUV is bearing down on me. I turn and kick the biker in the guts and he folds up. I take the bike handlebars and heave. The bike is no lightweight. I don't recognise the logo. Probably an old communist bloc make.

Some dirt explodes in a puff next to the front wheel of the bike. It takes me way too long to realise that I'm being shot at. I double the effort and pull the bike upright. I get on.

I haven't been on a bike since college. I pull in the clutch and feed the gears back to neutral. I find the kick-start and slam my foot on it. The engine coughs but doesn't burst into life. A bullet pings off the rear mudguard. The SUV slews to a halt with a suit leaning out of the passenger window, levelling his gun for a body shot. It's Buzz 1. His face is swollen. Blood cakes his face. The young man is trying to get up and I plunge my foot down once more on the kick start and the engine explodes into life. I flick up into first and let out the clutch, slowly, listening for the note drop – willing myself not to stall it.

The engine bites and the bike starts to move. The door of the SUV opens and Buzz 2 rolls out. He steadies his gun and a spurt of air just above my hand tells me that Buzz 2 isn't trying to warn me. He's trying to kill me.

Dirt spits up from behind me as the bike shoots forward. I haven't the skill to wheel the machine away from the SUV the way I've seen dirt bikers handle their machines. Instead I gun it and head straight for Buzz 2. He dives out of the way and I'm gone.

I point the bike down a worn track and wind up the throttle. The roar of the engine drowns any other sound. The situation demands speed.

I reach a bend in the track and flick my head round to see if the suits are following me. The SUV is much closer than I would have thought possible. I cut off the track and head in what I hope is the direction of the exit.

I crest a small ridge and spot the entrance we came in last night, about a quarter of a mile away. Next to it, nestled on a small hillock, is a red brick building. It's called Broadview, the Christian Science Nursing home that Lorraine's friend was in.

Another SUV slides into view and blocks the exit gate. I swing left and aim for the nursing home.

Once the second car is sure I'm not going to double back it sets off after me.

I reach the grounds of the nursing home and feed the bike onto a well tended path that leads to the gardens beyond. I slow down as I roll along the path. Passing a pond and a flagpole I have to swerve to avoid ploughing into a man pushing a wheelchair. I keep vertical and spin the throttle to maintain speed. The man's mouth is moving and I'm not sure they are very Christian Science words.

The place is a maze of paths. Designed to help you to lose yourself. I'm doing a fine job of that. The main building finally appears through a gap in the trees and I aim for it, cutting over newly-mown lawn and leaving deep tracks. A group of people stand chatting on the edge of the lawn and their heads all turn to me as I fly by.

I catch sight of a car moving beyond the building on what has to be the main road. I spray gravel as I round the building and drive into a blacktop parking lot. Squirting through a pair of six feet-high gates, past the gatehouse I wheel to my left. Low-rise detached houses start to flick by and I slow down to turn my head. No sign of the SUVs.

The freeway is to my right but I would be too easy to spot if they caught up with me. I'm conscious of my speed and the last thing I want is the police stopping me.

I hit a junction with an ATM at the corner. I need cash but not here. The road falls away in front of me and I try to balance legal and illegal on the speedometer.

I take lefts and rights at random. I don't know this area in any depth and the last thing I need is to be caught in a dead end, but I have to give myself some breathing space. Some thinking space.

I pass under the freeway and skirt the Dodgers stadium. A strip mall appears. It has a parking lot hidden from the road. Ideal. I park the bike next to a pick up - checking it can't be easily seen. I walk to the front of the shops and enter a mom and pop diner.

The restaurant is empty. Gingham cloths decorate the tables and I think of Lorraine and her gingham dress. The waitress wobbles up to me and I order a coffee and slice of apple pie. I need the caffeine and I need the sugar. More than that I need Lorraine. I have to see her. She could be dead. The payphone is in use. A slim woman is in full gab mode. I stare at her. Willing her to put the receiver down but she's in full flow. I wait.

For the first time since I entered the elevator I let my mind look at the carnage that unfolded as I escaped. The blinding headache, the blue world, the violence. I'm beginning to get a sense of what Lendl is after. In some way I was responsible for the spontaneous brutality. Iraq, Iraq again, the plane, the bar, the agency hideout. Me as the common link. What am I? A victim of circumstance? A catalyst for destruction? A freak? Or is there something else? Who would believe this stuff?

Lorraine would wrap some perspective around it all. I can't take it in. There has to be a simpler explanation. If I was some kind of freak I would have suspected something long before now. These things – whatever these things are – don't just creep up on you – or do they?

The thought continues to scuttle to the front of my frazzled brain. What if I really am the cause of all this? Look what it did to people. Look what it did to Lorraine. Hell, it could happen again. How would I know? I could be my wife's executioner in waiting. Sitting in the wings. Never knowing when I'm going to bring harm down on her.

Stupid. Just stupid. It makes no sense - but it does – just a little. Just enough to make me think twice about visiting her. Just enough to think about never seeing her again. God no! Not an option.

The waitress asks if I want more coffee and I nod.

Never seeing Lorraine. The words are painful. I can't accept them. I'm making more out of this than there is. I need to calm down.

First things first. Lorraine. The talker on the payphone has finished. I root around to make change and the waitress gives me a directory from beneath the counter. I flick through it to find the medical centre.

'St Vincent's. How can I help?' The voice is bright and cheery

'I'm trying to find out how Mrs Lorraine McIntrye is doing. I'm her husband. She was brought in last night.'

'Please hold sir.'

Light music fills the earpiece. The door to the diner swings open and two guys in jeans and T-shirts enter. They sit at the counter and the waitress pours coffee. Time ticks by. The music keeps pumping and ten minutes later I'm still on hold.

I tap the phone against the wall. Lorraine tells me I do this all the time with the cell phone – as if it will speed up the person on the other end.

The Bontempi organ player on the phone decides to give the Bee Gees' 'More Than a Woman' a hammering. Food arrives for the two guys. I see a black Buick Regal slipping into a space in the strip mall parking lot. No one emerges from it and then a second black Regal stops in the middle of parking lot.

A third Regal edges into view.

For Regals read SUVs.

Suit cars.

Shit.

I slam the phone down as the doors to all three cars open and suits pour out. Buzz 1 is leading from the front. I leap the counter. The waitress shouts and I push through the swing doors to the kitchen.

'They'll be out the back.' The thought skids across my brain.

'Is there any way out of here other than through the back door?' I say to the chef.

He looks to the front door as it flies open. At the same time the door behind him bounces off the wall and a pincer of black suits is on. Buzz 1 shouts for me to stand still. The chef lifts his finger and points to a cupboard door next to me. 'In there and through the window.'

I open the door and, once inside, slam it shut. The cupboard is a storeroom racked with shelving units. I grab the nearest one and pull. It comes away from the wall in a waterfall of tins and jars, crashing to the floor in front of the door. Someone reaches the door and tries to open it but the unit stops it travelling more than a few inches.

A fly-screened window sits about four feet off the ground at the back of the cupboard. A chest freezer sits below it. I jump on to it and push open the window. I stick my head out, expecting to see suits. The window opens onto the side of the mall with the parking lot on one side and the back of the mall on the other.

There are no suits.

I scramble through the gap and land on grass. I sprint into the bushes in front of me. Just as a suit rounds the corner. A shout goes up and I'm spotted. Emerging from the bushes I put my head down and run.

The street ahead is bordered with single-storey detached homes. Mid- market abodes with two and three-year-old cars peppered along the sidewalk. I jink to my right and up the first driveway and into the backyard. An old lady is sitting sipping a glass of something. I throw her a smile and leap the fence into the next garden. A sun-tanned old man with a deeply wrinkled face and a faded Dodgers sweat is tending a patch of dirt and I give him the same smile. I cut right and jump over a back fence into the alley beyond.

I'm faced with the rear of what looks like a small church and skirt round it and onto the next street. I have no plan. I just need to keep running.

A Regal screams into the road ahead and I leap into the garden directly across from the church and enter another backyard. This one is empty. I begin to hurdle up through the next four gardens. At the fifth fence I place my hand on a post for support and launch myself into the air. I come down on a woman lying on a sunbed. She screams and we both roll onto her lawn. I push to get up. She's wearing a bikini. My hand slips on the grass and I grab at her to stop me falling back to earth. I get a handful of breast and she yelps.

'What the fuck?' The man of the house emerges from the back door. He's wearing boxers and nothing else. I ignore him and head for the rear of the garden and into a back alley.

I can't keep this up for long. I'm not as fit as I need to be. I jump into another garden where a young boy in shorts and a striped shirt is washing a car. A Toyota Hilux. The driver's door is open and the boy is on the other side waxing the bonnet. I jog up to the open door and look in. A set of keys dangle from the ignition. I jump in. Slam the door. Turn the key. Select drive and plant my foot.

The pick-up jumps forward and I have to stand on the brakes to make the turn into the road. In the rear view mirror the boy is standing – jaw hanging open. I hurtle down the road and hang a left. A sign for the I10 takes me onto the freeway. I stay on for a couple of junctions, slip off and start to weave my way across town.

I have one destination in mind. The hospital.

Chapter 14

St Vincent's sits across from me. I've parked up the Hilux opposite the main entrance and I've already clocked four suits. Another Regal rolls up and I start the engine and cruise away. Circling to the back of the building brings another Regal into view.

I drive round once more and an SUV has joined the party. Buzz 1 gets out and I drive away. My focus is on Lorraine but getting myself caught won't help.

I head for Charlie's place.

* * *

The pub has boards across the main window. I see Charlie through the glass front door and I keep back into the shade of the bushes that guard the library. I've been watching for an hour and if there are suits around they are well hidden.

It sums up my life that the only person I can turn to is Charlie – a man who sells oblivion to people. Friends are thin on the ground. They peeled away as my time in the hospital stretched. The odd visit was the best I had.

Charlie is tidying up, but amazingly – despite the devastation - he's still open and couple of regulars seem to be earning beers by helping out.

I wait until the late afternoon light is gone and circle round to the back alley. There's no one here. Good news.

I push open the back door and slip in. There is noise from the bar but, before I enter, I check out both washrooms and Charlie's office. All are empty.

I stick my head into the bar and check the booths. There's a man in one but he is all T-shirt and jeans. Two more customers are sitting at the bar enjoying the reward for helping with the clean-up. Apart from the boarded window Charlie has done a remarkable job on the place. There are fewer tables and chairs than there used to be and the front of the bar has a crack in the woodwork running half the length, but the gantry behind is clean and tidy, the floor is swept and even the jukebox seems to be working – 'Chirpy Chirpy Cheep Cheep' by Middle of the Road.

Charlie spots me. 'Craig?'

I wave for him to come over. The three customers look up and dismiss me. Charlie walks over and I point to his office. He nods and we vanish into the cubbyhole.

'What the heck is going on?' he says, dropping into a battered leather office chair.

'I'd like to know the answer to that question too. Has anyone been asking about me?'

'Two men in suits have been in. Three times so far. Each time I tell them the same thing. I haven't seen you since last night. Each time they say they'll be back. Who are they?'

'I don't know. Not police that's for sure. Some agency.'

'FBI?'

'No. Not CIA either. Something else.'

'What do they want with you? Is it to do with Iraq?'

'Partly. I'm struggling to make sense of it all.'

A voice shouts from the bar and Charlie tells me he'll be back in a second. I look up at the battered picture that hangs above Charlie's desk. Stripped to a pair of leather briefs Charlie is in full-pose mode. All oiled up and flexing muscles. A certificate underneath announces his first place in a competition held in San Diego.

Charlie returns with a grimace on his face. 'Craig McIntyre, you're an expensive son-of-a-bitch. I had to double up the rounds for free or we wouldn't get five minutes to talk.'

'Shit happens.'

'So what gives?'

I'm not sure what to say to Charlie. I could do with another brain on this one and Charlie is smart. Far smarter than he makes out. Lorraine is also convinced he has a share in a few other places. She overheard him talk about a place in Florida one night and I asked him about it but he just laughed.

I need to make a call. I flip a coin in my head. It comes down heads. 'How much do you want to know?'

'All of it. I'm a barman remember – gossip is my trade – or rather keeping gossip quiet is my trade.'

'I'm being serious. Whoever these guys are this is not a kid's game. They've tortured me and Lorraine already.'

This brings a silence.

'Lorraine. When?'

'Thanks for the concern for me.'

'"I can see you're ok, but isn't Lorraine in hospital?'

'Yes, and they pushed a few hundred volts through her while she lay in her sick bed.'

'Fuck.'

'So you see I'm not kidding and I sure could do with some help.'

'Hang on.'

He's gone for five minutes and I'm left with the Charles Atlas picture for company. I lean back in the chair and can't get Lorraine out of my head. I'm just considering whether I should return to the hospital and leave the chat with Charlie until later when he returns. 'I just closed up. My regulars aren't too happy but I promised them a free night on the beer and they saw sense.'

The lights are out in the bar and Charlie pulls the office door shut. He reaches out to the small wire-meshed window that faces onto the alley and yanks a thick strip of material across the glass. 'That'll make the place look empty but if someone is listening in the alley they'll still hear us.'

He's whispering and I can't tell if he is doing it for effect or if he really believes we're in some danger.

'OK', Craig. Shoot.'

I give him what I know. Even the bits I missed out for Lorraine. Charlie asks the odd question and when we get to my escape from the park he whistles.

'Either you have the best imagination since Raymond Chandler or we're in a whole new land of hurt. Do you want a drink?'

The question catches me by surprise.

I think about it for an eighth of a second. 'Yes.'

'So do I.'

That does surprise me. Charlie is all but teetotal with the exception of his birthday and the odd celebration – like the time he won fifty thousand on the lottery. Once more he vanishes and returns with a large bottle of Coke, a bottle of Jack Daniels and a bucket of ice.

He pours two drinks. Mine's a triple and his a single. I polish off half of mine in one go.

'So?' He looks me and scratches at the side of his head. 'Three choices. Either all of this 'stuff' that went down is just coincidence. Or, someone is out to mix you up in something that makes no sense at the moment. Or...'

'Or?' I ask.

'Or you have something about you that has its rightful place in the Twilight Zone.'

'And where would your money lie?'

'The first two if I was being realistic. The latter if I was a betting man.'

'You think I'm responsible for all this?'

'I should say no, but look at it. Unless you've just made it all up or got the facts wrong it sure sounds like it.'

'How could I be?'

'Oh don't be so stupid. Listen to what you've just told me. Look at what has happened. Violence, headaches, a 'blue world', secret agency, miracle escapes.'

'I could be delusional.'

'True but that wouldn't explain the bikers last night or Mary sticking a bottle in your wife's eye or the two suits that keep asking after you.'

'Do you think that's what the experiments were about?'

'Run through what they did and said again.'

I sip at the JD. 'They tied me down and told me there were two subjects on the other side of the screen. Then they mentioned that I had been asleep or out for the count when Clegg and Johnston and Tom and his girl had been killed. When I woke up they talked about me being stressed. That's when they wired me up and ran the mains through me. Then they talked about me knowing the subjects, ran a spiel on the two down-and-outs, did a Frankenstein and then the same to Lorraine. After that they called it quits.'

'Sounds like they were trying to trigger whatever it is they think you do.'

'You figure?'

'Don't you?'

I take another slug and finish the glass. The JD is getting to work nicely but I don't want it to take over. It would be too easy to take that path. 'No it doesn't make sense but it's one explanation.'

Charlie leaves his drink untouched. 'Did anything ever happen like this outside of the last few days and the two soldiers back in '03?'

Another slug and I root around in my head for a minute. 'Not as such but...'

'But what?'

'Have you ever felt that there was something else going on around you that you didn't know about? That things weren't all they seemed?'

'All the time. When people are drunk they tell you all sorts of weird crap and sometimes, just sometimes, it rings a bell.'

'Well every so often I've been in places where I feel the world is operating without me. I'm there but I'm not.'

'Lost you.'

I decide a refill won't do any harm and pour a small one. 'I was witness to a car crash a year after I left the army. I was on day release and an RV broadsided a battered old Camero. The RV shot a red. The Camero had no chance. I went over to help but the passenger and driver in the Camero were at each other's throats as were the two in the RV. Neither were in the slightest interested in the crash. I tried to intervene but it was as if I wasn't there. Every so often stuff like that happens but nothing like the last few days.'

'Have you talked to Lorraine about it?'

'No way. She has to deal with the fact I was once an extra from the Mad Hatter's tea party. She married me and thinks I'm OK now. '

Charlie smiles.

'What?' I ask.

'Lorraine knows you're not OK. She's not stupid. Five years in the loony farm and you're going to flip to Mr Alright? No way.'

'It wasn't a loony farm.'

'Sorry. Anyway how long has this stuff be going on?'

'Since Iraq the first time.'

'What happened in Iraq?'

'I'd rather not say.'

Charlie takes a sip of his drink, licks his lips and drains the glass. 'You know you can't go back to Lorraine.'

I drop air from my lungs in one lump. 'What?'

'If these guys really want you they'll stop at nothing to get you. You need to vanish. '

'And what if they use Lorraine to get to me?'

'Leave that to me.'

'Look, I'm going to get Lorraine and that's it.' I fiddle with my drink.

'And then what? You can't move her. She'll be in need of care for a good few weeks. Didn't you also say they have the hospital staked out? They know you'll go for her. Come on Craig, these guys want you and want you bad. You try and get her and you're a dead man walking. Leave Lorraine to me.'

'You? How?'

'Well for a start I'm going to tell the police that the men in suits have been sniffing around. I'll mention they've threatened me and told me to tell you that if I see you they'll harm Lorraine.'

'I don't think the police will bother these guys.'

'Maybe not but it might make them think twice about hurting Lorraine. I'll drop a note to the local paper. Men in black suits, vague threats, bikers ripping up my bar – they'll love it.'

'And the fact your brother is the editor doesn't do any harm.'

'That as well.'

'Then?'

He pushes his untouched drink to one side. 'Then I set up shop at the hospital and when Lorraine is on the mend we get the hell out of there.'

'Hell Charlie they'll come after you. After both of you.'

'And they won't come after you?'

'Maybe but she's my wife. I'm not running.'

'And what if Mary was just the start of the pain you bring to her life?'

'What else can I do?' I lean back in the chair and stare at a picture of Gary Cooper on Charlie's wall. Charlie loves High Noon.

'Hide.'

'And just leave Lorraine?'

'Hanging around for the men in black suits to pick you up isn't the best idea on the planet.'

'Hiding isn't going to solve anything.'

'Might give you some space to figure a solution. If the men in black suits catch you and you're to blame for all this then I can think of a hundred uses for a ticking time bomb. But then again maybe it's not you making people flip out. Maybe, even if it is, it can be fixed.'

'Who by?'

'Try Ripley's 'Believe It or Not' website – they have a phone number.'

'Funny. Where do I go? I can't just hit the road. I need to have a plan - somewhere to stay - an objective.'

'You also need to act quickly.'

'No shit.'

'No I mean it. Listen.'

The sound of a single footstep bounces off the wire-meshed window.

Chapter 15

Charlie throws the light switch and plunges us into near perfect darkness.

A second step. Soft. Not someone out for a stroll. Someone trying not to be there.

A voice, so low it's a murmur. No words. Too indistinct. Then a second voice.

Charlie whispers, 'Time to go, Craig. We can finish this later.'

'How do I get out?'

'Female washroom. I'll draw them in and then you go.'

I stand up and feel my way round the wall to the door. It opens with a soft squeak and I wince. I cross the corridor. A shape blocks out the light in the doorway to the alley. I duck and push into the ladies' washroom.

It smells far fresher than the gents. The light from the alley casts shadows. There are two cubicles and a single bowl, with a hand dryer pinned to one wall.

The voices are talking again. Still too low to make out the words. The cold faucet on the sink is dripping. A single drop every four or five seconds. The extractor fan built into the window turns as a gust of air flows through the alley. I move behind the entrance door. Unless someone slams it open I'll be hidden if they do a quick check.

Someone is trying the back door. It clicks as the handle lowers. I can feel the change in air pressure as the door opens and the outside air slides in. I stiffen.

Light spills under the door and Charlie's voice booms out. 'I have a gun.'

The door clicks shut again. Charlie has changed plans on me. No one is going to come in with a gun waiting for them. The sound of retreating footsteps suggests they're leaving. Then the washroom door opens. Did one of them make it in? My eyes burn as light floods the room. I try to keep still but the door opens wide and catches my toes.

'Craig?' Charlie's voice.

'Are they gone?' I'm whispering.

'No. I had a peak through the drapes and there were four of them. All suited and booted. I figured that inviting them in might not be the best idea. If there are four out back there will be more out front. We need a plan B.'

'Like what?'

'This way and keep low.'

I follow him out of the washroom.

He grabs my hand. 'Keep your head down.'

I do as I am told.

We enter and Charlie points towards the bar. 'There's a trapdoor behind the bar. The stairs go straight down and mind your head.'

I walk over, find the handle on the floor and pull up the cover. The trapdoor is heavy and awkward to move but it finally gives and I swing it up and back to the floor.

Charlie follows me over and whispers. 'There's a small door at the rear of the cellar. The key's on a nail to the left. When you go through the door you'll find another trapdoor that's used for dropping in beer and spirits. It comes up under the fire escape in the alley. In this light you might get out without being seen. It's the best I can think of.'

'Thanks Charlie.'

I start to drop down and he grabs my shoulder. 'Here. It's not much but it will get you out of town. I wouldn't go using any ATMs or swiping credit cards in the near future.' He hands me a fistful of notes and I stuff them in my pocket. 'Charlie, I'm still going for Lorraine.'

'Don't be stupid. I'll take care of it. Trust me.' Charlie

closes the hatch and I fumble around until I find the door and the key.

The lock is tough to open and when it frees itself the door flies inward and I stumble into the space beyond. My shin cracks against a beer keg. I curse and stumble in the dark before I find the hatch. I undo the catch, all by feel, and lean upward, shoulder against the metal. The plate lifts into the alley. Catching it with my hand I put my head to the crack. I've seen the hatch often enough as Lorraine and I have lounged near the pub door. It sits hard against the wall under a metal fire escape.

I can't see anyone but my view is restricted. I listen for any telltale sounds but the rumble of traffic and the sounds of the city are all I can hear.

I heave, catching the metal handle before the hatch bangs on the ground. I haul myself up and close the hatch. The alley rolls into view. Clear.

A suit rounds the corner and then a second. I turn and find the other end of the alley blocked by three more. Buzz 1 leads them and he smiles. I think about diving down the hatch but I'd be trapped. The bar door is an option but I'd be back where I was. I look like I've been caught in a car's headlights.

'Ok Mr McIntyre, don't make this any harder than it needs to be.' Buzz 1 starts to close in.

I look up, more for inspiration than for any outreach to a higher authority. Either way it works. The fire escape. Jumping up I grab the pull-down ladder. It rattles down as my weight triggers the release mechanism. Buzz 1 starts to run and I start to climb.

Charlie's premises are part of a three-storey block and I gain the platform for the first floor as the suits converge at the bottom of the ladder. I try to pull it up but Buzz 1 is only feet behind me. I wait until his head is level with my feet and stamp down hard on his face. He twists to avoid the kick, but he's too slow. My foot catches him a side blow, he loses grip and falls into the suits below.

I fly the next twenty feet and at the top I'm faced with a flat roof. There are no other exits. I sprint to the far side and look down onto the street. Two suits are standing at either end of the alley and three more are standing at the front door to the bar. I duck back as Buzz 1 makes the top of the fire escape.

I run to the far end of the building and look out. The alley is below me and the next strip of buildings are two-storey. The roof beyond is flat, with a doorway about halfway along. The door is open and I can see stairs leading down.

I look back and Buzz 1 is on the roof and coming at me. I judge the gap between my building and the next at a good twelve feet with a ten foot difference in height. I'd never make the distance as a long jump but with the fall I might.

I need a long run-up but Buzz 1 will be on me in seconds. I run at the edge and leap knowing I'm not going to make it. I'm too slow and my leap too weak.

The far wall looms and I throw my hands up. The edge of the roof digs into my palms and I grab hold of it to stop me plunging to the alley floor. My chest hits the side wall, followed by my legs. Fuck. My hands find a grip and hold. I scrabble with my feet for some purchase and feel something jutting from the wall. I put my left foot on it and push.

'Jump. After him.'

'No way.'

The voices are coming from the roof I've just left.

I plant my other foot on the protruding object and shove myself onto the roof and I'm up. I run for the door, crash through it and fly down the stairs. There are two flights and then another door. I open it and fall into an empty space. It looks like a storage area. I scan the surroundings. A gap at the back leads out onto what looks like a balcony. I head for it.

I hear glass breaking from below and then voices.

I reach the balcony and find it's glassed in. This is no storage area. Someone has laid this out as a loft-style apartment. Three glass sliding doors protect a metal balcony. I try the sliding doors one by one, but they're all locked. I look around for something to break the glass with but there is nothing. The voices are closing in.

I run back to the entrance, up the stairs and onto the roof. I sprint to the edge where the balcony sits and drop myself onto the metal structure. Through the glass doors I see suits pour into the space beyond. One of them sees me and his mouth moves but the double-glazing stifles the shout. He raises a gun and I place my hand on the balcony railing and leap over. There is no alley below - just a stretch of scrubland. I fall ten feet, roll forward and I'm up and running again.

A muffled shot rings out and there's the sound of one of the glass doors exploding. I keep running and enter a small parking lot at the back of a commercial row of buildings at the other end of the scrub. I run into the gap between two buildings and out onto the street beyond.

Across the street there's a movie lot stuffed with cinema equipment. Flats, lighting covered in tarpaulins, a couple of trucks and range of props. I enter the lot and grab a handful of the tarpaulin from one of the lighting rigs and pull it over myself. The rig is a crisscross of aluminium tubing. I climb up a few rungs, settle myself into the nest of steel and try to stop breathing.

There is no point running further. I haven't the strength. This might be the most obvious place to hide in LA or it just might fool them. I just wish I didn't need air.

Breathing makes so much noise.

Chapter 16

'Did you see him?'

I hear Buzz 1 talking. He's only a few feet away.

'No but he can't have gone far.'

'You try that way. I'll try this way.'

They're talking too loud. You don't yak like you have just come out from a rock concert when you're hunting someone. You do it by signs not words. Not unless you want the prey to believe they are close to freedom.

I'm cramping up and the cold of the metal is creeping into me. Don't move. It's all I can do. Not to move. My ears are my defence. The slightest noise. Any sign that I'm not on my own. Anything. I start to count. Backwards from one thousand. If I get to zero with no sign then I'll move.

A car drives by. Chat and laughter and the car slows.

'Is he watching us?' A girl's voice - then she continues. 'He is.'

'Hey!' Now a man's voice. 'What are you looking at? You dressed for a funeral? Because it'll be yours if you don't fuck off.'

I'm guessing one of the suits is hanging around to see if I reappear.

'Let's go,' the girl sounds drunk. 'Maybe he likes to watch. Is that it – you like to watch?' The last few words are shouted.

More laughter and they move away.

I've lost count so I start again.

1,000-999-998.

I hit zero and wait for another count of one hundred before starting to unfurl my legs. The blood rushes back and I bite my tongue and clench my fists as the pain kicks in. The pins and needles are extreme. I flex my joints and try to ease the throbbing. My foot hits the ground and drop down. I'm still inside the tarpaulin tent. Dropping my head to the ground, the smell of damp concrete in my nose, I stretch my hand out and lift the corner of the material to reveal a slice of the road.

I crawl forward and lift the tarpaulin a little more. No one - but this is like shining a torch for light in a desert. You can see a few feet but someone a mile away can see you. I lift a little more and push my head into the gap.

No one.

I roll out, wait for the pins and needles to ease before standing up.

No one.

Time to walk – not run. No need to draw attention. Anyway I'm out of running at the moment. There's no cover to be had on the street but the next corner is only yards away. I hold my breath as I walk round and put my hiding place out of sight behind me. I cross the road and enter yet another alley.

A cab is sitting at the end of the next street and I walk up and jump in. The cabbie looks surprised to find he has a fare.

'St Vincent's Medical Centre.'

The driver takes off. I try to look behind in a manner that doesn't suggest I'm being followed. There is no one in sight. I settle into the seat as the driver takes an on-ramp to the I10 and heads downtown.

We hit the off-ramp and St Vincent's is a block away. Two SUVs sit at the next corner. I duck down as we pass them. Two more sit at the entrance with three suits on the door.

'Take me round the back.'

The cabbie nods.

A SUV, a regal and two suits sit at the back.

Fuck.

The cab stops.

'Not here.' I say.

'Where then?'

'The nearest payphone.'

Two blocks on the cabbie pulls up at a phone.

I jump out. 'I'll be two minutes.' The phone is working and I dial Charlie's pub.

'Michael's can I help you,' Charlie answers.

'Charlie it's me.'

'How are you?'

'How am I? How the hell do you think I am?'

Silence.

'Charlie are you alone?'

'I…'

I slam the phone down. Stupid. Just stupid. Of course he's not alone. A car burns rubber and I turn expecting to see a SUV or a Regal but it's an old Taurus pulling away from the lights too quickly.

I jump back in the cab. 'The Greyhound Bus Depot.'

I'm no use to Lorraine here. It's me they want. A little distance and figure things out. Then back for her when things have cooled off. I pull the bundle of notes that Charlie gave me from my pocket but it's not enough. Charlie has given me fifty notes. I need to get cash.

Shit.

I lean forward. 'Can you pull off the freeway and find an ATM?'

The driver doesn't look happy but I don't care. I have to get cash now. If I draw it out at the bus station it will be a giveaway as to where I am and I need money. Once I'm on the road I can't access more.

There's an ATM at the bottom of the next off-ramp and the machine only lets me draw four hundred dollars. I jump back in the cab and we take off again.

Twenty minutes later the taxi driver pulls up at the bus depot. The complex lies on a side street fronted by chain link. The vehicles are parked rear in and it's quiet. It's late but there are still buses pulling in and out. I strip forty bucks from my cash and pay the driver.

As I enter the depot I keep an eye out for suits. The good news is that they'll stand out a mile in here. Two-piece and ties are thin on the ground. The ticket office has a queue of one and I approach it trying to figure where I'm going.

Two police officers walk into the depot and, with the eyes of the well practised, scan the concourse. They stop when they see me. I look away and when I turn back one of them is on his walkie-talkie.

Can't be for me. Can it? The suits have some reach if the beat cops have me down pat already. I wander to the coffee machine and order up something to keep me awake. When the cup pops out I risk a glance at the cops and they're gone.

Time to go.

I approach the ticket booth. 'When is the next bus to New Orleans?'

'Ten to twelve tonight sir.'

The ticket man looks bored. His shirt is stained and his name badge tells me his name is Helmut.

'Helmut, how long does the journey take?'

'You arrive at ten to eight on Monday night. Change twice. Tomorrow morning at six-fifteen in El Paso and then again at Houston at eleven fifteen on Monday morning.'

Long trip. I reach for my money. 'A single to New Orleans.'

The man hits a few buttons on his screen. 'One hundred and ninety dollars.'

I step back. 'That the cheapest fare?'

'Book on the web and you'll get some off.'

As if. I start to count out the cash. 'OK. I'll go with it.'

He prints off the ticket and a receipt. 'Do you have a list of the stops in between?' I ask.

He plays with the screen again and a printer spits out a list of towns.

'Thanks.' I scan the list and count off the states. Arizona, New Mexico, Texas and Louisiana. 'How far is it?'

Helmut shakes his head and punches some more. 'Just under nineteen hundred miles. Most of it on the I10.'

I sip at the coffee and screw my face up at the taste. 'Last question. Will it be busy?'

This time he smiles. 'There are a few on board but if you're looking for company,' he winks as he says company, 'you may be disappointed.'

The phone next to him rings and I'm dismissed.

I check out the café and load up on doughnuts, candy and Coke. There's a small stand selling travel aids next to the cafe. Inflatable headrests, non-drip cups and the like. A shiny Leatherman hangs from the top of a small carousel. I'm a Boy Scout at heart and cough up for the tool and slip it into my pocket. I ask where the nearest liquor store is and I'm directed a few blocks away. A bottle of Jack Daniels and I'm back at the depot with ten minutes to spare before the bus departs.

I'm not sure I want to go all the way to New Orleans, but I need distance and there will be plenty of places en route to stop off if I change my mind.

The bus is waiting on the last but one stand. There's no one out front but the back seats seem heavy with people. I flash my ticket at the driver and find the front half empty. The rear is noisy. At a guess I would say we have entered 'little old lady' land. The chatter is loud and friendly. I count twenty women. Halfway down the bus two older men sit on their own. I choose a seat a few in front of them and flop. Then I'm bolt upright. No cup!

I jump off the bus and order a coffee I don't want from the machine, tip out the liquid and leap back on as the driver shuts the door and we pull out.

As we leave I scan for suits but it seems clear. I feel trapped in the metal shell. This is such a dumb thing to do. How easy will it be to figure where I have gone? Why am I leaving with Lorraine still in hospital? I mix up a drink and tip it down in one go.

What is the plan? I mix a second drink. Who are the suits? What do they want? I slug half the second drink.

What do I do next? Do I stay on the run? For how long? I finish the drink and pour another.

Chapter 17

'We stop here for an hour.' The voice cuts through the fug of booze and sleep.

'Sorry?'

The driver is standing over me. 'We stop over for an hour. You can stay on if you want but you might want to get a coffee.'

I rub my eyes and stare out of the window. There's a six-lane highway outside and little else. The bus is sitting in a double-storey concrete shell.

'Any good restaurants around?' I enquire.

The driver shakes his head. 'Depot café or nothing.'

An hour later I'm back in my seat, two coffees to the good and three doughnuts light from my bag. The gaggle of women are back on board, a little more subdued than when we left. The two older men have moved and are in the row behind me.

'You on your own son?' One of the men is talking to me but I'm not in the mood for chat.

'We don't bite.' The second man joins in. I still ignore them.

'You had a nice gab with Jack last night,' says the first man.

His bright blonde hair is an award winner in the bouffant category. It sits atop a suntanned face with more wrinkles than could be cleaned out with a pipe cleaner. He's wearing a cardigan, purple with 'sixty-nine' picked out in stitched panels. His teeth look store bought.

'Jack?' he says and points at my bag. He smells of expensive aftershave. I smell like crap. 'Jack Daniels?'

They both laugh.

'Up for sharing it?' he asks.

I shake my head.

'Long journey if you are going all the way to the Big Easy. Pays to be friends with people on a bus. You never know when you'll want company.' The second man is as bald as his friend is hirsute. He is equally tanned and is top to toe in black – a roll top hiding his neck.

I turn away.

'Company.' The Bouffant King rolls the word around his mouth as if he's chewing hot candyfloss.

'Company,' repeats the Man in Black.

I lean against the window as the bus pulls out and they lose interest in me.

At Tucson I crash the men's room and use a sink for a quick wash.

We cross into New Mexico around midday and the driver pulls over and tells us we have a half-hour stop over in Lordsburg. There's a McDonald's on the opposite corner to a gas station and I think I'll risk a Big Mac.

The place is busy. The little old ladies are ahead of me and have all decided to tuck into calories. The only spare seat is in the booth next to the Bouffant King and the Man in Black. I sigh, pick up my dead cow and take a seat. Thankfully they are too engrossed in each other to bother with me.

'So who's left?' The Bouffant King is talking.

'For me, Mary, Caroline and Jenny. You?' says the Man in Black.

'Caroline, Deborah and Enid.'

'Oh you'll love Enid. Kinky if you push it.'

'Really.'

'If you persuade her. Know what I mean?'

They're looking at the women as they talk and I'm not sure I want to hear this.

'Caroline is the real money,' says the Bouffant King.

'Hard nut to crack. Hell I've been on the case for over a year.'

'Worth it though.'

'No doubt.'

'How was Jenny?' the Man in Black stage whispers.

'Dull as dishwater. I think I was the first man in her pantyhose for a decade. It smelt that way anyway.'

They both laugh.

'So who's next?' The Man in the Black leans out of the booth and catches me listening. 'You looking for some old tail?'

I duck back in.

'Young man there fancies some aged pussy I think,' says the Bouffant King.

I slide out of the booth and take my meal into the morning heat. I'm followed by two of the old ladies. They sit down next to me.

'Hi, I'm Enid and this is Tanya.'

The 'kinky' one and friend. Great.

'I see you were talking to Bert and George,' says Enid.

'Is that the man in black and his friend?' I munch as I talk.

'That's them.'

'Can I ask what you're all doing on the bus?'

'Sure,' says Enid. 'We're off to a mystery convention in New Orleans.'

My look of confusion spurs her on.

'Mystery novels – you know, detective, crime. We go every year.'

'By bus?'

'Three of us are scared of flying. Anyway we're all retired. We're in no hurry. What are you doing on the bus?'

'Going to see a friend.'

'You should join us. Bert and George aren't much company.'

'Not unless you pull your knickers down.' It's the first words that Tanya has spoken.

'If you don't mind ladies I'd rather grab some sleep.'

'JD will do that to you.'

I'm not as anonymous I thought. 'I'll take that on advice.'

'Well, any time you want a chat we'll be at the back – you can't miss us.'

They get up and head for the bus as their friends troop out to join them. Bert and George are laughing as they leave.

* * *

El Paso comes into view at just after half-past five. We need to transfer buses and there's forty minutes to kill. I avoid the Mystery Mob.

The bus leaves carrying the same passengers who've been on board since Los Angeles. The last of the hop-ons left us at El Paso and it's just the Mystery Mob, the Bouffant King, the Man in Black and me.

The light is dropping and the land has a bad case of dry brushwood acne on either side of the highway. The odd oncoming headlight breaks the monotony but, as the light dips, there's little to see. A broken shell of a shack flies into view. A long-dead Dodge, rusting back to the earth it came from, guards the shack's front door. I check the printed itinerary that the ticket man produced and we're not far from the next stop. My Jack Daniels is burning a hole in my bag and I pull it out.

The laughter is like a gunshot in my ear.

'Bert, fuck off.'

Bert is laughing as Enid shouts after him. He returns to the seat behind me and sits down next to George.

'What did you say?' asks George.

'Asked if her ass was available for rent.'

They both laugh.

Bert hangs over my seat, his bouffant moving of its own accord. 'Want to split that bottle three ways? We're dry.'

'No.'

'Too good to drink with us old fogies?'

'No. I just want a quiet drink.'

'So do we son. I'll get you a fresh bottle at the next stop.'

'No thanks.'

'We insist.'

It dawns on me that he's drunk. They both are. George adds his two cents' worth. 'We only want a drink.'

I shake my head. 'Might have had one too many already.'

'You tellin' us how much we can drink son?' Bert has an edge to his voice.

'No. I just want a quiet time.'

George taps me on the shoulder. 'Look all we want is a drink and we'll be off your case.' His words are loud. A mean drunk. I seem to attract them.

'Look, I'm just going to slip down to the front of the bus and leave you two alone. You can pick up a bottle at the next stop and drink till you fall over. Ok?'

George pushes Bert to one side and exits onto the aisle. 'Look, son. You ain't going to down that bottle on your own – so just divvy up the fair way.'

I stand up. 'The bar is closed.'

George is a few inches shorter than me and I have earned-muscle on my side, but he's drunk and running on brave pills. He stands his ground. I place a hand on his shoulders and lean forward. He tenses. 'Get you hands off me son.'

'Or what?'

He tries to step back.

'Or what?' I repeat, leaning in close. I reach into my pocket and finger my Leatherman. I slip a blade from the handle.

The scene has the attention of the bus now. The Mystery Mob are fixed on us and George knows he's on a loser. He might get a punch in but I can take him, and he knows it. He can back down but his future sexual conquests are watching and his chances of bedding them are slipping away. He rocks a little from foot to foot.

Bert wades in. 'George you old fool. Let the boy be.' He turns to the Mystery Mob. 'Now ladies, has anyone squirreled away a little drink they would care to share?'

George backs off, glad of the exit. I slide down the bus and choose the seat behind the driver. Sitting down I twist the cap on the bottle and settle down for a drink.

An hour later and the noise from the back of the bus is akin to a school kids' outing. Sounds like Bert and George have mined some drink from someone and are winding up the Mystery Mob. The driver glances in the rear view mirror.

'Noisy for an old bunch,' I say, cup to my lips.

'Always the same,' he replies. 'Teenagers and the grey brigade – as bad as each other. I'll need to warn them though. Other passengers won't be happy.'

I was the only other passenger at the moment and I wasn't that fussed. 'I'm OK.'

'Yeah, but there will be others to get on and that's when it won't be OK.'

I think there's a suggestion that I might like to go have a quiet word. I'm having none of it. I sip at my drink.

A horn blast from a rig grabs my attention. My window lights up as a truck flicks its full beam at a car riding beside us. The car lays an inch of rubber on the blacktop as it's forced to duck back and fall in at our rear. The light reveals a black SUV and the alarm bells go off in my head. The headlight briefly picks out a man in a suit in the passenger seat. I think he might be looking up at me. I think it's Buzz 2.

I cross the bus, sit on the other side and wait. A few minutes later the top of the SUV glides up again - matching the bus's speed. It doesn't overtake; instead it hangs there - on the wrong side of the road. Another truck approaches and this time the

SUV accelerates and pulls in front of the bus. The bus driver hits the horn, swears and the SUV accelerates before slowing down fifty yards in front.

The SUV's rear window is lit up by the bus headlights - but the tint is heavy and I can only make out two shapes. My mind goes into overdrive.

I flick open up the itinerary and look for the next stop. Van Horn. I've never been there.

The SUV keeps ahead. Gaining none. Losing none. I check my watch. Twenty minutes and we're scheduled to pull in. I weigh up the options and don't like any of them. Waiting for the next stop is bottom of the list. Getting off early is a poor choice. It's still scrub desert outside and I won't get far on foot. There might be a chance to get off as we enter the town and make a break for it but for all I know the bus stops at the edge of town and I'll be toast. I wonder why they showed their hand early. Why not wait for the bus to pull in?

I lean forward to talk to the driver. 'Do we come off the highway for the next stop?'

The driver turns slightly to answer. 'Yes. Not long now.'

A second SUV drifts alongside and I cross the aisle and shift back to the seat behind the driver. 'Don't leave the highway at the junction.'

The driver turns round. 'What?'

I point at the road. 'Don't stop. Keep your foot on the gas and just drive.'

Chapter 18

The SUV in front begins to slow down.

'Kill the internal lights and keep up the speed.' I slide to the edge of the seat to get a better view.

'What?'

I slap him hard over the back of the head. I need control. 'Lights out. Foot down.'

He reaches down and flicks a switch and the bus descends into darkness. There's whooping from behind and the school kids think it's recess.

'What the hell do you want me to do?' The driver's shoulders are tensed up.

I yank out the Leatherman's blade and jam it into the back of his neck. Hard. 'Just drive.'

'We should turn off soon,' he says.

'No. Just keep going.'

'Where to?'

I have no idea. I look around the driver's seat. 'Do you have a map?'

'No. GPS.' He points to the small unit sitting on the dash.

'Pass it here.'

He pulls it off the dashboard and passes it up.

The SUV is less than ten yards in front.

'Pull out and overtake,' I order.

The driver signals and almost immediately the SUV swings to block us.

I push the blade into his skin a little more. 'Right up his ass. Get the bus up his fucking tail.'

The driver doesn't respond. I push the blade deeper and his skin splits. A drop of blood spreads down his neck - black in the light of the instruments.

He plants his foot and the bus surges forward. For a second

the SUV doesn't react then, with only feet to spare, it accelerates.

I try and play with the GPS, but with one hand holding the rail and the other on the knife I can't.

'I'm going to remove the knife. If you piss me off I'll stick it in your ear and slice open your eardrum.'

The GPS is touch screen and I flick around the area we're travelling through. I whizz by something and back it up. A small airport. It's marked up as Culberson County airport and is a three runway triangle set-up. One of thousands across the country. It's less than a mile beyond the town and three-quarters of a mile from the highway at its nearest point.

We pass the exit for Van Horn as two SUVs speed along the on-ramp and join us. We are now three to one.

The sat nav shows a road running parallel to us called the Old Bankhead Highway. It runs out just beyond the airport with the turnoff leading to it just ahead. 'Slow down. Right down,' I say.

The driver obeys. Two of the SUVs pull up beside us. A window winds down on the nearest one and Buzz 2 waves at the driver to pull over.

'Ignore him.' My heart rate racks up as I weigh up my options. The speed at which the two new SUVs joined in suggests they had the town loaded up. They still want me bad.

My head starts to thump but I shake it to try and concentrate on what I need to do.

A shout goes up from behind and the Mystery Mob seem to be having more fun. My headache explodes but I need to keep my mind on the job at hand.

A shout from behind. 'What the...?' Then a scream. A man's scream.

'Jesus what are you fucking doing?' Bert is shouting.

The driver turns round.

'Keep your eyes on the road,' I yell. My head is splitting down the middle.

'Fuck.' The word hammers down the length of the bus. 'Get off me you stupid cow.'

A muffled 'thwump' and another scream rises from the back of the bus.

One of the new SUVs tries to cut in front of us and the driver brakes. I lean forward and plant my hand on his foot and push down. The bus leaps forward and catches the SUV on the inside rear. The car flips to the right and the other SUV has to stand on the brakes to prevent ploughing into it. They both vanish from view leaving a lone escort out front.

I clip the driver's head. 'I told you not to fucking stop.'

Another scream from behind. 'How do you like a little persuasion? A little kinky, eh?' Enid's voice is strong. 'He talks dirty. I don't like it when he talks dirty. I tell you what? Tanya I've got scissors in my bag. Be a good girl and get them for me.'

What the hell is going on back there? I turn round but there's not enough light to see by. My headache is starting to blind me.

'No. Noooooo!' The scream from behind is desperate.

'There, got it,' says Enid.

'It's so gooey,' says Tanya.

George shouts out and I can't be sure what is going down but I can guess.

'You shut up. You're next,' shouts Enid.

'I got his cell and he has KY in a tube. Maybe George would like to see if it fits,' says Tanya.

I get back to the job in hand. I suspect that Bert and George are on the receiving end of a bad night but I can't cope with the headache, the suits and the nonsense on the bus. I tap the driver on the shoulder. 'I want you to take the next turn-off. Don't indicate; wait until the last minute. I'll tell you when. Do you understand?'

The driver nods as another SUV pulls up beside us. The tinted window is down and this time there's a gun pointing at the bus. The driver sees it and eases off the gas. I reach down and push his foot. 'They're not going to shoot with a bus full of passengers. But they will shoot if we stop. It's up to you.'

The driver stares ahead.

The junction emerges in the headlights of the SUV. It's unmarked.

'Now wait until you are on the junction - then hard left. Once you're round give it as much gas as you can.'

The white lines are no longer a blur as the driver eases off for the turn. Each looks like a stepping stone over a black sea. The SUV passes the junction and the bus looks like it will follow suit.

'Now,' I shout.

The driver pulls hard down on the wheel and we swing off the highway. I'm flung hard against the chair. I look at the highway and the following SUVs are caught out and miss the turn.

I smack the driver's head. 'Foot down.'

The road is no more than a dirt track and seconds later we're bouncing across a set of railway lines. There's still commotion from behind and, as we straighten up, I step out onto the aisle to try and look back. My foot slips and I fall onto the chair. I try to stand up and slip again. As we bounce along the dirt track I put my hand on the floor and it comes up wet, sticky... and warm.

What the hell?

I lift my hand into the light cast by the instruments in front of the driver and realize that Bert and George are having a very bad night.

Car lights appear in the giant wing mirrors of the bus. They gain at speed but the road is too narrow for the SUVs to get past and the terrain either side is lethal.

I haul myself back onto my seat. 'Another half mile and then take a left. There should be a road.'

The driver is hunched in concentration. He's driving too fast on a road that is not designed for the behemoth he's trying to control. Add to that the chasing cars, the nonsense going on in the rear and my knife, and his shoulders are rods of iron under his jacket.

One of the SUVs pulls out into the desert in an attempt to overtake. I reach out, grab the steering wheel and pull it towards the vehicle. The bus lurches off the road. The driver yells and pulls the wheel back. I hear a crunch and headlights spin away to our left.

I strain to see ahead. I haven't got this all figured out but action is better than inaction. The track twists and turns and, every so often, a pair of white eyes flick out of the dark as the headlights hit the back of some nocturnal beast's eye sockets. We crest a small rise and there's no sign of the road promised by the GPS. I play with the machine. 'Where the hell is the road?'

'What road?' the driver responds.

'It says on the map there's a road called the Old Bankhead Highway.'

'It's nothing but a dirt track. Gone long ago.'

'How would you know?'

'I live nearby.'

Shit.

Somebody grabs my leg and I leap. Twisting round I bring my fist down on an arm holding the material of my pants. Bert looks up at me. He tries to talk but it's muffled. His tongue is gone. I want to lash out. Push him away. Get him the fuck out of my face. His bouffant hair is a matt of blood and the cardigan with 'sixty-nine' on it is ripped and torn. His mouth opens. A dark hole. 'Mmmphhh.' Jesus.

I step back. We hit a large pothole and Bert flips over. His pants are gone as is his manhood. No tongue - no dick. There is a scream from behind and George is receiving the attention of the Mystery Mob. I push Bert's arm away. The Mystery Mob are getting their revenge big time and I'm the catalyst.

My head is pounding, a steam hammer, making it hard to think. My skull is in a vice and someone is turning it tighter notch by notch. The bus staggers to the left and I'm thrown sideways. I grab the rail and pull myself upright. The driver is staring at Bert. I slap him on the face. 'The road. Look at the fucking road.'

He turns back but we're off the track. The bus bounces out across the desert floor and suddenly another dirt track flashes into view at right angles to the way we're travelling.

'That must be it. Get on it!' The driver's shoulder gets a thump as I say this.

The driver hauls the wheel and if this is the Old Bankhead Highway then the GPS is having a laugh. The driver was right. This is no better than the road we were on.

My head is fit to split and I can feel bile rising in my throat. 'Open the door.'

The driver reaches down, flicks a lever and the doors slide apart. A light above the entrance flicks on. I take my knife and drive it into the light and kill it.

Mistake.

The driver spots the tiny blade.

'I can still kill you with it.' I need to shout over the noise coming through the doors. 'Listen carefully. Those guys out there are not your friends. If you stop here they'll take you out with me. Do you understand? They will kill you. You need to get back to town. This road runs back into Van Horn. Drive to the depot. Make sure there are plenty of people around before you stop. If you don't they WILL kill you. Do you understand?'

He nods.

'Good. What's in the bag?'

There's a sports bag sitting in the well next to him. He glances down at it. 'A change of clothes and my snack.'

'I'm taking it.' I reach down and lift the bag. Heavier than it looks. 'Swing right and slow right down. I'm jumping. As soon as I'm clear, get back on the road. With luck they'll follow you and not notice I'm gone.'

A last scream from behind and I turn. It's too dark to see but I don't fancy George's chances. Bert is lying at my feet. He isn't moving. I turn back to the driver.

'Do you know if there's a hospital in Van Horn?'

He nods.

'Change of plan. Go there instead of the depot.' It's the best I can do for Bert and George. 'Now – swing off.'

The driver hauls us out into the desert and slows down. I jump down the steps and look at the ground rushing by. I throw out the bag and pull up the training manual for landing after a parachute jump in my head, and leap. As I do the world drops blue and the headache vanishes. I hit the dirt and roll. The rear of the bus flashes by and I hear the driver gun the engine. I lie flat. The SUVs scream by feet from my head. I count to ten and look up. Three sets of tail-lights are chasing the bus. The road is keeping them back but they are swinging left and right trying to find a way past.

The blue world brings my own personal night vision. It could be midday. I spot the driver's bag and pick it up, cross the dirt track and head in the direction of the airport.

I look back and the bus is still rolling and this is good news. The longer it keeps moving the more distance I can gain.

I start to jog and the bag clinks. I stop and unzip it. A fresh shirt and pants are rolled up on top along with a plastic lunch box. Beneath there are bottles and I pull one out. Wild Turkey bourbon. It has five more brothers to keep it company. Not my favourite brand but good stuff, and not the sort of luggage that inspires me with confidence in my driver.

I break back into a jog and I'm amazed to see animals dotted around. A coyote stands not ten yards from me. Watching. It's eyes follow me and I smile at it. It's so clear I could draw it.

I chink my way down to a fast walk and flick my head to check that the SUVs aren't on their way back. The noise of the wild has replaced the noise of engines and the vehicles are out of sight. My breath is ragged and it occurs to me that this place isn't on sea level. I'm grabbing for air. Mexico lies not far behind me and I wonder if I would be safer trying for a foreign country.

I stumble onto concrete and realize that I'm standing on one of the airport's runways. In the middle distance a small group of buildings are huddled together with some planes parked on the apron. A taxi-way leads to the planes and beyond them another clump of buildings squat in the blue light.

The place looks deserted but that would be normal - most of these local airports are dawn to dusk affairs. I cut across the runway and begin to walk up the taxi-way, listening for any signs of life in front or behind me.

The main buildings are shut tight and the two planes sitting on the taxi-way are the only sign that the place is in use. I circle the buildings and the sound of a radio falls from the light breeze.

I freeze.

Baseball. I can't hear the words but the cadence and the rhythm suggests commentators going through a game. A few steps and I've located the source. Behind the buildings an RV is parked up. The window is all but blacked out but a slip of light is escaping from the corner. I walk round the vehicle. Two men are talking inside. The conversation seems to revolve around planes.

A car engine hums in the distance. Probably from the highway but the suits could have it figured by now. The blue world is fading and darkness is returning. I hit the door with my fist.

It opens and a bald man with a beer gut and a faded Texas Rangers sweat looks out. 'What?'

Nice greeting. Beer fumes and cigarette smoke rush into the night. I back off a step as I gag on the cloud. 'My car packed in a few miles back. Do you have a phone?'

'Who is it?' comes a shout from within.

'His car broke down.' Baldy turns to look into the RV as he says this.

'Does he have any booze on him?' the voice comes back.

Baldy looks at me. 'Do you have any booze on you?'

I step forward a little. 'I might.'

'He says he might.'

The voice inside warms up. 'Then invite him in. I'm as dry as a buzzard's ring-piece.'

Baldy steps back and beckons me to go in. The RV is a tip. A dozen Miller Lite cans are spread on the floor and three pizza boxes lie on the table. The place is awash with litter and my host sweeps a pile of porn to the floor to let me sit down.

'So, do you have booze?' The other man has wisps of long hair. Thin as a rake he burps and points to the can in his hand. 'Last one.'

'Either of you a pilot?' I ask.

'I am.' Baldy drops to a chair as he talks.

'So is one of the planes yours?'

'The Skycatcher.'

'Not all his,' says the thin one. 'Part share.'

'Still mine and less than six months old.' Baldy rubs his belly and smiles.

'How many does she seat?' I ask.

'Two. Pilot and passenger. Why? You looking for some lessons?'

'No, a ride.'

'Where?'

'Just a ride.'

'Come back tomorrow.'

'No tonight!'

They both laugh.

'No way, San Jose,' says Baldy. 'It's dark and, in case you haven't noticed, we've been on the juice.'

The thin man stands up. Unsteady. 'Federal Aviation Regulation 91.17 prohibits pilots from flying aircraft with an alcohol level of 0.04% or more, and/or within eight hours of consuming alcohol. Isn't that right?'

Baldy nods as the thin man falls back to the seat.

I think I can hear engines. I reach into the driver's sports bag and pull out a bottle of Wild Turkey. 'Would this change your mind?'

The thin one's eyes light up. He reaches over to grab the bottle.

I pull it away. 'A ride first. Ten minutes. No more.'

'Ain't going to happen,' says the Baldy.

I pull a second bottle out.

'Cornbread,' says the thin one. 'Matt just give him the once round. Ain't no one going to know.'

Matt eyes the bottle. 'Chip, it's not worth it.' I dip my hand in once more and pull out a third. 'Ten minutes.' I say.

Engines.

Matt's eyes are fixed on the booze.

'Come on Matt. Up and down for three bottles. How hard can it be?'

Matt rubs his gut again. 'Ok but no crap. Up and down.'

'You're the pilot,' I say.

I stand up wondering how bad your drink problem must be to agree to fly a stranger at night.

'Leave the booze here,' says the thin one and I throw one to him.

Matt grabs one of the others and leads the way out of the RV. I drop the third bottle in the sink as I leave. We circle the buildings. Matt is swaying as if the earth is trying to shake him loose but he's slugging hard on the Wild Turkey. We reach the aircraft. Matt points to the passenger door. 'Jump in and strap up.'

Louder engines.

Matt walks round the aircraft and gets in the other side. 'Up and down.'

I smile. 'Up and down.'

He starts to play with the plane's controls and I can hear the note of a gear change. The cars are close. Matt fires up the prop and I can see lights bouncing towards us. Matt is flipping and checking. I want to gun the throttle for him. He flips some more and the plane jerks forward. I hope he doesn't notice the headlights. My luck holds as he swings the nose of the plane away from the building and the advancing cars.

We taxi back to where I had entered the airport at the junction of two runways. One running parallel with the taxi-way and the other tracking at forty- five degrees. Both start at the end of the taxi-way. If Matt takes the parallel runway he can't fail to see the cars.

We wheel left and he advances onto the further away track. He looks at me and I pray the buildings hide the cars. He pushes the throttle and we zip forward. It's clear that the silence from Matt, since we got in the plane, is down to sheer concentration. I wonder again at how much he wants booze that he'll risk a flight rather than the drive to the liquor store.

A double bounce and we're airborne. Airtime. I look over my shoulder and see four cars converging on the airport.

'Where to?' Matt's first words since we started up.

I point away from the airport, keeping the tail towards the brewing trouble.

'So are we good?' Matt starts to bank the plane. 'Ten and down.'

I have two choices. Tell him what is going on or force him to fly. 'We can't go back to the airport.'

'What?'

'You'll be grounded.'

'Who by?'

'FBI.'

The plane takes on a swinging motion as he tries to look at me and steer at the same time. 'FBI?'

'Back at the airport. Lots of them. Have a look.'

He nudges the plane round a few degrees.

The airport is lit by a collection of car lights. We're far enough away for them to be a single burning flame on the ground.

Matt straightens the plane. 'You a wanted man?'

'Sort of.'

'Bad deal.'

'Go back and your license is history.'

He buries the bad news in another slug of bourbon. 'Bad deal. Bad deal.'

'How far can we fly?'

'A few hundred miles – the tanks aren't full.'

'Is there anywhere you can set down?'

'Maybe.'

'You can park the plane, spend the night and fly back tomorrow.'

'And what do I say when they come asking about you?'

'Whatever you want. Just leave out the bit about the booze and your willing participation. You took me up because I threatened you. I forced you to land. You didn't want to take off again in the dark. You waited until the morning before flying back.'

'Won't wash. Chip will have blabbed. He has a mouth like a motor about to throw a rod.'

'Blank it. Let him tell his story and you say when we got outside the RV you were going to change your mind and I got heavy. Puts you in the clear.'

'And the fact I have one hundred per cent proof running in my veins?'

'Quit drinking now and don't go back until you're sober.'

His eyes are darting from me to the windshield. I think the story works and I think he thinks it works.

He dips the plane and we head for the ground.

'What are you doing?'

'Getting below radar. There is a plateau up ahead. If we hug it they won't be able to pick us up.'

I'm about to go low-level flying with a drunk.

Chapter 19

The desert is a smear, picked out by the moon hanging in a clear sky. We top a hundred knots. Close to the plane's maximum. So low we're in danger of clipping the cacti. For a while the highway is company but Matt waits until it's clear of cars before crossing it and swinging south.

'Where are we going?' I try and keep my eyes from the hypnotic conveyor belt unfolding beneath us.

'Fort Davis.'

'Where?'

'Middle of nowhere. It's a ways from the highway but there are roads leading south to the border or you can try to make the coast at Corpus Christi.'

'How far is it from Van Horn?'

'As the crow flies maybe fifty miles. Sorry I'm not going any further.'

'It'll do. Do you have a map?'

'In the back.'

I reach over and pull out a large map of the area that's sitting between us. Fort Davis isn't the best choice for someone on the run but it'll give me a head start. I stuff the map into the holdall. 'Where are you going to land?'

'There's a disused landing strip to the south of the town. I use it when I spray crops. An old barn sits at one end. It has a bunk. There's no lights so it'll be tricky but it's far enough from town that no one will hear us landing. After that you're on your own.'

Matt nudges the plane a few degrees further east. We suddenly twist in the air and he shakes his head - trying to clear the bourbon. I can see the lights of the town to the right and we're circling to avoid the built-up area. His head starts to do a nodding dog. I thought he was just drunk. I now think he's wasted. We're flying on Matt's personal version of autopilot.

The plane skirts the town and we leave it behind. Matt dips us a few more feet and I grip the door handle. The ground is a smudge.

'Could be rough,' Matt says. 'Hold on.'

He pushes us down a little more and I can't see anything but wasteland. Then we zip over a fence and there's a rough strip of ground. The wheels hit the dirt. I might know shit about planes but we seem to be going way too fast. Back into the air and bounce down again. A barn rises from the dark as we take to the night air once more – there's no way that we are going to stop in time.

Matt is fighting the plane. His reactions are slow. The barn too close. I lift my hands to my face. The plane bounces, tries to lift once more and we plough into the building. The world is alive with noise as the prop rips through the barn's wooden door. The engine roars, dies and the plane continues to career forward. The nose dips, burying itself in the ground. The planet flips forward - slamming us to a halt. Windshield fills my face. The seat belt bites. Matt shouts.

The barn is a whirlwind of dust, wood and shredded hay. It spins a cloud around everything as the night tries to reclaim some calm.

Matt is still shouting. My gut tells me to get out of the plane. I fumble with my belt, push at the door and fall to the ground. Staggering away from the wreck, I climb over the shattered door and squeeze out into the field beyond. I walk a few yards and fall to the ground. To my surprise the sports bag is in my left hand.

Matt follows a few seconds later and joins me on the ground. 'This will take some explaining,' he coughs.

A mild understatement.

'Somebody will have heard that,' I say.

'Don't count on it. We're a good few miles from civilisation.'

He's wrong. A pair of headlights are sliding across the field toward us. I jump up. 'I need to go.'

It's hard to believe that the suits would be here but I can't risk it. I pat Matt on the head and sprint for the rear of the barn. If I'm not turned around, the town is a couple of miles along the road the car has just left. I watch the vehicle bump across the field and pull up beside Matt. I cross the road and start to walk against any oncoming traffic. Ten minutes later the car flies by. Matt's face in the window. He looks less than happy and I pray he's not on the way to the police.

No other vehicles pass and I reach the edge of town. When I hit a crossroads voices attract my attention. I walk to the far side of the intersection and approach a low-roofed, clapperboard house. It's still dark and a large van is sitting in front of the garage, rear door open, headlights on. A man walks into view, his arms full of what looks like wood. He is large. Bulked up. A pair of dungarees and heavy boots catch in the light of the van. He jumps into the rear of the van and re-emerges empty handed.

As he walks out of view I jog up the driveway and look into the back of the van. In the dark it is impossible to see what the man is loading but there's a heavy smell of freshly cut timber and the scent of wood stain. I hear the man approaching again and duck out of sight.

'Graham, you've left one.' The woman's voice is soft.

'I know. I'm putting it in the front. I promised Muzzle that I would drop it off on the way.'

More stuff is loaded in the van before he retreats.

'Long way, honey' she says.

Graham sighs. 'I know but the buyer has four people lined up. I could move all of this in one trip. It would get us through winter easily.'

125

'But Tampa's so far.'
'No choice.'
'Where are you going to stop on the way?'
'Probably Mobile. Depends how I'm doing.'
'I'll miss you.'
'I'll be back before the party.'

I jump into the back of the truck. The rear is full of wooden boxes all securely fixed to the floor. I crawl across them and hunker down at the back. In daylight I would be easily spotted but in the dark you would need to be standing on me to know I was there. Graham pulls down the shutter and a minute later the engine fires up.

Mobile sounds as good a destination as any and the suits would have to be psychic to know I had jumped in the back of a van heading that way. Unless of course they thought me important enough to spring road blocks across the south of the country. But that's all a bit too 'most wanted' for me. I crawl forward and sit down in the space between the rear door and the last of the boxes. Mobile has to be a good eighteen-hour drive. I doubt it will be non-stop but I need to get comfortable.

We've hardly picked up speed when the van turns sharp right, stops and the engine dies. I jump up and crawl to the back of the van but the door stays closed. The engine fires up and I figure Graham has just delivered Muzzle his package.

I crawl back and find my seat. Graham picks up the pace and I'm in for a few hours of rock'n'roll. Out of curiosity I reach into the nearest box, root around and pull out a wooden carving. It's about a foot long, a few inches wide and feels like the wing of a plane. I run my hands along the surface. Smooth and curved. One side swoops in, while the reverse sweeps out, giving the wing a fat belly. A small rod protrudes from the bottom and I scrabble around in the box and find a clutch of bases, each with a hole in the middle. I put two and two together and slot the rod home. The carving is a superb tactile experience. Along the edges it's carved in small waves and the whole item rotates twenty degrees or so from top to bottom. It's too dark to see it properly but I find myself turning and stroking the object.

I reach into the box again and find more of the same, each one a little different to the next.

I lie my head against the truck wall, stroking the carving and try to sleep.

Chapter 20

I wake to the sound of the engine winding down and feel the gentle deceleration of the brakes being applied. Check my watch. Midday. I've been out for eight hours. I stretch and scramble to the back of the truck. We rumble to a stop and I wait for the door to open. Nothing happens. I wait a further five minutes and crawl back over the boxes.

A little light creeps through the seal on the doors but I have no idea where I am. I do some math. Eight hours at sixty would put us five hundred miles west. San Antonio or maybe Houston.

I need a whizz and I don't fancy relieving myself in the truck. The thought of sloshing around in my own urine lacks appeal.

Reaching out I pull on the handle of the truck door and the catch gives. The door starts to move up. I hold it an inch from its home and a breeze blows in. Bathing my face. I open the door a little further, roll under and drop to the ground. As I stand I find myself facing a breezeblock wall. Reaching back I grab the sports bag, push the door down and twist the handle to lock it. The sports bag is lumped onto my shoulder as I walk round the truck.

The skyline of Houston dominates the scene. The driver has pulled into a truck stop a few miles short of the city. Semis and trucks are spread around like discarded toys in a kid's bedroom. A single-storey, low-slung building with plate glass ground to ceiling windows reveals a diner, and to the right there are signs for the washrooms. I choose the latter and a few seconds later I'm emptying my bladder.

Popping the sports bag on the toilet lid to rifle through I find a wash kit, fresh white shirt, boxers, jeans, socks, a lightweight blue rain-jacket and a baseball cap. I pull them all out. The bus driver matches me in height but not in girth.

There are pay-as-you-go showers at the back of the washroom. I repack the bag, pay the attendant, grab a towel and scrub myself raw.

The driver's wash kit is small but on the money. Toothpaste, toothbrush, mouthwash, deodorant, aftershave, mini shaver – the works. I dry myself and put on the driver's clothes, wincing a little at using someone else's boxers.

A shave and a splash later and, with the help of my belt pulling the oversized jeans tight, I'm feeling a little more human. Check my reflection - if the suits have a description of me it isn't in a white shirt, jeans and blue jacket. I ram the baseball cap on and I'm no longer the me that walked into the washroom.

Now for some food.

The diner is busy and I spot Graham in the corner tucking into some serious cholesterol. I order up coffee and a meatball sub, paying with my dwindling money supply. A slip of paper falls from between two tens and drifts to the floor. I pick it up and study it.

'2234 Irondale Lane, Fairway Oaks, Hudson. Key in the pelican's beak.'

It's written in Charlie's scrawl. I take my food to a window seat and check that there are no black SUVs before eating and studying the slip of paper. The address is alien.

The first bite of the meatballs and the taste floods my mouth. Rich and thick. Just the way mother would have done them. I slug some coffee and let the caffeine and food get to work. Fingering the index on the pilot's map the only Hudson I can find is about forty miles north of St Petersburg, in Florida on the Gulf coast. If Graham is Tampa-bound he has to skirt the town. If he takes US 19 he'll almost pass through it. If he opts for the freeway he'll pass about five miles east of it.

Maybe my luck is changing.

I weigh up the piece of paper. If the suits have decided to

ride Charlie then he might have given up the address. It's no mistake it's bundled in the cash. Charlie's giving me somewhere to hide out. The meatballs give way to sweet onion and I wonder if the suits will lean on Charlie. A few questions, sure, but would they get heavy? Maybe. If so Hudson is a no-go. But I need a destination and Charlie's address is the only place I have at the moment. I swallow the last of the sub and drain the coffee. Graham is reading USA Today. The waitress is refilling his coffee and my lift seems in no hurry to get back onto the road.

A small shop sits at the entrance to the diner and I go inside to stock up on chips, Coke and a large bottle of water. It'll get warm in the truck and I need something to drink and somewhere to piss in if we're in for a long drive. An inflatable neck rest, a blow-up cushion, a packet of Lifesavers and I'm set.

The Houston sun is on bake mode and I've no desire to cook in the rear of the truck before I have to. A coffee refill sounds good and Graham has yet to pay for his food.

Outside, the drivers play Tetris with their vehicles in the parking lot. My eyes keep a look out for SUVs or Regals and more than once a black car catches my eye, but when Graham stretches and pays the bill there's still no sign of the suits. I exit and I'm in the back of the truck and crouching at the rear before he has left the building.

As the engine fires up I blow up the cushion and neck rest. I have a thought and clamber to the back and, as we start to move, empty the sculptures from one of the boxes into the others. Once it's clear of wood I get in and I'm fairly sure that I can't be seen from the door if someone looks in. It's too cramped to stay in for long but it's a better hiding place than crouching at the back.

I crawl forward and lie down, letting the rocking movement play over me.

* * *

Bang…

My head hits the side of one of the boxes and I'm awake. Despite myself I've been out for the count and we've either hit something or come close. The truck has stopped moving and I sit up to check my watch. The luminous dial tells me it's gone four. The heat is intense and I crawl to the back and get into my box. Once settled I pop a Coke and down it in three gulps.

The sound of a siren cuts in.

The police.

My heart lurches into the starting blocks and I try and bury myself deeper in the box. I can hear talking before the door rattles up and light floods in.

'See,' says Graham. 'Wooden carvings.'

The vehicle rocks as he climbs into the truck and roots around in one of the boxes.

'OK sir,' says a voice used to giving orders. 'Do you mind if I take a look?'

'Be my guest.'

The truck moves as another body gets on board.

'Look officer,' Graham adds, 'I just lost concentration and slipped onto the meridian. No big deal. There's no damage.'

'Could you jump out sir?'

The truck moves again.

There are six rows of boxes in the truck from back to front. I hear the police officer dig into a box followed by the click of wood on wood. Then the truck rocks and I realize that he's crawling over the boxes to get at the ones in the back. Something has wound up his radar. He stops to check a few more boxes before crawling a little nearer. I can smell stale sweat and long-since applied antiperspirant. His breathing is laboured and I imagine a gut hanging out over the police-issue gunbelt.

'Fuck.' The word spits out as the truck rocks again. It sounds like he's fallen into one of the boxes. He's onto the last but one row and I know what he's after. If the driver is hiding anything it'll be at the back and that's where I am. I wait for a face to appear over the lip. I grab at my breath and hold it. Bury my head in my lap but that won't prevent me from being seen. I tense my legs. If he appears I have one choice. Up and away. I just hope I can take him by surprise.

More rooting and he's in the box next to mine. My muscles are starting to ache as I tense, ready to leap. My hands get ready to grab him. Click. He drops one of the carvings back into the box.

'Anything?' A new voice.

'No.' The policeman's voice is so close that I jump a little.

'We have a call,' says the new voice. 'A 10-67 in Starling St. We're the nearest.'

'OK. Coming.'

I let go of the breath as the police officer moves back to the door. There's some chat and the door slides down. A few more minutes and the truck starts to move again. We bump and grind to exit the meridian before smoothing out as the road takes over. I climb from the box and my back clicks. More bones find other bones to play with. Once back at the door I place the cushion at my head and leave the neck rest to one side.

I try to settle down again. There will be no sleep this time.

Chapter 21

The dim light from the gap in the door is gone as day drops to dusk. The driver is on a mission. No stops, foot down. He's smooth as well. No sudden turns and since the incident with the meridian we are, if anything, moving faster. I had expected him to pull in after the bump with the grass but he's on his second wind

The truck slows. We swing to the right, tumble over something rough and come to a halt. I crawl into my box and wait. Nothing. I crawl back and flip the door handle. The air outside floods in and my sweat dries in the coolness.

A Holiday Inn Express sign lights up the parking lot around me. I jump out and Graham is at the reception desk, checking in. One of the comfy beds inside could be mine too. But I've no idea when he is likely to set out, and rides to Hudson could be thin on the ground. I don't fancy spending a night in the truck and wait for an hour before approaching the check-in desk.

A young lad, maybe a couple of years past the peak of his acne, is manning the desk. He's neat in the company uniform but his hair is a mess or, more likely, it's his way of rebelling against the corporate world. He looks up as I approach. 'Can I help you sir?'

'Sure can. A friend of mine checked in an hour ago. He's driving the small truck.' I point as I say this. 'I've to meet him in the morning but I don't want to disturb him tonight. Will you be on in the morning?'

The change of direction with the last bit of the question throws him a little. 'Eh. Yes.'

'Good. I'd like to check in and I'd also like a wake-up call when my friend is ready to leave. Would this be possible?'

'What is your friend's name?'

Good question.

'Graham.'

'Graham what?'

Good question. I don't answer. 'Do you have a room?'

He checks with the computer and it confirms what is obvious from the lack of cars outside

'Yes sir. Will that be one night?'

I nod.

The phone next to him rings and he picks it up. 'Certainly Mr Laidlaw. 7.00am and Mr Laidlaw, I have a friend of yours here…'

I violently shake my head as he says this. He looks confused as hell. 'Eh… Sorry Mr Laidlaw my mistake. 7.00am. Have a good night.'

He replaces the phone.

I lean forward. Trying to make it look friendly. 'It's a bit complicated but I don't want to see him right now.'

He nods. 'Do you still want me to call you when Mr Laidlaw checks out?'

'You know what, just leave it. I'll phone him in the morning.'

He finishes checking me in and doesn't blink when I take the cash option for paying.

Once in my room I strip and place the clothes on a hanger. I run the faucet to hot, fill up the basin with water and take out my own boxers to give them a wash. I do the same for my socks and throw in the bus driver's shirt for good measure. I wring them out as best I can and hang them over the shower rail. Change my mind and hang them over the TV and take a shower. Change my mind and fill the tub for a bath and make myself a coffee. Change my mind and slip on my trousers and old shirt and empty the vending machine in the lobby of three Cokes. Return to the room, strip and slip into the tub with a glass and a bottle of Wild Turkey sitting on the floor next to me

- cola cans at the ready.

The tub is a touch too small for me to spread out in but it's luxury compared to the back of the truck.

As the hot water works its magic on the outside of my body the Wild Turkey does the trick inside. I'm hungry but, despite the sleep I have squeezed in today, I'm too tired to get dressed and hunt down food. Breakfast will have to be a big one.

The constant roar of traffic makes me wish I had flipped on the radio but now that I'm up to my chest in water I'm not for moving. It dawns on me that I don't know where I am. It also dawns on me that no one else knows either. Of course the smartass suits may have me all figured by now. SUVs rushing to the scene. Plastic cuffs at the ready. Standing outside the door as I lie in the tub. Metal battering ram at the ready or, to be less dramatic, a master key from the receptionist. Six of them and me dragged naked into the parking lot and back to Lendl.

I hear a bang from the corridor and the water chills around me. I strain to catch another sound and hear a man and a woman laughing. I relax. How the hell could the suits know I'm here?

But the relaxed mood is gone and I climb from the tub and towel down. The bed is inviting but I do the good boy thing and brush my teeth first only to undermine the action by pouring another drink. One more and I'll call it quits. I don't want to miss my ride in the morning.

I prop up a few pillows, lie down and wonder how Lorraine is. I want to call but I can't figure a way to do this without giving away my location. Not for the first time I'm left wondering at the lack of people I can turn to. LA is a desert as far as friends go and my old army colleagues are few and thin on the blacktop. My mom and dad are long since gone. My brother could be on the moon for all I know. I laugh. He really could be on the moon. He works for NASA - a trained astronaut. Home boy made good – unlike me. 'Disappointment' was what my dad thought my middle name should have been.

I let my head wander over recent events. The truth is something I don't want to face. I'm a catalyst. A freak of nature. An emotion engine. Driving people to commit acts of random violence or it could all still be a wave of coincidences. An unprecedented set of episodes. Unrelated. Unconnected. A mathematician's statistical nightmare. The last of the Wild Turkey slides down my throat and I pick up the phone and put in for an alarm call to the receptionist for 6.00am.

My head is ready for sleep but my body isn't. I scramble around the bed like a lovesick spider. I move my drying clothes, flick on the TV and find CNN, expecting to see my face above a caption telling the nation *Do not approach this man. He's dangerous. If you see him inform the police immediately.*

The top-of-the-hour headlines slide into view and the world is in a shit state. I wonder when the world wasn't a turkey shoot. I kill the TV, get up and pull back the drapes. The parking lot sits beyond my window and I can see the truck from here. Beyond it a strip of badly rutted road leads to the highway. A car pulls in, u-turns and exits. A run of trees blocks out any other view.

A glow in the sky suggests I'm near a major city. I flick on the light over the dressing table, pick up a short brochure on the hotel chain and discover I am in, or near, Mobile. Graham's not hanging around.

I'm pulling the drapes shut when I catch sight of some movement. Two men pass under the Holiday Inn Express ad sign, dressed head to foot in black. They walk to the front of Graham's truck. They're too far away to make out much detail but both look short of six feet and skinny with it. One of them flips at the handle of the truck. His friend tries the other door and they wander back to the hood. A chat and they're off to the rear.

Shit.

I can't let them do the truck over. My little ruse with the receptionist is stacking up to be a bad idea. Follow the logic. The two thieves raid the back of the truck. The next morning my driver discovers the break-in. The police are called. They interview the receptionist and I appear on the police note pad. The police ask after me. I'm gone. On the run. They have a description and I'm wanted. If the suits are worth their salt then I'll pop up and they'll know where I am.

Strike that - scenario two. The two thieves raid the back of the truck. The next morning the driver doesn't do a check. I ride along and somewhere between here and Tampa he checks the load. He calls the police, mentions his stop in Mobile. A phone call and I'm there again. The suits close in and know I am somewhere between Mobile and wherever my driver discovers he has been done.

Scenario three. Same as Scenario two but my driver doesn't check until he reaches his destination. I'm history as a stowaway but he calls the police, mentions Mobile and there I am once more. The suits close in and know I'm somewhere between Mobile and Tampa.

The truck getting done over is not going to help me stay on the run. How hard can it be to just vanish? Don't thousands of people do it every year? Why the hell is this so hard?

Because there isn't some black ops agency tracking them down!

I need to stop the thieves. I flick off the light, throw on my pants and my old shirt. I'm pulling on my shoes as I return to keep a watch on the parking lot.

They're gone. I breathe a sigh of relief and swallow it again when I see the truck rock. They're inside. Why the hell didn't the driver lock it? Stupid question. I was the one that left it open.

I grab the room keycard and head for reception. I could use the fire escape but it will be alarmed. The receptionist looks up as I walk out and I realize that I'm wearing the same shirt I left LA in.

Too late to do anything about it.

I pull up a tuneless whistle and slap my feet on the wet concrete as I walk towards the truck. Trying to scare them off. The truck door rattles down as I approach. The front of the truck is bathed in light but the tail is in shade. I slide along the vehicle. No whistling now. No slapping. Either they're gone or they're still inside.

Rain starts to fall. Light drizzle works down my neck collar. I'm halfway along the side when the truck moves. Enough to suggest that at least one of them is still inside. Basic training one-o-one would have been to riddle the truck with bullets and then go in. Get real. I scan the bush behind the truck for any sign of movement and back off, circle round to the other side and then back to the front.

Dropping to my knees I lie in the damp and crawl under the truck - aiming for the rear. A large puddle has formed in a dip halfway down the truck. I have no choice but to crawl through it. My pants soak up the water, followed by my boxers, my shirt, my shoes and my socks. I grab at my belt and tighten it a notch to stop the water-heavy pants from paying a visit to my ankles. Keeping my eyes fixed on the gap between the truck rear and the ground I grind out the next few feet. A wet sponge belly-flopping forward.

I stop short of emerging from underneath.

Time to wait.

Raindrops bounce a few inches in front of my nose. The night is warm but the rain is cool. Heat starts to seep from me. It's uncomfortable but hardly life- threatening. The truck vibrates and a scrape echoes down through the drive- shaft above my head.

The latch is being turned.

I tense and the roller is lifted a few inches. There's no movement from the bushes. The door winds up and a leg drops over the edge. The heel swings back and I have to roll to the side to avoid being kicked. A second leg appears and one of the thieves drops to the parking lot. A third leg appears and I take a breath. They must have bedded down when they heard me coming.

The fourth leg drops into sight.

'What in the grease bucket is this?' The accent is heavy southern.

'Ain't nothin' but lumps of wood.' Another deep south drawl.

'Worth anythin'?'

'Who knows?'

'There's enough of it to fill ma ma's barn.'

'Let's dump it all in the pick-up and go. We can figure for it later.'

'Go get the wheels.'

I watch one of them walk off and the other lifts his leg to jump back in the truck. I wait until he's inside and I slide out from underneath. Standing up slowly I find the man in the truck with his back to me. I check that the other one is out of sight and reach in, grab the thief's jacket and pull. He catapults from the rear and flies over my shoulder. I turn to jump on him but find empty air. Something slams into the side of my head. My head lights up and he's on top of me.

He drops his knee onto my chest as I hit the ground and lets me have some good news with his right fist. I roll my head with the blow. The second punch is already incoming. Boxer-quick. I snap my head to the right and he grazes my chin. A third blow and I snap my head back and to the side. The strike misses and he uses the ground as punchbag. He howls and pulls his hand back. I push up and dislodge him from my chest. As I try and roll free I lash out with my foot and, more by luck than design, I catch him high on the hip. He screams.

I roll onto my front, raise my backside in the air and I'm hit from behind with a kick that dead-legs me on the thigh.

Shit but he's real quick.

He follows up with another kick and I think he has just separated two of my ribs. My breath vanishes and I'm back on the floor. I feel his weight as he drops from a height and drives his knee into my side. I try to spin away but he catches me on the back of the head with the side of his fist.

The rev of an engine suggests that his friend is back. A flash of headlights and another blow slams my head off the parking lot black. Another hit and sparks fly across my vision. My hearing dulls. My ribs are throbbing and I'm losing the battle to stay conscious.

A door slams. 'Corey, what the hell?'

The attack stops and Corey stands up. 'He jumped me.'

'Need a hand?'

'Nope.' Corey bends down. The blows start again.

I curl up to minimize the target. It is all I can do. Corey gets bored, jumps off me, stands up and lands a kick in my stomach. 'What should we do with 'im?'

His friend strolls over. Casual. 'Get the duct tape outta the pick-up.'

Another kick from Corey as he leaves and my head explodes. Above my neck, below the centre of my head, a small bomb goes off as the kernel cracks. A grenade spreads shrapnel and I cry out. The pain comes in waves. Deep, deep pain that caves in my vision, my thinking. I'm flicking in and out of the dark. I pull up as tight as I can. Corey's friend looks down at me but with little more than mild interest. I'm battling to stay conscious as

Corey returns with a roll of tape. 'He's seen us. Maybe we should take care of him a bit more permanent. Make it look like an accident though. You know - like Carl.'

'Over some wood?' Corey's friend says.

'He's seen us,' says Corey.

'True.'

Not good.

I place a virtual hand in my skull and try and get a hold of the chaos. Amidst the pain I have a single thought. If I'm a catalyst. If I really am a freak can I set off people – mano a mano – can I? If so why isn't it happening now? When I need it. Why aren't the attackers tearing lumps out of each other? Corey starts to unroll the tape. Iraq, the plane, the agency, the bus – why not now? Screaming hot metal is flowing through my head.

Corey bends down to tape me.

I shout over the noise in my skull and my voice is loud in the parking lot. *'Now. Why not now?'*

Corey stops at the outburst. He stands up again and rocks his head from side to side. His friend looks at him. 'Whatcha waiting on?'

Corey keeps rolling his head back and forth for a few more seconds before stopping – his head at an angle. His eyes are narrowing. Slits against an invisible wind. Then they snap open. His head straightens and he leans forward. A twist around the horizontal and his head settles side-on to me.

'Get on with it!' Corey's friend senses something is off kilter.

Corey turns on his heel, dropping the tape on the ground. It bounces twice and rolls under the truck, coming to rest on the same spot I had been lying in not five minutes ago. It tips on its side. Corey's friend watches it vanish from view. He lifts his head – trying to figure what's going on. Corey takes a step towards him and pivots, left foot planted - right foot trailing. He crouches, only a few inches, priming the spring. His shoulders come back and his head goes down. He swings on his hip and his trailing foot lifts from the ground, supporting knee bent, hip leaning out and over, keeping the centre of balance, working his muscles to build momentum and keeping the movement smooth. The trailing foot overtakes his body, knee still bent, the foot rising as it does so, turned inwards. His eyes are fixed on his friend. The right hand swings out to counterbalance the flying leg. Low down his hand is less than a foot from the ground. Bending at his stomach, his flying leg unfurling - he drives forward, gut muscles pulling tight, foot now extended, supporting knee springing straight.

His foot connects with his friend's face, heel to chin. A powerful blow. Practiced. This is no amateur attempt. His friend's head bounces back as far as his neck will allow. No time for surprise in his eyes. They are blank. He starts to go down, his feet flying from under him. His arm flies out. A reflex action but he's close to the rear of the truck. Too close. His hand misses the edge of the loading strip and he keeps falling.

Corey is still spinning. Unwinding the attack. Using the kick to make a three- sixty. Before he can complete the circle there is a sickening smack as Corey's friend's head meets the metal edge of the truck. His body tries to keep going - gravity pulling it to the ground - his head is a brake.

Corey watches as his friend's head bounces hard and rolls from the truck - the light gone from his eyes. His body a rag doll as it tumbles onto the wet asphalt. Corey settles from the roundhouse kick and has to squat to resist the forward motion.

'Nick.' Single word. Quiet. From the back of Corey's throat.

Nick's head lolls to one side and his tongue pushes through his lips. A single drop of blood squeezes through the space created by his tongue – pushed by his last breath escaping.

My headache vanishes as the blue world takes hold. My

night vision is acute – bringing everything into perspective with a flash of stage lights going up. Corey is still rocking from the kick as Nick's left foot twitches. The final act of a man with no future.

The roar of the traffic from the highway fades. A gentle twist of the volume dial and it's background noise. The pick-up is kicking out exhaust. Dirt black /blue - suggesting the engine was due for a service in the late eighties. The driver's door is open – the interior light a cobalt wash. High above a silver blue bullet glides by with a wink of wing lights.

Corey has stopped rocking and his shoulders have slumped. His body giving way to the recognition of what he has just done. He lets go at the knees and drops to the ground – reaching for his friend. Cold, unmoving eyes tell him the truth of his actions but still he reaches for him, unsure what else to do. He touches Nick's neck looking for a pulse because that's what they do in Law and Order. Then the wrist because he's seen it on The Wire. Now he's at a loss.

I watch him fall to his backside. The man on the ground is dead because of me. Not by my hand. But by my mind. The blue is becoming a bruise then a blood clot, then dark.

And now I need to act again. To take control. To figure out what to do next. I want to run but I can't leave. The chain would kick in. Police, death, interviews, the driver and then I would appear – courtesy of the receptionist.

I stand up and place a hand on the Corey's shoulder. He doesn't react. I bend down and he turns his head towards me. His eyes are vacant, uncomprehending. I point to the truck and he gets up. I grab his shoulder and indicate towards his freshly dead friend. 'In the truck.'

Somehow I know he'll obey. No questions.

He sighs. A sound out of place. He sighs again and reaches down to grab his friend by the arms. I check that no one is watching and grab Nick's feet. Three steps and he's in the back of the pick-up. I step back. 'As far as you can. Just drive.' Corey nods at my words, gets in and with the speed of a snail on dope drives from the parking lot.

I return to the truck and pull down the door. I check the lip of the loading strip and see a small clot of hair and blood. I wipe it with the arm of my shirt and head back to the hotel.

The receptionist is missing and for that I'm grateful.

Once back in the room I take off the shirt and scrub it until my hands hurt. I do the same for the pants and fall on the bed.

An hour before my alarm call I am still awake.

Chapter 22

The phone rings. I knock it from the cradle and let the automated voice talk to the carpet. My eyes can't have been shut for more than ten minutes. I try to sit up and pain enters my life as the kicking from last night stacks up a nice range of options for my brain to focus on. Top of the charts is my jaw. Not broken. I don't think. But sore from the punches. A shower doesn't help and putting on damp clothes doesn't improve the situation.

While packing the bag and checking the room before leaving I decide to make sure that we're police-free and that the pick-up driver hasn't been picked up.

Turning away from the truck as I exit the hotel – just in case someone is looking - I start to circle the building. A grass vista of neatly-mown yard rolls in front of me. I pass ground floor bedroom windows. If anyone is looking out I'll be a bit of a surprise. Reaching the far end of the hotel I stop, push my head round the corner. The truck is sitting quietly. There's no swarm of police around it. No CSI team. No SUVs. No suits. Of course they could be hiding, waiting for me. But taking me in my room would have been a far more sensible option than waiting until I was in the open. After all you can't run when your hotel room has only one exit.

I make my way back round the hotel again - just in case - and approach the truck from the other side. I check for any blood and hair I may have missed on the lip of the loading strip. It's clean. I examine the ground where Corey's head had lain. Clean. Another quick look round and I yank up the roller door. As I climb to the back and settle into my box I roll the night's events over in my head.

The implications are massive. I'm not only a freak but a dangerous freak. A dangerous freak that could be used as a weapon?

Last night I wanted it to happen. Wanted the grinding head pain to appear. Willed it to happen. Screamed for it to happen. And it did. Wasn't that the way it went down? Wasn't that the way it all rolled out in front of me? My own red carpet to a new world. A bad world. An incomprehensible world - because these things don't happen. Can't happen. People don't reach out through thin air and turn others into killing machines. They just don't.

But I did. Just when I needed it. Stressed to high heaven. When I was stressed... and there's the rub. Is that when it happens? Stress?

Iraq. I was on the ground. A blank to the planet. Both times. So that's that. It's not stress. We're back in the good old world of coincidence. None of this is explainable in the everyday world. So what in the hell is the blue world? Where does that fit into the new mathematically-challenging life that I am coursing through?

My thoughts are interrupted by the sound of Graham getting in the cab. The engine fires and we are back on the road to Tampa. Still no police and this makes me wonder what has happened to Corey. Maybe he's still on the road. On a mission to nowhere but if he is – why? If this is all coincidence then why would he get in his truck, dead friend in the back, and drive off?

The heat in the truck is already building. I clamber from the box and lie down at the back of the truck. The motion suggests that my driver is in a hurry He sees his destination and wants to be there today. No more layovers.

Two hours in and the truck pulls over. I'm shoved from a stupor and forced back in the box. My body complains big time at the movement but we are only filling with gas and are soon on the move again.

Hours begin to sew together like long tough strips. Each one stretching to join to the next but never far enough. Always a little further to go than would make sense. Time as a rubber band. Snapping together when I drift off to sleep. Moving forward in leaps and fits. Awake - a minute is an hour.

My mind turns to getting off the truck. I have no intention of finishing the journey with Graham in Tampa. Charlie's house in Hudson is worth checking out. It's either that or a few nights in a hotel before my cash runs out. I'm hoping the driver sees US 19 as an option. Traffic lights will make it easy to jump off. If he chooses the freeway I'm in for a long trek back from Tampa.

A few more hours crawl away and we leave the endless drone of the freeway and hit a start/stop motion. I twist onto my front and grab the release handle for the door. My ribs bitch but I ignore them. I hope there's no door alarm in the cab. If there is I need to be ready to run.

I pull the handle up and it releases from the catch. I let the roller take hold and push up, keeping my weight behind the action in case the door springs wide. The road is vanishing into the distance - unwinding beneath me. The highway is bordered with a succession of stores and businesses. We are talking six lanes wide at this point and through the buildings I can see the sun starting its journey into the Gulf of Mexico.

We hit a set of lights and I lean out. There's a road sign but from this angle I can't read it. I wonder why Graham has left the freeway. Are we in Tampa already? I do some mental math but I reckon we are still a good few hours away.

I'm caught napping when we hang a left and I let go of the door. It hangs for a second and then slams down. I breathe in. I don't fancy trying to close the thing while on the move. I grab the handle again and lift it. Once more air rushes in but this time it's slower. We're off the main road and in a backwater estate. The houses are typical Florida for the less well-off – all board and peeling paint. Streets creep past but there's no indication as to the area we're driving through.

The truck slows at the next four-way stop and crosses it at a crawl. Brakes are hit and we stop. I jump back, climb over the boxes and dive into my hiding place. I hear the door fly up and the noise of a box being scraped across the truck floor. Graham grunts as the box drops to the ground. The door stays open.

I wait before sticking my head up. Hold or go. It's an age-old problem in the field. Hold or go. I go. If I'm caught now I'll need to bullshit my way out.

Dropping to the ground there's little sign of life but a lot of wear and tear around me. Pick-ups and ten year-old SUVs outnumber cars three to one. Every third house has a flag waving on the front yard. We are deep in Schlitz and Old Milwaukee land.

My driver is staggering up the drive of a house that has had some out of the ordinary TLC applied to it. The paint is fresh and grass covers the front yard , mowed into neat lines. The small fence that borders the lawn is white and unbroken. An oasis in a Home and Garden desert.

The front door opens and I duck out of sight. There's chatter but nothing I can make sense of. Laughter and the door closes. I jump back into the truck and hide – waiting for Graham to return but ten minutes later and I'm still on my own. I get out again, wondering at the man's attention to security. Not only does he not lock the truck door but he also feels it's OK to leave the thing open in an area where even the packing boxes could be used to turn a buck. I almost feel a duty to stay and play guard to his goods.

I nip round the truck, keeping it between the house and me. The passenger door is open and I reach in and pull out a battered Rand McNally road atlas - no GPS for my boy. The pilot's map is useless for up-close detail. I walk back to the cross walk. Christine and 2nd. I flip through the map and track down the possibles for the two road names and come up with only one town with both. The town is called Shady Hills and I'm not much more than ten miles from Hudson.

A young man with jeans so low it's hard to tell if he's lost ten pounds in the last ten minutes or is just too lazy to pull them up walks up to me. His ears are full of white as an iPod pumps music intravenously. Hair hides his eyes. 'Dude, got a flame?'

I shake my head.

'Know where I can get one, man?'

Hippy meets Hip Hop. He's white with a black voice and Haight-Ashbury lyrics. Go figure. 'Sorry.'

'Bummer. You sure, man.'

'Positive.'

'Bummer.'

He likes the word.

I turn back to the truck but he isn't finished.

'Could you get me one, man?'

I start walking and shake my head.

'Hey man, no need for the rude walk, man.'

I keep walking.

'Bummer. Could you tell me what I need to do next?'

The question stops me in my tracks. I don't want to turn round and re-engage but I am intrigued.

He keeps talking. 'Could you? My life could be better. Much better.'

The down in the grit accent is slipping. A southern lilt of a well educated boy creeping through. I still don't want to turn. Turning will mean speaking and speaking will mean I might miss my ride. Although I'm already thinking my time with the truck is done. My driver will head for the Suncoast Parkway and bypass Hudson – the bible according to Rand McNally says there is no other choice that makes sense.

The boy steps towards me. 'Could you? I mean you kind of look like you might know about these things.'

My driver exits the house. A man with a neatly trimmed goatee waves him goodbyes. There's no way I can make the back of the truck now even if I wanted. I feel sad. I had intended to take one of the sculptures as a memento. Leaving twenty bucks of course. Assuming they were worth that much or maybe that would have been too little. Graham slams the truck door shut and he's history.

Shit.

My bag. My clothes. The Wild Turkey.

Shit.

Fingerprints. DNA.

Shit.

'Excuse me sir? Can you help? My life seems to have gone wrong somewhere.' The boys voice is close.

What the hell is this kid on?

There is enough in the truck to tie me to the Greyhound bus and from there to the plane and from there to the truck and from there to Florida.

Shit.

The boy keeps going. 'I did very well at school. I did well at college but I met up with some cool guys. At least they were cool when I met them. Now I think about it I'm not sure they were cool. Too much drugs. Too much of everything really.'

I turn. I don't want to but I can't see the downside now. He's standing a few feet away. Head down. 'My ma is worried sick. She thinks I'm going to end up in prison. I think I might. What do I do?'

The boy is a little different to a few minutes ago. His pants are up round his waist. His shirt is tucked in. His hair pulled back from his eyes and he's holding it in a ponytail with his left hand. The false accent is gone and he stands straight – the street slump gone.

'Look,' I say. 'I'm not sure what you want but if you want a bit of advice - smarten up, get back to College and work hard. Get a part-time job and knuckle down. Will that do?'

His face lights up. 'Wonderful.'

He screws round on his heels. A military turn and marches off – whistling.

What in the hell was that all about?

But I know. At least I know he's going to march all the way home. He's going to walk into his house. Up the stairs. Into his room. He's going to throw off the street clothes and pull on an Izod polo shirt, a pair of chinos and a set of Payless brogues. He's going to flush the smack he has hidden in among his childhood Lego, down the toilet. He'll go to the barber's and get a number two. He'll walk to the College and wait until the doors open tomorrow and sign up again. Then he'll go down to McDonald's and ask if they need anyone to flip burgers or clean the john. After that he'll try and ace the first year at college.

How do I know this? I don't. Somehow it's the only thing that makes sense and this in itself doesn't make sense – but it does.

I feel good about it. Real good. Like I've just saved a life. A One Republic moment – only I didn't have to stay up all night to do it. I turn west and look to the dipping sun. Hudson lies ten miles that way and ten miles is a three hour walk. A walk I am looking forward to.

The bag is history. The truck is history. The nonsense around me is history. For a bit. It may not go away but for the next three hours it can sit on the shelf. I may even blow a few dollars on a beer or two.

Chapter 23

The neon bar-light wraps a warm welcome around my shoulders and carries me in. It has echoes of Charlie's place but heavier with locals, although, thankfully, there is no brushwood moment as I cross the threshold. No one cares. Two barmen are on call. The younger asks what I want and I ask for a Coors Light. JD is too heavy for the moment. He cracks one from the cooler and pops the top. I decline the frosted glass and neck a third of the contents.

The feelgood sensation is still lingering. So much so that I made a point of looking for waifs and strays on my walk. A walking Oprah meets Jerry thing.

I sit on one of the stools guarding the bar and relax into my drink. Cool time. The first real cool time since the back alley at Charlie's place. This brings up Lorraine and the cool moment passes. I can see her lying on the bar floor. Face pouring with blood. Mary being carried away screaming. I look at the payphone on the wall. It is heart-achingly hard not to get in touch. Not to pick up the receiver and dial the hospital number. Not to listen to her voice telling me she's fine and, by the way, what are you talking about – electrocution – me?

'New boy?'

The question comes from my neighbor - a suited and booted man with slicked-back hair and a faint air of decline about him. I half smile at him. 'Just stopping for one.'

'I used to say that. He returns the smile and flips a hand at the nearest barman for another. 'Where are you from?'

'New York,' I lie.

'Never been. Kind of a Florida State man me. Tim Askovitz.'

He reaches out a hand.

'Paul Dearham.' Paul was my medical liaison officer when I

was discharged from the army.

'Knew a Dearham once. In the army I think.'

I think he notices the double take on my face. 'Really. Never been in the army,' I reply.

'Me neither. What do you do?'

'Freelance security. You?'

'Anything that pays.' He laughs. 'Used to be the sales director for a big software company but I got canned. Downsizing. Recession – you know the drill.'

'And now?'

'On the road. Sales. Bag in hand. Hand on bell. Foot in door. Mostly cleaning stuff.' He points to a sample case squeezed between his legs and the bar. 'You don't happen to need a couple of hundred gallons of 'Mr Kleen - Number 1'?'

I shake my head.

'Same story everywhere.'

My good mood has evaporated and I want to be out of here. The change is sudden, dramatic. I slug the Coors but there's too much to finish in one go.

'Your face looks a little familiar.' He is leaning towards me.

'Can't think why,' I say.

'Bit like a friend of mine. You have that look. Lost. Not sure of what's going on.'

I make the effort and drain the bottle before standing up. 'Time to go.'

'You just got here!'

'A quick visit. Nice meeting you.'

'Have one more?'

'I can't.'

'Why? Where do you need to be?'

'Somewhere.'

'No you don't. You don't have to be anywhere. You don't need to be two yards from here in the next week.' His voice has an aggressive edge.

'Yeah, well I'm off. Nice meeting you.'

'No it wasn't. You think I'm a waster.'

I get up.

He stands. 'Can see it in your eyes. Waster. Used to be big time – now a waster.'

'Tim. Leave the man alone.' The barman is on his shoulder.

I push open the door and Tim shouts out. 'Ain't no waster. I know where I am. Where are you? Where are you?'

The door cuts him off and I regret going for the beer. I walk out into the parking lot. US 19 hums along in front of me and I begin walking. If I have my directions correct it can't be more than a couple of miles or so to Hudson.

The day is closing off and the traffic winding up. I cross strip mall after strip mall. Parking lot after parking lot. The sign for Hudson appears and now I'm looking for Hudson Avenue. I find it. A Regions Bank on one corner and a Walgreens on the other. There is a Win-Dixie in the mall behind the bank and I enter the world of A/C and ask where Fairway Oaks is.

'When you hit two gas stations keep going - it's on your left.' So says the man stacking the trolleys.

I wander along the road and find the gas stations sitting next to another mall. I start to hunt down Irondale Lane. The whole name thing is a giveaway. Golf course development. I enter the estate and glimpse a golf hole in between the homes. The area is nice. Large, well kept, stand-alone houses. Each stands in its own plot and most are in good condition. The odd house sits in an overgrown garden but since the credit crunch nowhere has got off. Probably repossessions that won't sell.

A sign telling me to beware of golf buggies signals a crossing point between green and tee. After a few false starts I find the street I'm looking for and finally the house. I walk by – trying to look like I belong there. There are no SUVs. No Regals. No suits. I walk up the blockwork drive. A large stone pelican sits next to the front door. I take a look round. Clear. I put my hand in the pelican's beak. Nothing. I dig a little deeper and feel metal, grasp it and pull it out.

The front door opens onto a sitting room. The house is well kept. To my right is a dining area and, beyond this, a large open-plan kitchen sits next to the TV lounge. In the corner of the lounge sliding doors lead out to a meshed-in pool. A quick wander and I count four bedrooms, three bathrooms and a walk-in changing room in the master bedroom to back up the sitting room, dining area, kitchen and lounge.

The decoration is neutral and the smell suggests it's been uninhabited for a while. Although someone is keeping the garden neat and the dust off the furniture. I flip the fridge. Empty. I spotted a Publix in the mall next to the gas stations. I do a fly round once more and leave. Pocketing the key, I head for the supermarket, stock up on chips, chocolate, a bottle of JD, Coke and something for breakfast.

On my return I slump into a large corner unit that is wrapped around the TV and crack a packet of Lays and a Hershey. I flick on the TV. The Tampa Bay Devil Rays are at home to the Toronto Blue Jays and the first of a three-game series is into the bottom of the second inning. I watch the game unfold and switch it off at the top of the fifth with the Devil Rays two to zip and looking good.

I enter the master bedroom and strip off. My clothes are fit for the trash but I search out the washing machine, load everything I have into it and tip in some powder that might or might not be for washing. As it starts to work I walk back to the bedroom and through to the shower.

Fifteen minutes later I'm lying on the bed. A JD and Coke in one hand, my dick in the other. I'm not doing anything with it – just a comfort thing. There are paperbacks stacked in a display unit and I pull down a Stephen King I haven't read and try and give it some attention. I fail.

I go for another wander and see a red light flashing on the telephone. Pressing the play button brings Charlie's voice into the house.

'Each day at ten o'clock in the morning. I'll phone each day at ten o'clock until I get you.'

There are two more of the same messages on the machine. Each timed at ten o'clock. Twelve hours before the next one. Time for another drink and maybe bed.

Three drinks later and bed is still a distant objective. I fire up the TV again. The Rays win four to one and the late-night news doesn't have my face on it. I think about a late night dip but I have no costume and I'm not sure who can see in.

I lie on the bed and drain another and another and - good night.

...

The phone cuts through and I roll over and lift it.

'Craig?'

'Charlie?'

'You made it OK?'

I'm trying to clear my head. 'Yes.'

'Everything all right?'

'Where are you calling from?'

'A cell. Prepaid. Fresh out of the wrapper. Don't want the men in black listening in.'

'Lorraine. How is Lorraine?'

'Fine. I saw her last night. She's a bit groggy and I think your boys gave her something to keep her quiet.'

'What?'

'She doesn't have much recollection of the last few days.'

'But she's OK?'

'She's as OK as you get when you've had your face caved in

by a beer bottle. But the doc thinks it will heal well enough. She might need a minor op to correct the breaks but all in all she's a lot better than she could have been.'

'Thank God.' I roll back on the bed. The sense of relief is stunning. Simply stunning. 'When will she get out?'

'She hasn't been told.'

'The suits?'

'Nowhere to be seen at the hospital.'

'Do you think they'll leave her alone?'

'How the hell would I know but it would be hard to get to her. She's in a busy ward.'

It didn't stop the bastards electrocuting her.

'What are you going to do now?' asks Charlie.

'I don't know. Lie low?'

'You think that'll work?'

'No idea but the suits are serious. Deadly serious. Where are you?'

'Down on Santa Monica pier. Only place I could think of where I can get a clear view. Your boys have been back and I had a hell of a job losing the tail they put on me.'

'They're following you?'

'Craig I haven't always been injecting alcohol into the needy. I can tell when someone is playing my shadow.'

'And you're clear of them?'

'Not for long. How are you for cash?'

'Busted. Won't last another few days.'

'I can't send you cash. Too easy to trace but I might be able to get you a job. A bouncer. Private club. Not on the street. Discreet. Interested?'

'Charlie I can't. Whoever the suits are they'll find out.'

'They won't. There's no connection to me. Trust me. OK, if they tie me down and slice off my testicles a ham slice at a time I might talk but if they're that desperate you're fucked anyway.'

'Where is the job?'

'Tampa.'

'Let me think.'

'I'll call tonight. Seven o'clock.'

'OK.'

'I need to go.'

'Do me a favour?'

'What?'

'Pop in and see Lorraine for me.'

'Deal.'

The line drops dead and my first thought is a vision of Charlie standing in a ring of suits, the man in white linen nodding, telling him how well he has done. How clever he has been in tying me to the house while they arrange to have me lifted.

Only they would have been here by now. This is not a game. I pull back the blinds and at least it's a quiet road with no SUVs.

I'm going to take the job. I knew it as soon as Charlie mentioned it. I need the time to think. I need the cash. Lorraine is OK. For the moment. It's a risk keeping the tie with Charlie. House, job, phone calls but I need a line to my wife and the world is a crap place when you have no cash.

Tampa is straight down the US 19 and I'll need to figure the public transport system. Not that I'm a fan. The Greyhound was my first bus in ten years but public transport is as anonymous as you get. And it's cheap.

I take a trip to the washing machine and curse. I forgot to take the stuff out and dry it. I put it in the spin dryer, give it ten minutes and use the door that leads to the garage. Down in Florida the garage is a great place to dry stuff. Always hot and no chance of the sudden downpours that are part of Floridian life.

The garage would hold two cars and a party if need be and, much to my surprise, there is a vehicle taking up some of the space. It's wrapped in a white tarpaulin with just the wheels jutting out below. I pull the cover off and reveal a late nineties Toyota Corolla. White and a little dented it's the perfect runabout. If the keys are around I could be mobile. I have to assume that it's Charlie's, and my insurance is still good.

I try the doors. Locked. I search around the car. Behind the wheels. On top of the tires. I do a scan of the garage but it's clear of junk and there are no keys hanging up. I return to the house and begin a search. Systematically. I start with the master bedroom and check all the drawers and cupboards. I work my way room by room and strike lucky in the kitchen. Beneath the light switch there's a key hanging on a hook with the telltale Toyota bull sign embossed on it.

The remote is working and the car's lights flash at me as I press the tit. I flip the driver's door and heat barrels out. I let the interior equalize with the exterior and get in. Sticking the key in the slot I find a full tank. It's a stick shift but I'll get by. I start her up and she fires first time.

I'm still naked and my wardrobe is limited. I saw a sign for Walmart back at the main junction on my way in. Back in the bedroom I dig out a pair of shorts, an old T-shirt and a pair of flip-flops that are lying at the bottom of a drawer. Not exactly de rigueur but it will do until I can get to the store. I hit the remote on the garage door and I'm away.

The journey isn't far but it's a little bumpy. Not down to the lack of road maintenance. More down to me trying to work a stick shift in an unfamiliar car. I kangaroo for the first few turns and stall at every light. I park a country mile from the front door of the Walmart. Too scared to try and park anywhere near other cars.

I'm a cheap shopper. Ten dollar jeans, a pack of three white

T-shirts for seven dollars and unbranded trainers for fifteen bucks. The rest of my cash goes on a cheap suit, a shirt, tie and a pair of shoes. Along with boxers and a few other essentials it all but cleans me out. I'm taking the car for the job interview. I haven't the bus fare left.

On the way back I hang a left rather than a right at the main intersection. I slide down a road bordered on either side by houses backing onto row after row of canals. A boatyard appears and the road circles round on itself and meets the road coming in. A small beach borders the road with a bar as a full stop. It's a wooden affair and sits with its face towards the gulf. The sign above the door tells me it's called Sam's and they're advertising meals with a spectacular sunset over the sea.

Twenty yards from the beach a boat is exiting one of the canals. I eye the bar and wish I had a few more bucks in my pocket. A couple of beers watching the boat people do their business sounds fine. I pull into the parking lot that lines the beach and leave the engine running to power the A/C. On a whim I root around in the glove box with visions of finding a few dollars squirreled away.

Nothing.

I reach over into the back and flip down the split seat. The trunk has a black jacket lying on the floor. I pull it out and rifle the pockets. Andrew Jackson is crumpled up and hiding in an inside pocket. Andrew is worth a couple of beers of anybody's money. Well Sam, let's see how good the view is.

I stuff the twenty-dollar bill into my pocket and rip open the T-shirt packet to remove one. Jeans, T-shirt, boxers, socks and sneakers in tow I enter Sam's washroom and emerge – the thirty dollar man.

The bar opens out to an area corralled by a low fence. Colorful pictures of fish are fixed to it low down and an outdoor bar sits to the right. I choose one of the cut benches that border the fence. A narrow boardwalk flows from the fence to the water and then it's liquid all the way to Mexico.

A boat cuts through the swell to meet the main channel and a series of markers point the way to the sea.

A waitress bounds up and I ask for a Miller on draft. She smiles, vanishes and re-appears with a glass fresh out of the freezer, froth bubbling from the top. Ice cold and just perfect for a day like today. I lick at the white bubbles and inhale a few inches of the beer. With a satisfied sigh I lean back and fix my eyes on the departing boat.

The bar is quiet but I suspect that at night this will change.

A second boat cuts through the channel and falls in behind the first. A third and there's a convoy heading for a day of fun. I compose myself at the wheel of the boat and take a few minutes to suck in the salt air and feel the sea spitting in my face. I close my eyes and drift, the sun as my personal heater, the shallow breeze a pre-ordered cooler.

'Craig McIntyre?'

I snap out of the day dream and twist round to find the voice.

'Craig. What on earth are you doing here?'

Chapter 24

The girl is small. Five feet max. Short blonde hair. Tight white T-shirt and tighter jeans. She's rocking on high heels. Maybe a few inches short of five feet. I have no idea who she is. Pretty though.

She flicks her hair. 'You don't remember me?'

'Not really.'

She laughs. A friendly 'me I'm likeable' laugh. She sits down across from me. A little too premature for my liking.

'Can't say I'm surprised. Hatch Roll?' she says.

'Hatch Roll?'

'Sharon. Sharon Davies. Day nurse?'

Hatch Roll. Not a great time in my life but I still can't place her.

'A good few years ago. When I left you were still under observation.'

'You worked there?'

'Yip. Day nurse. Do you mind if I sit a while? Huh. I'm supposed to be meeting someone but they're running late.'

I wave my hand and she settles in. She flicks her hair again. 'How have you been?'

'Good.'

'When did you get out?' She makes it sound like I was in prison.

'A few years back.'

'You look good on it.'

I know she's lying. My clothes might be bright and shiny but the person inside is dull and muted. 'What are you doing here?'

She doesn't answer at first, her eye drawn to the departing boats. She looks back at me. 'I moved down here after I quit at Hatch Roll. You?'

'Taking a break.'

'On your own?'

I don't want to go there. She's a link to a past I want buried. She's also a connection to a world that the suits know all about.

'Yes,' I say.

'No girlfriend?'

Strange thing to ask. 'I need to be going,'

'You've hardly touched your beer.'

'I've been feeling a bit off. Thought this was a good idea. It isn't.'

'Where are you staying?'

I shuffle in my seat. Feel like I'm being interrogated. 'Hotel up the road. Days Inn. Just for last night. I'm moving on.'

'Where to?'

Give me a break. 'Don't know.'

'You have a car?'

Hells teeth. 'Yip.'

'Which one?'

'Sorry?'

'Which one's yours?'

"What is it with the twenty questions?'

'Just being friendly.'

She looks put out. Her face screws up. A pretty sort of screw-up.

'And what are you doing these days?'

'Same old, same old. New place though. Not far from here. Straight up the road and across the 19. Huh. You can't miss it and I never do.'

I'd seen the signs for the hospital on the way to the house. 'And I take it you stay local?'

"Fairway Oaks.'

Shit.

'It's not far from my work. Nice place. My boyfriend owns

it. Huh. It backs onto the golf course.'

I have a sinking feeling as I speak. 'What street?'

'Twenty questions.'

'Sorry?'

'Your turn. Twenty questions. It's Irondale Lane. Why?'

Double shit. 'No reason.'

A sun filled-silence descends. Count to twenty and still no talking.

'I thought you had to go?'

I can't. Unless I leave my car and walk. Sharon will see me get in and later on could spot the car when I get back to the house. 'You've cheered me up. Maybe I'll finish my beer.'

The waitress appears and Sharon orders an orange juice. 'So you feel Hatch Roll is in the past? Huh.'

She fixes her eyes on me as she speaks. There is a sparkle there that gives her real warmth.

''Yes and no. A lot of the time was a haze but when it was bad it was bad.'

'How long were you there?'

'Three years and a few months on weekend release.'

'Long time. What are you doing now?'

'This and that. I'm surprised you remember me.'

'When you've changed a man's clothes, cleaned him up and spoon-fed him you've done more than most wives ever do. Huh. My boss used to call you the hurricane.'

'Why?'

'You had a way of being at the centre of a storm. Usually when you were out of it on the meds – and you had some heavy meds at times. Fights on the ward, arguments – we even had a couple of stabbings. All in your ward. We moved you around to see what the heck was going on and you just kept being the eye. Calm, serene and nonsense all around.'

'No one ever said.'

'When you were awake and on low dosage it didn't happen so often. I had a couple of colleagues who wouldn't work nights on your ward. Thought you were some sort of jinx. Huh.'

The 'Huhs' were a cute habit. Probably something you would grow to ignore or hate - but at the moment it was cute.

'I never knew.'

'Why should you?'

Why indeed?

'So are you staying or going?' she asks.

My beer is dead. 'One more.'

I order up another cold one and she joins me.

We shoot the breeze for a while. She's into skateboarding and watercolors. Her boyfriend was into real estate but the recession put paid to that and he's now an admin clerk with a car rental firm. They've been together for a couple of years. There is no talk of marriage and the way she skips over the detail doesn't make him sound like the love of her life.

My second beer fades into memory and I switch to a soft drink. Adding DUI to my life might just be a bad idea.

I get the impression that there's no friend coming to meet Sharon. She doesn't make or receive a cell call and seems at ease with being stood up. When I mention it she tells me it happens all the time.

'How did you get here?' I ask.

'Car. How else? There next to yours.'

'Mine?'

'The Corolla.'

'How do you know it's mine?'

'I saw you drive up.'

'I thought you came in after me?'

'Nope. Huh. I was in the ladies' washroom. Saw you park up.'

I decide enough is enough. 'I really must go.'

'Oh well it was nice to meet you Craig McIntyre. Maybe we'll bump into each other again?'

'Maybe.'

I'm too quick to my feet and too quick to the car but if I'd known she had spotted me earlier I would never have spent the time chatting. Cute as she is.

As I complete the loop and get back on the road to the highway I keep an eye on the rear view mirror. A small blue Chevy zooms into view and it was a blue Chevy that had been sitting next to my car in the parking lot. I reach the main junction and indicate right - hoping there's a Days Inn close by.

I join the late afternoon traffic and head south, the blue Chevy six or seven cars behind me. I stop/start down the 19 and, as I cross into the town of Port Richey, I am relieved to see a Days Inn on my left. I indicate to cross over the oncoming lanes and the blue Chevy pulls into the parking lot of the Mattress Giant opposite. I park up and make for the reception. Unfortunately the hotel is the type where the doors to the rooms open onto an outside balcony or onto the parking lot. As such I can't walk in and lose myself inside the building.

The receptionist looks up as I enter. Early twenties. Tight-cropped hair. Tanned. 'Can I help?'

'Do you have rooms that don't face the road?'

'Yes sir. Through the large arch and the rooms at the back face the rear.'

'Could I have a look at one? I'm a very light sleeper.'

His face says what he won't. *Why in the hell would you pick a roadside hotel in the first place then?*

He hands me a key and I make my way out and round to the back. Slowly. Making sure that Sharon has enough time to see me.

The room is a carbon copy of every hotel room I have ever been in and I sit on the bed, counting to one thousand. I get up and exit. As I reach the large arch that leads to the front I stop. I drop to my knees and push my head round the corner.

The receptionist is standing in front of me. He looks down and I pretend to tie my shoelaces.

'Is the room to your liking, sir?"

'No. Too noisy.'

'Can I take the key?'

'Certainly.'

I step back and force him to walk out of sight of the highway. I hand him the key and he waits for me to leave. With me not willing to leave it gets awkward. I stare at the ground and he stares at me. This is going nowhere.

'Look,' I say. 'I need your help. My business partner is being an idiot and he's having me followed. A blue Chevy parked across the road. I'm trying to lose it and I thought if I stopped here for a while they might leave. You couldn't check if the car is still there?'

He wants rid of me, so he walks out into the arch and comes back. 'There's a blue Chevy sitting in the Mattress Giant parking lot.'

'Thanks.'

More awkwardness.

'I'd prefer it if you were to leave, sir.'

I know he would and so would I but Sharon is giving out all the wrong signals. You don't trail someone to a hotel unless you have an ulterior motive. I step back a little more. 'I need to stay here until the car leaves.'

'I can't let you do that,' he replies.

'Come on. Ten minutes and I'll be gone.'

'Sir, I need you to leave or I'll call the police.'

Now that isn't good news.

'There's no need for the police,' I say. 'Look she might be gone already. Have another look.'

He steps back and looks through the arch. 'The car's still there.'

'Five minutes.'

'I'm calling the police.'

'John?' The voice comes from beyond the arch and out of sight. 'John, are you OK?'

'No problem, Sam. I'm just asking this man to leave.'

Sam appears at John's shoulder. They could be twins. I reckon they are gym buddies. Cropped hair and all.

'What's the problem?' he asks.

'I've asked this man to leave and he's refusing.' His voice is stronger now he has back up.

'I'll go in five minutes,' I say.

'Why not leave now?' asks Sam.

John turns to his friend. 'He says the blue Chevy in the Mattress Giants' parking lot is following him.'

Sam turns to look at the Chevy. I start to walk away. I need to pull them out of sight and let Sharon get bored. John isn't happy at this. 'Sir, this is my last warning.' They both follow me.

At least they've both stepped out of view of the Chevy. The afternoon heat is turning this situation into something quite ugly. Neither John nor Sam look like they have the patience I need at the moment.

'Go phone. I'll keep an eye on him,' says Sam to John.

John nods in agreement.

'Give me a fucking break,' I spit. The swear-word seems to change the atmosphere.

'Use your cell,' says Sam.

John reaches for his pocket.

I step towards them and they tense. Two on one and I need this like a hole in the eyeball. John pulls out his cell. I hold up my hand. 'For fuck's sake I'll go.'

John ignores me and dials. I jump forward and slap the phone from his hand. Sam tries to block the move but he's too slow and I step back as the cell bounces off the ground with a crack. John stares at the phone. 'What the…'

Sam moves for me and I back off. John takes a step and I back up some more. The lot ends in a ring of brush. My head is motoring. None of this is good. 'OK, I'll go. Just let me get to my car.'

Sam smiles. 'A bit late for that, isn't it?'

Chapter 25

Sam has the look of someone who has been here before. His gait has changed and his head is down, eyes to the top of his sockets. His smile is fixed. John starts to circle to my left. I back up another few feet. 'I said I would go.'

John matches my move. 'You had your chance. Maybe we should teach you a little lesson.'

'Is there anyone in the rooms?' Sam asks John.

'It's all clear.'

'Time to dance darling?' Sam says.

'Why I thought you would never ask.' replies John.

They're both grinning. This is not their first time. Good old boys on a mission. Probably 'down-and-out' season. A bit of bum bashing on a Wednesday night. A few Colt 45s – 'Works Every Time' – and time to take your partner for the headbone dance floor.

Worse still they're both sober. Drunks can be brave but they're sloppy. Sam moves in and I'm being backed into a corner. I judge the moment and jump to my right, dummy and go left. I was the worst wide receiver in the history of our college but at least I made the team. I scrape along the wall of the hotel as Sam dives for me. His eyes are alight. This is good-time stuff for him.

I'm almost past him when he grabs at my T-shirt. You would think that a couple of bucks of material would rip easily but it holds just fine and he leaps at me. I duck the swinging fist and try to bury one of my own in his stomach. It's like hitting the Hoover Dam. Serious six-pack going on there. He grunts but doesn't let go. John moves to grab my arm and I bring my foot up but there's no room to get a swing on and I do little more than brush his thigh.

Sam tries another haymaker and takes me high on the

shoulder. I stamp on his foot and catch his shin bone on the way down. This time he shouts and the first blood is mine. John is on me and we both fall to the ground.

I swing my fists and kick like I am having a fit and some of the blows connect but so do some of the incoming. I'm only going to keep an upper hand because they're not working together. The beating from the night before has slowed me down. I aim a punch straight up and catch John on the chin. He lurches skyward and it gives me a chance to grab him and pin him to the ground. I head butt him with everything my neck muscles can find. His nose explodes and my head does the same.

Sam shouts again, tries to stand up and I lash out with my foot. I miss and he lands an elbow in my groin. I fall back on John as my balls detonate under the blow. John wraps his arms around me and I flip my head back and catch his broken nose. He lets go with a howl and Sam falls onto me.

I feel my head building up pressure – the headache winding up – and I know what's coming when a horn sounds. We all freeze and it sounds again. An engine revs close by and the horn is now going off like an alarm. Sam turns to look and finds the grill of a car inches from his face. He leaps up and I follow suit. John stays on the ground.

'Get in.' The passenger door of the blue Chevy is open. I can see Sharon's face through the windshield. I don't have time for questions and hobble into the car. Sam stares me down and looks at John, bewilderment in his face. He starts to raise a foot and I think he's going to plant it in John's gut but he lowers it as my headache vanishes. I wait for the blue world but it doesn't feel close. Sharon reverses to the arch and through. She brakes next to my car.

'Get your car and follow me back to Fairway Oaks,' she shouts.

I hesitate.

'Now! Before they get their act together and decide to beat up on both of us. Huh.'

I still don't move.

'Charlie sent me, OK?. So move,' she says.

I leap out the car. Sam is walking into the arch and a second later John emerges, clutching his nose. I jog to my car and pull open the Corolla door, keeping an eye on the pair as I jump in, kick the engine into life and follow Sharon into the traffic.

Cruising back up the highway she weaves her way north. At the next set of lights I pull level and hit the window button to talk to Sharon.

I'm slammed forward in my seat as the car is smacked from the rear. I turn round and Sam and John are sitting high in a Toyota Hilux staring down on me. Sam flips the bird and John points to his nose. The pick-up rolls forward and catches my bumper in its bull bars and begins to push. I stick my foot on the brake but we are three to one here in terms of horsepower. The lights are still red and the crossroad is busy. My tires squeal as the pick-up shoves me across the white line of the intersection.

I glance over at Sharon and she's struggling to catch up on what is going down. Her face creased with puzzlement. I open my mouth to shout when the car lurches forward another few feet. I'm gripping the steering wheel so hard it hurts but it isn't going to stop the forward motion. The car jerks again as the power of the pick-up overcomes the friction of my tires and I'm only inches from being broadsided by the crossing cars.

I try to calm down. Think and act – not the other way round. If this was an automatic I would plunge it into reverse and try and fight the pick-up but in a stick shift I need to take my foot off the brake to hit the clutch. That will send me into the crossing cars. The car lurches again. Why in the hell don't the lights change? How long can they stay at red?

A horn fires off as a car slashes across the front of my fender. The Corolla continues to slide onward. The pick-up engine is roaring in my ear. A few more feet and I'll be midstream. A second car has to swerve to avoid my nose. I make a choice. Another car is bearing down and I whip my foot from the brake, ram the car into first and floor it.

I jump forward and catch the pick-up driver by surprise. We both shoot into the traffic. A car misses my tail but can't miss Sam and John. The sound of grinding metal falls away as the other cars signal their warning with a clutch of horns and brakes. I clear the crossing and keep my foot down.

I look in the mirror and the doors to the pick-up are opening up. Sam and John are leaping out and then they're lost to the distance. The next junction rears up and I almost forget to brake. As I stop I expect a crumpled Hilux to rush into my life again. Instead a blue Chevy cruises up on my right.

I wind down the window.

'What the hell?' shouts Sharon. 'Just follow me.'

As the lights change I check the rear-view and pull in behind the Chevy. At the next junction Sharon hangs a right and navigates a back way towards the house. I'm not that surprised when she indicates to turn into my driveway and parks, with enough space to let me into the garage.

I hit the remote and the garage door wheels up.

A minute later and I'm letting Sharon in the front door. I have a bunch of questions and she has a thousand. 'Coffee?'

She nods and I start to cook up some strong and black stuff. 'You want to tell me how you know where I live?'

'You want to tell me why you lied?'

'You first.'

'Charlie told me.'

'And you know Charlie how?'

'He used to be a patient at Hatch Roll.'

'He did?'

'Do you think he hands out cash to complete strangers? How big is your bar bill?'

'A few dollars?'

'And the rest,' she says. 'The day you walked into the bar and told him you had been at Hatch Roll he phoned me to check. When he knew you were coming here he phoned me. I moved to St Pete's two years ago and he's kept in touch. It wasn't hard for me to check on you.'

'Why did he phone you?'

'We were friends when he was at Hatch Roll.'

I place the cups on the coffee table in the sitting room and we sit down opposite each other.

'What was he in for?'

'Same as you.'

'He was in the army?'

'Special forces.'

'No shit.'

'Good soldier as well. Just one too many missions in one too many bad places.'

'He never said.'

'He wants to forget it.'

'And you kept in touch why?'

'We were an item.'

Lucky Charlie. I sip at the black stuff. 'What were you supposed to do? Watch me? Protect me from the baddies?'

'Just check you out and let him know how you're doing.'

'You do know I'm being hunted?'

'Charlie said there were some people after you. Huh. Was that them back at the hotel?'

'No. That was a pair of idiots.'

'Just as well I turned up when I did.'

'How did you know I was in trouble?'

'I knew you weren't staying at the hotel and I saw the two guys walk out of sight. I thought they might be the people Charlie had warned me about.'

'You're not lacking guts.'

'Maybe you mean brains.' She smiles. 'Are you going for the job at the club?'

'Charlie has a big mouth.'

'It's my brother who hires the muscle. Charlie doesn't know anyone down here.'

'I thought this was Charlie's house?'

'Nope. Mine.'

'I thought you lived in St Pete's?'

'I do. This used to belong to my parents and when they passed on I couldn't move it. Huh. The credit crunch was on us. So I mothballed it.'

'So the house has no connection to Charlie?' Well maybe the suits won't find me just yet. 'Charlie said he would phone at seven to see if I want the job.'

'Do you?'

'Do I what?'

'Want the job.'

'No choice. I need the cash and time to get my head together. Where is it.'

'You can trail me and I'll show you. Now do you want something to eat?'

'I do but I'm afraid your larder is empty.'

'Yes but the telephone works and there's a wonderful Italian that delivers.'

Chapter 26

Charlie phones and we talk. We wander around his past, Sharon and the way to the moon. Sharon is more than an ex from the way he talks.

An hour later and I'm following Sharon's Chevy down the Suncoast Parkway with a pound of lasagne nesting in my gut. I feel better. An appetite from the wild and extra garlic bread will do that. I'm wearing the cheapest suit I have ever owned but I've been seen in worse. Anyway, bouncers need suits that are practical. Machine-washable is good.

We hit Tampa as the rush hour falls off and pick up signs for the Tropicana Stadium, passing a sign advertising the second game in the Blue Jays series. I'm lost but Sharon weaves her way through the town with purpose. We hit a strip of bars and restaurants and she pulls up in a fire zone. I draw level and hit the down button on the window. She tells me to park in a multistorey next to the fire zone and walk back to where she's illegally parked.

I have a sweat on by the time I get back to her.

She points to a small blue door that sits between a Mexican restaurant and a sports bar. 'Knock on the door and ask for Jake. If they give you any grief tell them Sharon sent you. I'll wait and see you in.'

The door could be a door to anywhere. There are no markings on it. I knock and it opens within a couple of fast heartbeats. 'I'm looking for Jake.'

'And?'

'Sharon sent me.' I step to the side and Sharon waves at the doorman. He nods his head and moves to let me in.

The corridor beyond is dimly lit and heavily carpeted. An airport scanner stands in front of me and, beyond this, another door. I step through the metal arch and the doorman raps on the second door. It opens and a man in a grey suit looks at me.

'For Jake,' says the doorman.

I'm ushered in and find myself in a small vestibule. A wooden table sits to the left and a stunning brunette sits behind it, protected by a computer screen. She's wearing a Bluetooth and pressing away at the keyboard. I'm conscious of the bruises on my face.

She looks up. 'Name?'

'Craig McIntyre.'

'And you're here to see who?'

'Jake.'

'Is he expecting you?'

'Yes.'

She hits a few more keys and speaks into the Bluetooth. Then to me. 'Go on through. He's waiting.'

There's a buzz and a double door swings inwards to reveal a large bar and restaurant, empty save for a couple of men behind the bar and a woman pushing a vacuum cleaner across the floor. I step in and the doors close behind me.

'So you're Sharon's new man?' The voice is loud and I turn to find a guy whose eyes connect him to Sharon. 'I believe I'm supposed to give you a job.'

Jake is six feet six at least. His shoulders have the look of an athlete.

'I was told you might have a vacancy,' I venture.

'Sit down.' He throws his hand towards one of the room's large sofas. "I haven't got much time and you have even less to impress me. Done any of this kind of work before?'

'I was on a few doors before I joined the army.'

'Army is good. What else?'

'I'm a personal security expert.'

'A bodyguard then.'

I nod.

'Better. And do you know anything about the club?'

'No.'

'Good, the less you know the better. You start tonight and you work with Clyde. You do what Clyde says. You walk where Clyde tells you to walk and you talk when Clyde tells you to talk. The pay is better than anywhere else in town and it's cash at the end of the night. You sort out the IRS. You'll find Clyde upstairs.'

He lifts his massive frame from the chair and leaves.

It appears I have the job. Whatever the job is.

A spiral staircase lifts from the centre of the room. I climb it. The next floor up is more of the same except there's a dance floor in one corner. A small man with an eighties ponytail and a taste for tight suits is leaning against the bar. He has a sheet of paper in one hand and a pen in the other.

'Clyde?' I ask as I walk up to him.

'Who's asking?'

'Jake sent me up. I've to work with you.'

'Sure. Virgin?'

'Sorry?'

'Thick too. We open at ten. That suit is crap. Far door – code is 98789 – pick out something better to wear and be back here in ten. Figured!'

'Eh?'

'Just go.' He points at a door.

I go.

The door is padded and once I punch in the code I'm allowed to enter a small offshoot of Saks of 5th Avenue. Suits to the left, shirts to the right, shoes at the back and ties in a carousel in the middle. A small changing-room sits in one corner. I flick through the suits and find a black Versace in my size, a brilliant white Ralph Lauren shirt, a pair of Cole Haan Chukka boots and a Brioni striped tie. Total cost – probably north of three thousand bucks. What kind of club keeps this stuff as spare change?

Back with Clyde he nods approvingly. 'Any damage is out of your wages. Hand it back at the end of the night. Figured.'

I think I know what he means.

'First up. Coffee. Black.' He waves at the other end of the bar where there's an industrial coffee-making machine. I worry it for a while and he stomps over and shows me how it works. 'Thick.'

Maybe I am.

'Bar duty,' he says.

'Sorry?'

'Bar duty. Not serving. Watching. Too naïve for door or VIP club. Maybe in a few weeks.'

'What do I do?'

'You watch.'

'For what?'

'What do bouncers watch for?'

'Trouble?'

'Figured.'

It's half an hour until opening and I brew up a coffee for me. A couple of girls appear wearing so little that I can't keep my eye on the job. They introduce themselves as Caroline and Nell. They don't seem to be interested in the new boy and start setting up the bar. I can't see a cash register but I'm thinking this is not a cash club.

Twenty minutes later a small alarm goes off and the girls straighten their hair and push the belts, which double as skirts, down a quarter of an inch. I drop down the spiral staircase to see the guests arrive.

Nothing happens. The door doesn't heave open and no thronging crowd fills the place. An hour crawls away and hangs itself before a man with the girth of the Louisiana Superdome walks in. He has four ladies in tow and none of them has less than five-inch heels. I climb back to my perch, not expecting the large man to make it up, but there's an elevator in the corner disguised as a mirror and he emerges.

He collapses on the nearest sofa, wet patches under his armpits despite the ice cold A/C. Caroline takes an order and returns with two bottles of Krug in two silver ice buckets. The man pops one and pours for the girls. He opens the other one and grabs a straw from the silver tray that the glasses sit on. He pushes the straw into the neck of the champagne and sucks.

A hell of an expensive soda.

The night is slow to build. I should have asked when my shift finished. I should have asked what the wages were. I know neither. At two o'clock the place is gearing up to flying. There's not a spare seat in the house. The dance floor is switched on and crammed. I can see why the A/C is so heavy – it has to fight hard to win in this atmosphere.

No one is drinking the cheap stuff. Mainly because there is no cheap stuff. Payment is through a club card. No cash. Caroline and Nell have been joined by six others and so far I've done nothing but people watch.

The elevator opens and a man in casual slacks and a polo shirt rolls in. I recognise his face from TV. Senator Bob Tampoline. The Tambourine Man. His surname having helped christen him when he took up a tambourine at his inauguration ball and joined in with the band. I saw it on the news. Some say his surname is made up. That he's really called Bob Schmucker. Of course he denies it. An orphan. No mother or father save a note that said, 'the son of Mr and Mrs Tampoline'. As if. But he's done well on it.

I don't recognize the girl he is with and I'm fairly sure there is a Mrs Tampoline back at the ranch. He squeezes through the crowd throwing a few nods and handshakes as he goes.

The VIP room is at the far end of the bar and Clyde is on the door. He tilts his head at the Senator as he vanishes inside. With no trouble on the horizon I walk up to Clyde. 'Can I get ten minutes for some fresh air?' I have to shout to be heard.

He looks at his watch and nods. 'Ten. No more. Go through the bar. Down the stairs. Out the back.'

I thank him.

'Figured,' he says.

The alley at the back takes my head back to Charlie's place. A fellow bouncer is dragging a cigarette to death next to the fire door. 'Jools.' He offers a hand.

'Craig.' I shake.

'Quiet night.'

'Club's busy.'

'Club's quiet. Wait till ya get the weekend. That's busy.'

'Who owns the place?'

'Mr White.'

'Who's he?'

'Rich and ya don't ask questions like *'who's he?'*'

'OK. Can I ask about you?'

'Sure. Born on Treasure Island. Live on Treasure Island. Went to school on Treasure Island. Had a job on Treasure Island. Got married on Treasure Island. Got divorced on Treasure Island. Ma and dad died on Treasure Island. You?'

'Drifting. Always drifting.' My mother's face tries to take shape in my head. A fuzzy ball that has more to do with the one old photograph that used to sit in my wallet than from any real memory.

Jools speaks. 'Where's ya home?'

My mother's face fades. 'Nowhere really. I'm from Springfield, New Jersey.'

'The Simpsons.' He sings the words.

'Not the first time I've heard that.'

He ignores the response. 'Ma and da from there?'

'No. My dad was from Brooklyn and my mother was from Glasgow in Scotland.'

'Scotland?'

'I've never been. My mother came over when she was three.'

'How did they die?'

Odd question.

'How did you know they were dead?'

'I didn't. Mine got hit by a train. Unmarked crossing. I was in the back of the car. Nine months old ya know. They tell me that the police photos show the car sliced in two but I've never wanted to see them. You?'

'Complicated.'

And it was. Very.

'I got five minutes. Don't ya?'

'I don't want to talk about it.'

'Why not?'

Because I might have killed them. I look at his face in case I have just spoken out loud. 'They died in a fire. Our house. OK?'

'Sure.'

He finishes the cigarette in silence and waves as he goes back to work. I inhale the last dregs of the second hand smoke and a familiar craving creeps over me. I gave up smoking the day I left Hatch Roll but I could slip back with such ease.

I return to my post. I have no idea how you could fit in more people, but while I was away another stream of humanity has risen up the spiral staircase and we're all breathing less fresh air.

Half an hour later I get my first taste of action. To be fair I see it coming. A young man has been leaning into a girl at the bar for a while. She has her back turned towards him but he isn't taking the hint. She's trying to blank him by talking to her friend. A couple of times she's pushed the young man away but he is drunk and persistent – a bad combination. I push through the crowd, trying not to get a drink over my wage-arresting suit. I stand a few yards away and watch.

It kicks off when the young man, tired of the knock-backs, grabs the girl by the shoulders and tries to turn her towards him. If I had been her I would have walked an age ago but he would have probably followed. She tries to shrug him off. I look towards Clyde and he's spotted it. He nods his head for me to intervene.

'I think the lady wants a little space,' I shout into the young man's ear.

He flicks round to look at me. 'Fuck off.'

'Let her go.'

'I said fuck off.'

This is not going to go well. 'Look take it easy. All I'm saying…'

He swings his fist at me but he telegraphs it. I step back, catching a customer who tips his drink down my back.

Shit, that'll cost.

I grab the young man's arm, swing him round and force his wrist up his back. He squeals above the hubbub. It's too busy to march him through the club so I take him down the back way and out into the alley.

'Do you know who my father is?' He has to hold onto the alley wall to stay upright.

'No sir, I do not.'

'You will if you don't let me back in.'

'That isn't going to happen.'

I close the door but he takes a run at it and I hear him make contact.

Clyde is waiting at the top of the stairs. 'Not bad. Spell me on the VIP room. Slash time. Only go in if the bell goes. Got it?'

'Yip. Do you know the guy I threw out?'

'Colin Mark's son.'

'Is that bad?'

'No. Colin would have chucked him first. Hates him. Figured.'

I've been promoted to VIP status. I walk to the door and realize I have no idea who should get in. I stop Nell and ask her how I'll know.

'Black membership cards only. Blue and Gold don't count.'

Easy.

A few rubberneckers walk up but I make sure they leave with their tails between their legs.

Clyde returns. 'Stay on. Boss wants to see me. Any trouble use this.'

He hands me a walkie-talkie with an earpiece which I insert. I hear the doorman inform everyone that Juan Revez is in the building. I think he's the short stop for a big team up north.

The edge is off the night. The peak is past and dawn is on its way. The dance floor has daylight and, although there are no seats to be had, there is standing room. I check for Clyde, push at the VIP door and look in. A short corridor stretches out and there are three doors either side. All are shut. Private means private around here. One of them opens and I get a glimpse of a small room mostly filled with a bed.

Very private then.

A man walks out and I hold the door for him. He doesn't even look at me. I hear a shout from one of the rooms but there's no bell. I start to close the door and there's another shout. A woman's shout and one that means pain. I keep the door open a crack and there's a scream.

Enough.

I step into the short corridor. I think the shouting came from the last door on the right and when another cry goes out I'm certain. I place my hand on the door handle and swing it open.

The senator is naked and standing with his flabby backside towards me. The young girl he came in with is on her knees on the bed. She is tied to the headboard by rope, and a stool has been placed under her stomach, lifting her rear into the air. The senator is holding something but his body is hiding it from my view.

The girl looks at me through her arms. There's a red stain on the white duvet beneath her raised backside.

'Stop him,' she says.

The senator turns. He has one hand round his cock. In the other hand he has an oversized vibrator. Its end is red and as he steps back blood drips from the girl's rear. 'Turn around and walk out. You're history,' he growls.

I don't move. I can't move.

He isn't fazed by the situation in the slightest. 'I said turn round and leave.'

My head explodes. No warning. The pain sends me to the floor. I feel a hand on my head and then under my chin. The senator brings my eyes up to meet his and I'm inches from his engorged member. 'I said…'

He pauses, tenses and steps back. My head pounds out a new rhythm of pain. The girl is struggling but the bonds are too tight. The make-up that made her look older has run with tears and sweat. She can't be more than sixteen.

The senator stands up and drops my head. Then he picks it up again. I'm frozen. Unable to think. The headache is everything.

He slams my head into the shag pile. It doesn't add to the pain, just to my lack of action. He takes the vibrator and plunges it into the girl's rectum. She screams but he doesn't stop pushing, the muscles in his arms trembling with the strain. He leans into the girl with devastating force. There is a tearing sound and she flops down. The senator shoves the device in up to the hilt. Blood drips from the girl's mouth. I can't move for the pain in my head. I roll over as the senator stands up and views his handiwork. His aggression turns into a look of confusion and 'boom' – the world is blue – headache gone.

The door behind me bursts open and Clyde is standing there. 'Jesus Christ.'

The stop-start nature of the blue world is back and the words come out as Jeeeeeeeeeeesssssssssssusssss. Chriiiisst. Clyde's lower jaw hangs loose.

I start to stand up and Clyde looks down on me and then at the girl and finally at the senator. He has the sort of hesitancy of action I saw in my short time in Iraq as a soldier. Multiple choices but none of them solving the problem you're facing.

The senator suddenly collapses on the floor. Spent. I want to kick his head into pulp for what he's just done but I know I need to be a hundred miles from here. I turn and Clyde is blocking my way but he sees something in my eyes. Something he doesn't like. He stands to one side. I don't think it is voluntary. It's reflex.

I wonder if it would be better to wait for the police but I'm in the frame for the young girl if they want. Even if I run it will be me, not the senator, who killed the girl. If I stay it will still be me. An ex mental patient wanted by a government agency for his involvement in multiple deaths versus an elected official of the state. I'm dead meat.

I put my foot to the floor and I'm gone. I turn so quickly towards the exit that I need to hang onto the door frame to make the ninety degree move. I push at the padded door and fly into the club. A few faces turn to see who is exiting the VIP room. I blank them as I skirt the bar and take to the stairs.

The alley is empty. Déjà vu. A back alley and I'm on the run again. The only way out lies next to the sports bar and a lone ciggie junkie is drawing in the bad stuff as I sprint into the night.

The blue world vanishes.

Chapter 27

I climb the car park stairs three at a time. The building is a graveyard, with a few of the late night revellers' cars in random slots. My car is on the second level and I'm sure there will be police waiting at the bottom when I exit. I'm wrong. There isn't even any activity at the club door as I pass by and pick up speed. Starting to put distance between the nightclub and myself.

I don't know the area and it takes a while to pick up the signs for the road north. I know the police will be involved soon. Not yet though. Not just yet. The crime scene will need to be altered to blank the senator and put me in the picture. Only then will the police be called.

As the car bites freeway dirt I wonder what the hell to do. The miles slip away and the panic doesn't. I play out the scene in the VIP room and run it back into the previous days. It jumbles up, taking on a new level of confusion and adding to the panic.

I can feel another headache beginning to build and I need to back off. A car in front of me flashes its brake lights and I swing out to overtake. The man in the car flips me the bird, a snarl on his face. I keep my foot down and he drifts backwards, vanishing with the headache.

The relationship between the headaches and violence is clear. How it works? Why it works? None of that makes sense. Common patterns in the last few days are thin and few. That the violence is focused on others and not me seemed clear until the Days Inn duo decided to chase me down. But maybe they were just the exception that proves the rule.

The sight of the senator ramming home the vibrator was testament to the extremes of behavior I seem to be able to generate.

A couple of dollar tolls and I reach my turn-off. I

contemplate not returning to the house. After all, the car may be tied to that address and the police would be waiting. Maybe even the suits. But there are no blue and white flashing welcome lights. Once in the garage I take a few breaths and make for the house.

The cool air hits me and I wish I had put a few beers in the fridge.

'Hi.'

The voice makes me leap.

Sharon pops up from the sofa. 'Did you have a good first day?'

My wife has never used those words. My only job was in Iraq. 'Not really,' I reply.

'Pray tell.'

I walk her through the evening. When I reach the death of the girl she draws her feet up and gasps.

'What?' It's the only word she can find. She isn't buying it. I can't blame her. I'm ex Hatch Roll. An ex lunatic. A trained killer with a screw loose. As far as she knows the whole thing is a fantasy. Or I'm the killer?

''The police will be here soon,' I say.

'Probably.'

'And they'll be after you as well.'

'Yip. After all, I recommended you for the job.'

'They'll blame me.'

'Yip.'

'But I didn't do it.'

'Yip.'

'You believe me?'

'I should say yes and make some excuse to go to the washroom. Huh. Then run. If what you say is true things will get messy. If you're lying I should get the hell out of here anyway.'

'But you're not going to?'

'No. I told Charlie I'd help. So let's say the senator did what you say. I'd say the chances of you staying out of jail are nil. Huh.'

'No kidding.'

'But I don't think the police will come.'

'Why?'

'A senator caught in a brothel with a dead hooker. I don't see the club being quick to dial 911. I see them cleaning up the mess or maybe phoning some guys from the FBI, CIA or even KFC first. Senators don't go down that easily. What I do see is someone else turning up here soon. If I were you I'd probably want it to be the police. Anyone else and I don't fancy your chances.'

'You seem surprisingly well versed.'

'Maybe. Five years in a military nuthouse can teach you a lot about how the world really works.'

I drop on a chair and lean forward, placing my head in my hands. I'm so out of my depth I can't see up from down.

'I don't think self-pity is a good call. Huh.'

I lift my head up. 'What would you suggest?'

'We need space to think.'

'We?'

'I told Charlie I would look out for you.'

'You must really like him.'

'A lot.'

'Were you an item?'

'Were?'

'You still are?'

'On the nose Mr McIntyre.'

'But he's in LA and you're here?'

'No dodging the bullets when you're around is there? Huh. Things are bad on the job front unless you hadn't noticed.'

'So you work here and Charlie in LA?'

'I work in St Pete's.'

'Not Hudson?'

'I made that up. I've a senior administrator's job with a health company. The pay is too good to quit.'

'How long have you been doing this?'

'About a year and a half. I used to work in LA but the company closed the office. It was St Pete's or nothing and they offered me a promotion. Charlie's looking for a place out here but he can't sell the LA bar.'

'He never mentioned you.'

'Maybe you didn't ask.'

'Maybe I didn't.'

'Anyway, do you think getting my life story is a good use of time? We need to move.'

'Where to?'

'No idea.'

She gets up and I follow.

There's a thump and the window that looks out onto the front lawn shatters and a smoke bomb bounces into our lives.

Chapter 28

The lights die and a second smoke bomb follows the first. I grab Sharon around the waist and pull her back into the TV room. 'Hit the floor and follow me.'

I start to crawl towards the door that leads to the garage and she follows.

'Where are we going?' coughs Sharon.

'They'll be ready for us. The garage is our only chance.'

'Who'll be ready for us?'

'Crawl, don't talk.'

There's a small gap between the back of the kitchen and the master bedroom and it's clear of smoke. Rising to a crouch I fumble for Sharon's hand and pull her into the laundry room, slamming the door behind us. I grab the door to the garage and throw it open. The darkness beyond could hide an army but it seems quiet. I hear footsteps from the front and a smash as the front door is caved in.

'The car,' I whisper.

Sharon obeys and jumps into the passenger seat. I leap into the driver's seat and nearly drop the key as I try to insert it into the ignition. I miss the keyhole and miss it again. Sharon looks at me and I draw a breath and use my other hand to guide the key into its slot. I turn it enough to switch on the electrics and the dashboard lights up. I look for the garage door remote.

Shit. It's in the house. There's no time to go back. The noise from outside is now inside the house. I have seconds. Twisting the key I fire up the engine, push down on the clutch, take the revs up to the limit, slide the car into reverse and wheel-spin the car backwards. Ten feet of space to cover before we hit the garage door and I'm not sure that the small car will have the momentum to punch through the aluminium shell.

Sharon screams as we hit the door and it gives – crashing

from its mountings – but not enough and I'm forced to shoot forward and try again. The car makes it further on the second hit but the metal door is strong and we get jammed. Our rear is in the driveway and the front still in the garage. I floor it but generate tire smoke and little else.

Guns click and a million lights surround the car. I kill the engine. We're going nowhere.

Chapter 29

'Hands where we can see them. Don't move.'

The order is loud as men with guns appear through the door to the house and flood onto the driveway. I lift my hands into the air and urge Sharon to do the same. Her face is white and she stares at the men. A hand grabs the door handle and yanks it open. A gun barrel appears next to my head.

'Quick. Give it to him now,' a voice spits.

A gloved hand grabs my forearm. I try to pull away. The hand holds firm and a needle is rammed home.

* * *

There is no slow slide from oblivion. One moment I'm in the car, the next I'm in a room, strapped once more to a bed. The ceiling lighting is low and the air-conditioning hums. The restraints feel the same as the ones used in Iraq. I test them but there's no give.

'Welcome back, Mr McIntyre.'

The voice is way too familiar. 'Still wearing the crumpled white linen suits?' I ask.

'I don't know about the crumpled bit - but yes. Mr McIntyre you are, and I say this with the greatest of respect, a very, very dangerous man to be around.'

'Pop in and we can chat about it.'

'You'd like that wouldn't you?'

'You don't know how much. Where am I?'

'Safe.'

'Who from?'

'From yourself.'

'Bullshit.'

He blanks me. 'So down to business. You possess an ability

that we find interesting.'

'Do I?'

'Oh you do, Mr McIntyre. You do. And I have a lot of very excited people who can't wait to stick some probes into you, wire you up, open your head and play around inside. You're highly unusual and in my experience, and believe me when I tell you that my experience is very extensive, I would say you are close to being unique.'

'Wow.' My sarcasm misses the mark.

'Before I let my colleagues have their fun with you I need to test a few things.'

'Fuck off.'

'I'm not sure that this'll be as bad as you think.'

'So tying me up, torturing me, torturing my wife, hunting me down, drugging me - not bad?'

'Let me make this plain. You work with us and we work with you.'

'Or?'

'Switch on the monitor.' The words aren't for me.

A large TV monitor replaces the ceiling lights above me. The screen is blank save for a small white dot pulsing in the top left. I try to twist my head but the restraints hold tight.

The monitor fires up and splits into two images – divided down the centre. Two rooms come into view. The camera angle suggests that the CCTVs are high up in the corner. Each room has a single occupant. One is sitting on the floor – the other is standing in the corner.

Both are familiar. Way too familiar.

'No.' I shout and deny what I'm seeing. I close my eyes and pray, and for the first time in an eon, really pray, that what I am seeing is not real.

Energy flees my body, leaving me boneless, devoid of blood – a sack of nothing.

Lendl interrupts my panic. 'So Mr McIntyre, here's how I read the whole game. You have a special talent for bringing out the worst in people. In your presence people seem to lose their inhibitions – an inhibition amoeba you might say. Whatever it is that you do takes individuals, strips them of their usual social norms and leaves them free to vent violence on others. After the event it would seem that they have little recollection or at best remember the incident but seem to see no wrong in their actions. Almost as if they never actually did anything. As far as we can tell from interviewing our colleagues back in Iraq and the senator there is little more that they can tell us.'

I open my eyes and look at the TV. Lorraine is in one room. Charlie is in the other.

'So,' Lendl continues. 'A bit of deductive reasoning leads me to wonder what triggers your little incidents and – and this is key – to whom. For only some seem to succumb to your abilities.'

Lorraine doesn't look well. She's ghostly pale and a bandage covers most of the right side of her face. Charlie has his head down and I can't see his face.

'I have a theory.' Lendl is in lecture mode now. 'Stop me if you think I'm going astray. Let's take all the incidents that we know of. Iraq 2003, Iraq this week, the plane, our offices, the bus and the senator. Did I miss any?'

At least they're not omnipresent – the Days Inn duo are missing.

'So what do they all have in common? Well the real clue was in the mess that you left in our offices. Twenty-one wounded but, when you break it down, each one was wounded by someone they knew. No stranger-on-stranger action. And then you begin to see the picture. Your two buddies in Iraq. Mr Taylor and his on/off girlfriend. The bus – well they were all old friends of a sort - and then we have the senator and his aide. She has been working for him for a few years.'

Lorraine twists her neck and looks up at the camera.

'But friends isn't enough.' Lendl continues. 'Why would friends let loose on each other? I'll put a few bucks on the fact that buried deep in most friendships is something that isn't so friendly. Something that wants to get out into the open but the friendship stops it rising to the surface. I think that's what you set free Mr McIntyre.'

Lorraine lies down, curling into a ball.

Lendl keeps his foot down. 'So we have friends as a common denominator. Friends with something dark in their communal cupboard. What else do we have? What is the trigger? What sets it all off? What sets you off? I'm guessing a little stress might work but I'm also wondering about the times you were out for the count. They're harder to figure but in every case you were under some form of stress during or not long before the incidents.'

Charlie lifts his head and the bruises on his face suggest he didn't come quietly.

'Here's the rub, Mr McIntyre. I need to give my hypothesis a test. Run it up the flagpole as I used to say in the old days. As you see, we have your wife in one room and in room two your friendly neighborhood barman. I know they know each other and I understand that Charlie has a thing for your wife. So let's see if there's something else buried in there. Let's see if you can unlock a little secret or two, shall we?'

'You can fuck off,' I shout. 'Let them go and I'll help you.'

'Time is against me and I need some answers now. So we'll play by my rules. Put the barman in with the woman.'

A door opens in Charlie's room and a man with a gun enters – a partner covering his back. Charlie is ushered out. A door in Lorraine's room opens and Charlie flies in, landing against the far wall. Lorraine stands up and walks over to him.

'I need to know if proximity is an issue so we'll start this on a remote basis first.'

I hear someone walk in.

They stick a knife into the back of my hand.

I scream.

They push the knife down and through the bone and into the table beyond.

Hot lead runs up my arm. It feels like someone is dipping my hand in boiling water. I scream.

They pull the knife out and drop a pad on the wound to stem the blood flow.

For a good minute I do nothing but writhe in the restraints. Lorraine and Charlie are talking.

'Nothing.' Lendl sounds pissed off. 'Again.'

Same hole, same knife only this time it's twisted as it goes in.

More screaming from me and no reaction from Lorraine and Charlie.

'Zip,' says Lendl. 'OK, pull up the grill.'

There's a grinding sound and Lorraine's voice is in the room. 'Craig. Oh, Craig.'

'Lorraine?' I try and turn to see her.

'Craig, what are they doing?'

The pain in my hand is acting like Prozac. I have no focus – no sense of what to do for the good. 'Lorraine stay away from Charlie. Charlie stay away from Lorraine.'

'Craig.' Her voice is followed by a gasp as the man in my room takes the knife and clips off the top of the index finger on my injured hand. This is like no pain that I have ever felt before. This is new. This is something on a different level and my scream is primeval.

'Stop it. Stop it.' Lorraine is shouting and Charlie joins in. 'What the hell do you want?'

The kernel deep in my head cracks and, despite everything, I'm aware that this is bad news. I try to shout a warning. It comes out as a hoarse cry. The headache trumps the clipped finger and I nearly pass out.

I look up at the monitor and see Charlie lift his head and stare at the camera. He looks at me. Not at the camera but through the camera and right at me.

I scream 'No' as he turns to Lorraine. 'Stop him.' My shout is extreme.

Charlie grabs Lorraine by the hair. The hair I so love to stroke. He takes a handful and jumps into the air. His knees curl up and he raises Lorraine's head high. I can see the first signs of realization from Lorraine as Charlie fails to overcome gravity and starts back down to earth. At the same time he wrenches his arm down – taking Lorraine's head with him. The combination of his fall and the pull snaps her head forward.

I'm still shouting but the headache is louder.

At the last possible moment Charlie twists his arm and body to the left and directs Lorraine's head towards the edge of the bed. The metal-rimmed edge of the bed.

I hear the crack. Feel the crack. Sense the crack. Bone losing out to steel. The thin layer of flesh no barrier. There is a grunt from Lorraine. A last noise from my wife? I don't want to watch but I can't stop. Her head rocks back on the top of her spine and she drops to the floor.

'Very good.' A new voice in the room. I can't turn my mind to it as I watch my wife. Motionless on the floor.

The monitor above me flashes and dies. The grinding sound returns and no matter how hard I shout there is no response from the next room. I'm back on my own.

'Very good indeed,' says the new voice.

'Bastards.' My voice is losing power. My vocal chords scraped and worn.

'Well Mr McIntyre,' says Lendl. It seems there might be some history between your wife and the barman that you don't know about.'

'Bastards,' I shout but my voice is down to a hoarse croak. 'I'll kill you. All of you. Every fucking one of you.'

'I don't think so.' The new voice is back. Smug, southern. I recognize it.

'Tampoline. You murdering bastard.'

'I don't think so.'

The word 'so' is drawn out to sound like sow.

Tampoline sounds calm. 'I would say that you're the murderer. You might not see it that way but think about it. All those dead people and you're the one at the centre each time.'

'My wife. You killed my wife.'

'Wrong again. Your friend did or was it you? Hard to say but I never thought it would work quite as well - you performed like a Trojan. Her blood is on your hands. Not mine.'

I can't think what to say. What to do. The headache is still growing. There is no sign of the blue world. My vision is blurring. Sounds are fading.

Chapter 30

I come round. My ties have gone. I'm in a new room but the headache is too much. Too painful.

* * *

I come round again. A cool, calm, peaceful blue world. The lights are out but, with the night vision, I can see clearly. I sit up and the death of my wife is somehow distant. A thing that happened a long time ago or maybe something that never really happened.

I walk over to the door. There's no handle. I push at it but it has no intention of moving. The rest of the room is a metal cube. Bare concrete floor, no wall coverings - a single panel in the ceiling that no doubt supplies the light.

I return to the bed.

The light flicks on.

'Good morning Mr McIntyre.' In the blue world the voice races forward and then slows down. 'Good morning' took a few seconds to roll out of Lendl's mouth while my name was an express train. 'I need a few more answers.'

'I need to use the toilet,' I say.

'Feel free.'

'Where?'

'On the floor. We don't mind.'

'You're joking.'

'Mr McIntyre, given your talents I have no intention of letting you out. Until I know how to control you, you'll pee on the floor.'

'What about food?'

'There's a bottle of water under the bed. You don't need to eat.'

'What about my rights? You know, the Constitution. The Bill of Rights. The rest of the amendments. US law.'

'As was once said by Mr Spock – the needs of the many outweigh the needs of the one.'

'What?'

'I have a duty to protect the citizens of this country and you are a threat. A clear and present danger. That changes things. Think of this as Guantanamo Bay. Think of your stay here as being a guest of our fine country.'

'What do you mean YOUR country. I am a fucking US citizen. It's my country as well.'

'As you say. Anyway to work.'

There is a hiss and I begin to cough. A cloud passes over my eyes and I try to fight the gas. I collapse onto the bed and then I'm gone.

* * *

I'm back in the restraints. TV monitor above my head. Two rooms. Two people. No Lorraine this time. Charlie. Sharon. The blue world has gone.

A voice crackles from a speaker. 'Ok Mr McIntyre, let's see if we can dispense with the knife.' Lendl is enjoying this. 'Pay a bit of attention. I want you to concentrate on the barman and his girlfriend. Do whatever it is that you do and we'll have made some progress.'

'Fuck off.'

'You need a new vocabulary.'

I look at my bandaged hand. Neat and tidy. Must have been done when I was out of it.

'Simple really Mr McIntyre–I don't want to send someone in with a knife.'

'Then don't.'

'It would make things a lot easier if you co-operate.'

The grinding sound of the grill rolling back rings out and Charlie is led into the room with Sharon. Charlie looks cool. A man who didn't murder my wife. Sharon looks confused. A woman not aware of what's bearing down on her.

I close my eyes.

'Craig?' Sharon's voice.

'Craig?' Charlie's voice.

Rising rage at Charlie's actions builds in my gut. He killed my wife. Took her head in his hands and dropped her like a fresh egg.

There's a small beep.

'At least you're trying,' says Lendl.

'Craig, why are you tied up?' Sharon is shrill.

'Craig, where the hell?' Charlie's voice stops with a slap. On the monitor two suits have entered the room and Charlie is lying on the floor.

'I'd appreciate some quiet,' says Lendl.

'I swear…' but I have no more words.

'You were doing well. Raised heartbeat. Good vitals.'

I must be wired up to something.

'We benchmarked you yesterday Mr McIntyre. Heart rate one seventy. BP elevated by ten points. Hit that again and we'll see what we will see.'

I breathe deeply. Calming myself. Fixing my head on a grass-covered hill. Looking down on a lush valley. A few white clouds dotting a perfect blue sky. Seventy-five in the shade.

'Hit him,' Lendl orders.

A hand grabs me from behind and I wait on the knife. A jab in my arm tells me that this is a new approach. My heart starts to race. I feel a rush. A solid wave of good-time rolls in. I want to talk. So I talk. 'My mother once told me that the only way to tell a good man from a bad one was to ask him when he last told his mother he loved her. Bet you haven't told your mother that in a long while.'

I want to rant. ' I love the mother thing. I want the mother thing. Mother gone. Do you know that? Gone. Real gone. Not coming back. Whoah I need a drink. Water. Now. Can I? Would you? Dead. She's dead. Not me. Not me. Was it me? Was it? Tell me.'

My heart is flying. A trip hammer fed by whatever they've injected me with. I want up. Away from the bed. In the sky. Somewhere that isn't here.

I look at the monitor and Charlie is standing over Sharon. She isn't moving.

'Good.' Lendl's voice sounds smug. The grill vanishes. The monitor dies. Another needle and lights out.

* * *

I'm not sure how long I've been out. I'm not sure how often I've been back with real time. More than once. More than twice. Much more? Much less? Hard to tell. Hard to know. A strobe goes off in my memory. A flashbulb followed by a flashbulb followed by a flashbulb. Each one less distinct. Further away. Softer. Less important.

Needles are the norm. Needles to perk me up. Needles to calm me down. Needles to make me sleep. Needles to change my mood. My arm is not so much a pin cushion as a collection of tiny little access tunnels to my ever-changing world. Liquid flowing in. Bubbling beneath my skin. Entering my bloodstream. Another delivery. Another mystery to be revealed.

The TV monitors and the restraints are no more. A soft chair sitting in front of a small stage is my world. People are brought out for someone else's entertainment and I am the catalyst. Such a good word. Catalyst. Has real grit while being round at the edges.

Tests flow and people die. Not always but most times. The

chair is moved to another room but they seem unhappy with the results and I am back in front of the stage. Proximity is a variable. So I'm told.

I don't know the people. No more Charlie, and of course Lorraine and Sharon are dead. I want to care but the drugs never let me. I sleep the sleep of the innocent. But I am not innocent.

The days draw out. Merge into a strip cartoon with Craig McIntyre as the central character. Never involved in the action. Never part of the story but always there. I hold sway over the world. A king upon a poor throne, dispensing my kingly duties but always to the tune of another.

Once there was a cast of thousands on the small stage. Too many bodies to count but the play was cut short. The carnage too great to control and I was given an injection well before the curtain came down.

I know I'm being used to bring pain and suffering to others. I know I'm being primed like a pump. Ready for something in the future. I know they are working out the kinks. Finding out ways to make me jump through the right hoops at the right time. Tuning in to me. Creating a cocktail of drugs and instructions that will act as a remote control when they require it. Press 'play' for the action. 'Pause' to check things are going their way. 'Stop' to put me away for another day.

I never see the same person twice, not on the stage nor in the wings. Faces are random. The suits are the most random. I'm sure they must be running out of new people to administer the drugs. They're careful. The restraints were released in stages. Each time testing that I had no influence over the suits. Once, a suit tried to inject another suit and now they only come alone. It seems that in my world two is the magic number. Solo and I'm no threat.

Friends, acquaintances, knowing. These are variables as well. Lendl says that proximity and friendship are key. The prime variables. The two locks I have the key for. Close and personal. A deadly combination. Don't underestimate what I can do if I'm in the right mood and the victims know each other.

There is a third variable. Lendl hit another home run. Moments in the past that run sour in the good blood of friends, sometimes hidden, rarely talked about - but always there.

Moments that need out and want out. And one day when I'm not there it would have leaked. A drunken argument. A slurred set of words that dredge the river the cohorts swim in. A minor indiscretion or maybe a major one. Something from the past that spills out into the daylight and then the friendship takes up the strain. Often surviving but never as it was before. Maybe weaker, maybe stronger. Never the same though. I just nudge it along. Amplify it. Give it permission to breathe. Then it stretches its rotten wings and people die. Sharon. Lorraine. People.

The tests continue.

There is no day. There is no night. There is but pre, during and post needle. I need the needle. I can feel it calling in the morning. I desire its few millilitres of liquid. Wish them into my system. I adore the rush. Crave the world in overdrive. I book an appointment in my head each time for the next time. For the upper, for the downer, for the sleeper. Three needles. Three points in my life to look forward to.

The stage is long since gone. They take me outside. Never the same people. Often more than one but they don't know each other. It is essential in my drugged-up new universe. I walk among others ripping inhibition from their souls. Exposing old wounds.

We drive through the suburbs of Tampa and fights break out as I pass. Road rage makes Eyewitness News. I'm harder to control in the open and they experiment with new drugs. Looking for the switch. On and off. It's all they want.

Then they find it. A rush and I am live. A fall and I am neutral. I suspect I am more artificial, synthesised fluid than plasma now. You could sell me to the junkies downtown and they would auction off my blood. I don't know what they are giving me. Nor do I care. I just want more and they're happy to oblige.

New targets are found - in the park - in the mall. Trial and error as I'm dropped in as many places as they feel fit. Always figuring out the main plan. How to control me, direct me - make me work for them.

I have no idea what people see when they look at me. There are no mirrors in my world. No dressing rooms. I am the white T-shirt and blue jean man with a beard and eyes that scare. People look away. I've lost weight. A lot. I can circle my upper arm with my forefinger and thumb. My hard-earned muscle is gone. I am wasting away. Deep down I know this is a one-way trip. Much more and there is no coming back.

My teeth are loose and occasionally clumps of hair fall to the floor, and my head now feels smooth. Walking is hard. My feet blister with surprising ease. My skin splits at the slightest of contacts.

Soon I am moved around in a wheelchair. Soon I will die. I am a drug addict with no way back. I cannot stop and nor would they want me to. I am being primed for one last act. One major event. They won't tell me what or when but it has to be soon.

My body tells me this.

Chapter 31

'Craig?'

I want the voice to stop. I want the needle to begin.

'Craig?'

The slap does little to penetrate. My nerves are fried. Useless wires, dead to the touch.

'Craig?'

A needle. I'm happy.

Then I'm not. No rush. No welcome high-voltage planet. Just awareness. Frightening awareness. Lights too bright. Sound too loud. The real world knocks hard and I don't want it to come in.

'No.' It's so long since I used my voice it sounds alien.

'Craig. You need to come back to us.' Lendl is standing over me. I'm Craig to him now. So nice.

'No. Take me away.'

'Give him another shot,' he says.

I try to pull away but there's no strength in my arms.

'Craig.' A bullet in my ear. 'Craig are you with us?'

'Yes. Please stop it.'

'I can't stop the real world, Craig. This is where most of us live all of the time. Time to wake up. No more Oz for you.'

'Just one shot.'

'Not going to happen.'

I want to scream and shout. I want to vomit up the words that will make them obey but the old world is crowding out my senses – what's left of them.

'How long before we can get sense out of him?' he asks someone.

'Hard to tell. I'm amazed he's still here.' An unknown voice.

'But he is and he's primed.'

'Yes, but much more and I think he'll be history. Once

more up the hill. Once more down and then he's gone.'

'I only need one more turn,' says Lendl. 'Craig, can you understand what I'm saying?'

I nod but I'm not sure if this means yes or no.

'We leave in twenty minutes. You're about to meet two old and dear friends. Friends with a dreadful yesteryear that they share. Just do your stuff and we're all home free. After that you can have as many shots of uppers and downers as you want.'

I like the last bit.

'But I need you to act normally for a little while. Best bib and tucker. Shave. The works. A suit. Five minutes on your feet and then it'll all be over.'

I am violated in this new world. Scrubbed and I bleed. Shaved and I bleed. New clothes and they cut me. The creases in the shirt staining red.

I cry. I can do nothing but cry.

Hands lift me and I'm dropped into a wheelchair and strangers take me to a car. Black. Another SUV. My buttocks split as I sit on the leather. I leak fluid into my pants.

A drive. Not long but full of pain. We stop at a ball of fire. Lights dance around doors and I'm spat from the car into the pit of hell. People around me stare but the suits rush me to the stairs and up. We plunge into a box overlooking a stage. Two chairs and a lectern sit in the centre.

The theatre fills and I wonder when the needle is coming. The sound of the crowd hurts my ears and they bleed. Silence and the lights dim. Two men walk onto the stage. Both are dressed in suits that try to hide their fat. Both men speak and both sound African. One black and one white.

The crowd applauds at words that mean nothing to me. The men sit down and a third man walks on. He talks to each and they answer. Questions lead to questions and more applause.

Then a suit leans towards me and the needle is back. My

world returns to normal. I embrace the charge. I grab the charge.

Chaos descends. The black man rises from the chair and leaps on the white man. They fall to the ground and a roar goes up from the audience. I don't care. I just wrap my arms around the electricity running through my body. Sucking it in.

Beneath me the theatre begins to boil as fights break out. Violence and violence meet violence and violence. I'm a conductor in a world of pain. Directing the electricity. Sending it to the seats and watching the people as they jump. Fists, legs, heads. Handbags, pens, hairbrushes. All weapons.

I spray the electricity in larger waves and the noise becomes one of death. Voices way beyond the norm. Sounds that belong in a war not downtown Tampa. People doing unto people the worst they can. A storm of hate rolling across the seats. There's no hiding place in the hurricane. No one is untouched.

I revel in my isolation as blood flows, blows fly and teeth bite. On the stage the black man has reduced the white man's face to pulp and has no intention of stopping. The guards – no doubt expected to intervene – have little interest in stopping the black man's pumping fists. They're too busy. As the electricity burns bright one of them reaches out and snaps his colleague's fingers with the ease of pulling a dead branch from a tree. He holds on to the hand, pops it into his mouth, bites down and starts chewing on the fingers.

There's movement from behind me. Panicked, quick movement and a needle is pressed home. I stop rising and fall back. Caught in the smooth hairless arms of the downer drug. I'm lifted from the chair and dragged down the stairs and into the night. The door to the SUV is open and I am flung inside.

We take off as the narcotic tells me all is right and nothing is wrong.

'Fucking mess.'

I don't know the voice but it's coming from the front

passenger seat.

'I thought he had this shit figured.'

I can guess who he is.

'Did you see what the hell was going on?'

'The whole place went crazy. God knows how many are dead.'

The words stop as the world moves sideways in an instant. The car spins and mounts the sidewalk. I am flung against the door and bounce back, my head coming to rest on the seat.

Warm evening air invades the car's interior as the door is ripped open. A hand reaches around my leg and pulls. Even if I wanted to there's nothing I can do to stop me being hauled from the car.

The suit next to me is trying to react but with a pop his face explodes and he bounces back, his head bursting into the car's interior like a rotten firework. The hand keeps pulling and my skin rips.

I bounce off the running-board and fall to the sidewalk.

'Help me.'

I recognize this voice but I'm in no position to help anyone. Arms cup under my armpits and I'm lifted. I try to place some weight on my legs but the drugs have softened my bones and I dangle.

I see the SUV, hard against a shop window, a giant pane of glass crazed but not yet collapsed. Another car is welded to the side of the SUV. Nose in. Creating an L-shaped vehicle with seven wheels. The second vehicle is a pick-up and loaded into the back is a mud-splattered trail bike.

The hands drag me to the back of the pick-up and let me fall to the road. The tailgate drops above me and the bike is tugged across my line of vision. A second pop and there's a scream and I see a gun in the hand of the man heaving the bike.

He bounces the rear tire of the bike to the ground and

guides the front tire down, inches from my head. Another pop from his gun and the engine fires up.

'Can you hold on?' I still can't see his face.

Hands lift me to the bike and onto the back. The man struggles to keep the bike upright while holding me by the waist as he leaps on in front. I start to fall and he reaches round and pulls my arms around his waist. I try and snuggle in but I need his hand to keep me upright.

'Shit, Craig. You need to help.'

I grab his stomach. I don't want to help. It is not on my agenda. I live in the needle world and people help me.

The bike leaps forward and I start to fall back. Hands whip round my arms and pull me tight. The driver lets go to change gear and grabs me after flexing the clutch. He does this three times and hits top gear. A set of lights flick red as we approach but he keeps on the speed and we zip through. Five blocks down he slows and takes a left – the engine moaning at the lack of gear change. If he lets me go I'll be roadkill in seconds.

Another turn. Another, and we hit the interstate and roar up the on-ramp. Four junctions later we're off and into a small town. A couple of rows of shops flicker by and the bike is forced down a small road. Open fields ride beside us and a small wood drifts into view. We take a dirt track into the trees and out the other side.

The field beyond is barren and at the edge sits a trailer. At one time it was someone's pride and joy – now it's slumped at an angle – silver aluminium faded to gunmetal grey.

The man parks the bike behind the trailer and lifts me off. He carries me to the trailer door and fumbles for keys. Once inside he drops me on a foam-covered bench seat.

I look up as Charlie leaves me on my own.

Chapter 32

I don't sleep. I don't think I can without my 'out' drug. The trailer is dark. I hear movement outside and the door opens. I try to smile as Charlie walks in. 'Craig, you're a mess.'

I need some more liquid in my veins. Up, down or out – I don't care. 'You killed my wife.'

'No I didn't.'

I want to argue but I also want drugs. 'Got any of the stuff?'

'What stuff?'

'You know. Needles. Drugs.'

'Ain't none of that shit in here.'

'Need it.'

'I'm sure you do.'

'Can't do without.'

'You'll have to.'

Cold turkey is a phrase that means nothing to me. Words from a novel or a TV show. 'Can't.'

'Sorry, you have no choice. Not unless you want me to take you back to your hosts?'

I don't and I do. 'Something?'

'I can give you Coca-Cola, food, a blanket and sympathy. How much shit have they been pumping into you?'

'It's not shit.'

'Coke?' He fetches a can and I drain it in three gulps.

'Again.'

He hits me again and I need a third before I can talk. 'Charlie what happened?'

'You tell me. Last I know I was running my bar and then whack, and I'm being bundled into a car and driven across most of the USA.'

'Not to you. To me?'

He sits on the bench seat opposite. 'I've no idea. I'm not

even sure what you are. Other than bad news.'

'How did you escape?'

'Carelessness. After the thing with Sharon I was taken to a new block. I'm not sure they knew what to do with me. I asked for fresh air and they assigned someone to watch me. One day they let me walk round the compound on my own. Then they stopped accompanying me. The pound was chain link and razor wire but I've been there before and it didn't take much to use the metal on the bed to make a cutter. Once I had that I just picked my time and one night never came back.'

I slump to one side and the craving for the drugs is building. I have no idea how bad it will get but it doesn't feel good. Normally I'm gone by now.

Charlie takes a blanket from an overhead cover and places it on me. It smells of damp and dirt.

'Please.'

He ignores me and I curl up into a ball.

Chapter 33

I'm bathed in sweat. My trousers are slick with urine and something else. Charlie is gone. Cans of coke stand in a line and are backed up by large bags of chips. I'm shivering despite the warmth inside the trailer. I have a single thought. Needle world. It is all I can focus on. I try to stand up but my legs won't carry any weight. I stuff the blanket in my mouth and bite down hard.

I have no breath to scream. I have no way to move and I want a needle in a way that my heart needs blood. I'll die without the drugs.

A large packet of own-brand headache pills stands next to the Coke cans. I pick it up and discover only four pills sitting in the box. I eat them all. Crunching and chewing with the few teeth I have left simply to avoid having to reach out and open a can of Coke.

I curl up tight as a wave of shivering flows through me. Ice cold one moment – burning hot the next. My stomach churns and a blowtorch is lit. I vomit and the painkillers mix with the small puddle of yellow fluid as it drips from my bed.

I stick my head into the bench seat. Driving my skull hard against the wood that lies beneath the foam. Wanting pain that will distract from the pain.

The door opens and Charlie walks in. I see his nose wrinkle and a young girl and boy trail in after him. They seem less bothered by the smell. Both are fresh-faced and vaguely familiar. The girl is pretty. Short red hair and a set of diamond-white teeth. The boy is no more than twenty. Curly hair and the same teeth as his partner. They could be the Osmonds' grandkids.

They get to work on me. I'm stripped and cleaned with a bowl of water and a collection of damp cloths. My wounds are bandaged and I'm given pills to swallow. The sick feeling falls away. The girl makes broth on the trailer ring and they force-feed it into me. Five glucose tablets are dessert.

'What did they have you on, man?' asks the boy.

'No idea.'

'Not good. It's hard to help when you don't know what you've been into.'

Not good when they take it away either.

'You look as bad as I've seen and I've seen plenty,' says the girl.

Great.

'Take these.'

I swallow more pills and the world starts to dull.

* * *

Days start to crawl away. Twenty-four hours - each one full of sixty minutes – each minute full of sixty seconds and each second lasting for a week.

The girl and boy appear twice a day but they don't chat much. Charlie thinks I might not die. So does the boy. The girl is not so sure. I'm with the girl.

'Do you do much of this sort of thing?' I ask them both one day.

The girl and the boy are called Tina and Gary. Stage names.

'More than we would like to. We work in a rehab clinic in Laguna Beach. You're quite the privileged one getting house calls.'

Long way for a house call. 'Charlie must pay well.'

A smile. 'Not really his style, paying.'

'You're doing this for free?'

'Kind of.'

You have to love someone who'll clean up your shit for free.

Broth, pills – then solid food. The pills to dull the craving. But the craving is strong. The solid food helps. I can't remember the last time I had any.

***

'I want to get up.' It's been a few days since I asked about the pay.

'On you go,' says Tina. This time she's alone.

'Just like that?'

'Just like that.'

'I could run away.'

'Who cares?'

Nice.

I swing my legs onto the trailer floor. I don't recognize them as my own. Stick-thin and white as chalk. They don't look like they could support a balloon. I press down and Tina catches my arm as I push up. My emaciated body is less of a burden than I thought and my legs hold. Then the world spins and I fall back before I faint.

'Still feel like hitting the road?'

Funny ha ha she is.

…

By the end of the week I'm on my feet and able to go to the toilet for myself. Which makes Tina and Gary happier. Charlie has been noticeable by his absence.

'Where's Charlie?' I ask the girl. I'm sitting on the edge of the bed. Shoes on. Dressed. Ready to take some air.

'He calls but he doesn't say from where.'

'Tell me again why you're doing this?'

'We love the job.'

'Bullshit.'

'You asked.'

'I need some air.'

I step out into the evening and the cool air feels like it has just leaked from heaven. I draw in a deep one and cough myself into a sitting position on the stairs that lead to the trailer door.

The trees sit close by, the leaves fighting their last round against nature. Winter is nearly here. I miss not having an autumn but that's LA for you. Then I remember I'm not in LA and that brings back Lorraine.

'Can I have a mirror?' I shout.

Tina comes out of the trailer, rooting around in her purse. 'Are you ready for this?'

'Just give me the thing.'

She hands me a compact and I flick it open.

The man in the mirror is not me. My face has no substance. My cheeks look like they should meet on the inside. My eyes are sunk so deep that a baseball cap won't be needed to keep the sun out of them. Wafer-thin parchment paper has replaced my skin – the color of weak tea. A few tufts of white hair cling to the cratered moon that is my head. I was thinning before I met the suits but at least I could still style my hair for a night out. Now I'd be better with Pledge.

'Not exactly your strong handsome type.' I say.

Tina smiles. There's something familiar in the smile.

'You're doing well. You're lucky to be here.'

'What were they giving me?'

'I've no idea. Describe what it felt like.'

I tell her.

'Hard to tell. A mix. Something to get you up. Something to bring you down and something to make you sleep.'

'I still want it.'

'Of course you do. You had an express course in becoming an addict. Most people slide into it slowly. You had front row seats by the sound of it.'

'Aren't you interested in what this is all about?'

'In our business we don't ask. Discretion is writ large upon our front door.'

'Tell me again why you're doing this?'

'No.'

That night I dream for the first time in an age. Not a long dream. A simple dream of standing on the edge of a lake. Water lapping at my ankles. The lake is warm and inviting. The wood behind cold and far away. I want to walk into the lake.

I don't need Freud to decipher this one for me.

I wake, drop to the floor and try a press up. I fail but feel good that I tried.

I'd kill for a burger.

Chapter 34

'Charlie, I want to kill them.'

The sun is low in the sky and Charlie hands me a beer. I sigh. 'Are you sure this is good for me?' My arms are still thin but I'm up to three press-ups today and I could have done one more if I'd pushed.

'If we're going to talk about Lorraine, essential.'

The wind blows leaves around and a dust-devil picks some up and wheels them under the trailer.

'Why would we talk about Lorraine?' I crack the tin and sip at the liquid. I'd still prefer a needle but the beer and a few of Tina and Gary's tablets help keep the craving at bay.

'Craig, what did they do to you?'

I look at him and instead of avoiding the question I offload. The whole shebang. When I'm finished he looks at me. 'Brings back the old times. Me serving you beer and you wringing yourself dry.'

'This is cheaper.'

'For you, maybe.'

'Charlie, why the hell are you helping me?'

'Hatch Roll.'

'Garbage. Thousands of people cycle through there. I'm nothing special.'

'You want to know about Lorraine?'

I don't want to know about Lorraine. I don't want to remember the sound of her skull cracking like a busted snail shell. This is the man who took her away from me and I'm sitting on the stoop sipping suds and chewing air with him.

'I know that you didn't mean to kill her. Let's leave it there.'

'No.'

'My rules. We play by my fucking rules. OK?'

'My beer. My rules.'

'Charlie, this isn't the time.'

'It's exactly the time. You know what it felt like?'

I don't answer.

'Like nothing. Like the biggest nothing on earth. That's what. I didn't even believe I'd done it. Not right after. It was a blank but the suits played me the tape. Again and again. At first I thought it was a James Cameron moment. CGI and all that. Not me. Not me with Lorraine. But they had it on tape and I have to accept it. I didn't want to believe it but it was me. I still don't want to believe it. I loved your wife.'

'I know.'

'I mean I really loved her. Ever since the day you walked into the bar. I saw her and I didn't see you until an hour after you sat down. There was Lorraine and there was everyone else. Except you had her. Not me. The joke about the money. A thousand and one dollars! I would have given you every cent in my bank if I thought she would have chosen me. But it was never going to happen. She loved you. And that was that.'

'So why did you kill her?

'Because you made me. Isn't that the way it works?'

'All I know is that I'm somehow responsible for you killing her.' I stop. The words are harsh and too real. 'I pushed you to do it but there was a reason. I haven't figured out all the angles yet but I only set off people with bad history. Something nasty in the past that I bring to the surface. Not bad blood. Something hidden. Something that's rotten at the core of the apple. All rosy on the surface but deep down? Buried. So what happened with you and Lorraine?'

Charlie sits back and drains the can he's holding. There is something and the pause is enough to tell him that I know there is something. He leans away from me. 'You know what, maybe it doesn't matter.'

I shake my head. 'You wanted this. You dug me from the

grave and decided I was worth saving. You wanted this conversation and now I want to know what happened between you and my wife.'

'I tried it on with her.' He lets the words hang in the evening air and I watch them blow around our heads.

'What?'

'I tried it on with her. One night after closing. You were back at Hatch Roll for a check-up. She had come down for a late-night chat. She didn't even have a drink. Just coffee. On the other hand I had been drinking. Stupid. I pushed, she pushed back. I pushed too hard and she ran.'

How hard did you push?'

'It was enough. I overstepped the mark. I tried to kiss her.' Pause. 'And then a little more.'

I hit him square on the chin and then I'm on top of him. Raining down blows. But I'm weak. He pushes up and rolls me off. I try to stand up and he pushes me back down. 'Bastard. Is that why you're helping me? Is it? You kill my wife and then tell me you tried to rape her. So this is your 'Get Out of Jail Free' card is it? Save poor Craig and bang goes your guilty conscience.'

I'm shouting and the power in my voice feels good. 'Is that IT?

'I never tried to rape her.'

'But you weren't far away.'

He drops his head.

'Fuck you,' I say. I stand up and he backs off. I spit in his face, turn away and begin to walk towards the woods.

'I'd never have hurt her,' he shouts after me.

I turn. 'You killed her.'

He takes a step towards me. 'Craig. You killed her and you know it. I might have been there but without you it would never have happened. '

I start to run. It hurts but I need to be away from Charlie. I hit the edge of the wood and feel dead leaves slap me in the face. It feels good. I take another twenty steps and fall to the ground. I struggle to get up. I want to run. I want Lorraine back. I want my life back. My legs won't support me and I start to crawl. Anything to keep moving. I fall to my stomach and slither forward a few feet. I scream in frustration.

I'm not going anywhere. The scent of the dying leaves buries itself in my nose. I roll on my back and see Charlie standing over me. He reaches out and I ignore the offer. I flip my face away and try to crawl but I'm spent. Charlie's hands grab my waist and I try and wriggle free. Charlie lifts me clean from the ground and wraps me over his shoulder.

Tears flow as I thump on his back. He walks to the trailer and his back is damp by the time he lays me in my bed.

He walks out. I try to get up, fall back and slide into sleep.

Chapter 35

'I really do want to kill them.'

Charlie is sitting next to me on the bed.

My anger with Charlie comes and goes. It's been a week since I tried to run. A week of tearing my head apart. Trying to figure what to do. 'What you did to Lorraine was wrong.'

He says nothing. I want him to say sorry again. Just to let me have another pop but there is no mileage in this. I need to make a decision.

'I'm going to kill them. Lendl, Tampoline – then maybe you.'

'Food and rest first.

* * *

I pass thirty press-ups in the next week. Sixty in two weeks. I go for a walk each day. On the day I do one hundred press ups and walk two miles I am on the way back.

I shave my head each day. My dream of thick, offensive hair has gone for good. Tina and Gary are like clockwork toys. They arrive every day at eight in the morning and then again at six. Conversation is random but never useful. Baseball scores. World news. Small requests – I'm back reading again. Charlie is in and out. I ask what he's doing. Where he goes. He tells me has sold the pub and is tidying up a few things. He tells me how hard it is to do stuff when you have a government agency trying to track you down. And then he tells me if the Unabomber could evade the FBI for seventeen years then a few months should be easy.

I'm not sure I care and I'm not so sure he's right. The suits don't seem to dance to the same tune as the FBI.

I've work through a thousand scenarios in my head. All involving the death of Lendl and the senator. None holds water.

For a start I'm not sure where Lendl is. I have a rough idea of where I was held but it was a secure facility and wouldn't be easy to get into. Anyway he could be anywhere on the planet. I first met him in Iraq after all.

The senator is easier. He has a public diary but I want both and, given my talent, I know if I can get them in the same room things may well take care of themselves.

Charlie comes into the trailer. 'Time to move on.'

'Why?'

Tina and Gary are just finishing up breakfast around us. I won't need them much longer. I'm still a shadow of my previous self but I'm in no need of babysitting.

'I caught sight of a couple of suits.'

Charlie has refused to tell me where he's staying. All I know is that it isn't Hudson or Sharon's place.

'Where?'

'Too close for comfort.'

'So where do we go?'

He throws a paper on the table. It's the Tampa Tribune. 'I thought you might like to see this. Try the sports pages.'

I flick through and see that the Devil Rays are at home tonight. The second in a series against the Boston Red Sox. 'What am I looking for?'

'Look who's throwing the first pitch tonight.'

'Tampoline.'

'Thought you might like to know.'

'Pity that Lendl won't be there.'

'Won't he?'

Charlie drops a small leaflet on the table to join the paper. It's an invitation to buy into the Tampa Bay Devil Rays. At the bottom there is a bunch of faces and names of current shareholders.

Lendl's face is dead centre.

'He has a share in the baseball team?'

Charlie nods. 'Clive Lendl's one of the minor players.'

Tampoline and Lendl. Tonight. In the same place. Assuming Lendl attends.

But of course he'll attend. He knows Tampoline. He might even be funded by him. After all, Tampoline was there the night they started my experiments.

I look up at Charlie. 'When is the first pitch?'

'8.00pm.'

'Tonight. I'm going after them tonight.'

'And what are you going to do once you get there?'

'Let nature take its course.'

'Great plan.'

'Best I have.'

The window shatters, something bounces off the far side of the trailer and smoke pours from the object. Charlie looks at the object, at me and then to Gary and Tina. I drop to my knees and shut my eyes. These bastards are nothing if not consistent. In the confined space of the trailer we have seconds before the gas forces us from the trailer.

'Gary, Tina – get out.'

I hear Charlie push Gary and Tina to the door – his eyes will be streaming. There's a scuffle, coughing and then the door opens. I hear a voice and the word 'fire' and Charlie joins me on the floor.

'Under the bed,' he coughs.

I want to point out that this is useless just as a second missile flies in. I don't see it – just hear it smack off a surface and start hissing.

Charlie drags me under the bed and fumbles around. There's a click and I fall into a hole. He joins me then reaches up and closes the trapdoor we've just fallen through.

'Here.' He hands me a mask and small metal bottle.

'Oxygen.'

I strap the mask to my face and fiddle with the bottle until I start the oxygen flow.

We are lying side by side in a metal box maybe eight feet long by four wide. At a couple of feet deep the tip of my mask touches the top of the box as I lie on my back.

'What is this?' My voice is muffled and amplified at the same time. Muffled from the mask and amplified in the metal coffin.

'A back-up plan. You can't see the box from the outside. I had it installed when I decided I was coming for you. A modern day priest's hole.'

'It won't take five minutes for them to find us.'

'This is only part one of a three-part plan.'

'What's part two?

'This.'

I hear a click in the dark. There is a few seconds' silence and then a dull whoomph from above.

'What was that?' I ask.

'It's going to get hot in here. Stay with it. The trapdoor has a strip of Pyroblanket on it.'

'What?'

'To give protection from heat.'

'What heat?'

'I've just set the trailer on fire.'

Chapter 36

Charlie coughs as the fumes he breathed in still rattle around his chest. I feel him shudder with the effort.

I turn to him. 'What do you mean you set fire to the trailer?'

'I set up a firebomb in the trailer. I'm betting that once the trailer is a molten mass they'll assume we're dead.'

'Are you kidding? We WILL be dead in here.'

'Not if I've thought this through.'

'Have you?'

'If you're asking if I've ever done anything like this before – the answer is no.'

'Great.'

The temperature is rising. Whether this is because of our body heat or the fire above I can't tell. I try to move but there's little room and as I wriggle, I feel the metal box bend beneath me.

'Charlie, the box is moving.'

'Metal one-o-one was never my strong point. Had to guess at what was needed. This is hardly in the Home Depot manual.'

There's a roaring sound from above and light leaks in from the edge of the trapdoor. I turn my head and Charlie is coming into view.

'Not good,' he says. 'I thought the seal on the trapdoor was airtight.'

'Charlie, this is insane. At best the heat will seal us in here. At worst we'll bake to death.'

'There's still part three. But we need to wait.'

'For what?'

'Just wait.'

Something shatters above us and there's a crash as an object falls to the floor. Another crash and the whole trailer rocks. The box-floor dips a little more. The light around the trapdoor is bright – a constant glare and I can now see the inside of the box. It's made of the non-slip metal sheets that started life in industrial complexes and are now used as a shorthand by theme parks to indicate danger. The raised surface is a criss-cross of short strips, and the welding that keeps the whole thing together would fail a freshman's first exam.

Heat is coming in waves. Each one hotter than the last. The air has been sucked from the space and my exposed skin is starting to smart. I try to draw slowly on the bottle of air. It doesn't look like it holds much and without it I'll be dead in seconds.

'We can't take much more,' I yell.

'A couple of minutes. Just hold on.'

'For what, Charlie – for what?'

'Just hang on.'

An explosion from above suggests that the fire is having fun. The noise is now making it difficult to hear. A series of mini bombs go off as my home for the past few weeks is reduced to little more than ashes and bent metal. Each bang, each explosion, each sound vibrates in the coffin and all the time the heat is rising.

We lurch downwards and I roll into Charlie as we settle at an angle. I hear a faint grunt and realize Charlie is shouting. 'I can't get to the release.'

The words are a whisper against the hurricane. I lean over to try and press my ear to Charlie's mask.

'Lever. Pull the lever,' he shouts.

I reach around but all I can feel is the rough texture of the metal. We lurch again and a blast of heat flows in as the corner of the trapdoor bends towards us.

'It's under me,' shouts Charlie.

I push beneath his back and feel a rubber-tipped object. I wrap my hand around it and pull. Nothing happens.

'I can't pull it up while you're on it,' I scream.

Charlie arches his back and I try again, but nothing happens. He rolls on to his side and the handle is free. I pull hard and we fall.

We land in dirt. Charlie pushes me away and a blanket flies over my head. I can feel the cool, damp sensation of lying on moist earth. The blanket kills the light and dulls the sound of the fire.

'Is this part three?'

Charlie coughs. 'Yes. I dug the pit before I moved the trailer in. I'd hoped we wouldn't have to use it. Anyone watching the trailer would have seen us fall.'

'I doubt it. The whole thing must have settled a couple of feet. What now – part four?'

'I was lucky to get to part three.'

'Well at least they won't have to dig our grave.'

'The blanket is the same stuff I used on the floor. As long as something large doesn't fall on us we should be OK.'

'What, like a trailer?'

'That could happen.'

I want to laugh. 'Charlie, if we survive they'll still find us. They'll have seen us go in and if they don't Tina and Grieg will tell them we were inside.'

'Not a problem. They both know what to do.'

'They're kids. The suits will make beef-chuck out of them.'

'They may be kids but they're my kids and they'll do the right thing.'

'Your kids?'

'Sharon's and mine.'

I knew there was something familiar about the pair.

'Look Charlie, we need to get out. This is fucking serious. They know we aren't David Copperfield.'

Above the roar of the fire I hear sirens.

Charlie rolls onto his side. 'I told the kids to phone the authorities before I joined you.'

'The police and fire won't make any odds. The suits are way beyond them.'

'Station twenty. I just hope they're on call.'

'What?'

'Station twenty. A couple of friends.'

'What are you on about?'

'I chose this place because it's in station twenty's area. I have some friends who work there.'

'Station twenty?'

'The local fire station.'

Sirens are closing in.

'And they know about us?'

'Kind of.'

I'm at a loss. Charlie has put his own kids on the line for me with the ropiest of 'outs' if things go wrong.

'You know the suits will search for us?'

'I'm counting on it.'

'Then what?'

'No idea.'

The fire is starting to die down. The noise is falling away and I can hear some voices where there had only been a din before.

Water starts to flow in from above. In seconds the hole starts to fill with it as the hoses are turned on the fire.

'We need to get out. We'll drown,' I shout.

Charlie nods and pushes the blanket away. We're faced with a metal ceiling.

The floor of the coffin has fallen and sealed us in tight.

Chapter 37

'The trailer has collapsed on us!' Stating the obvious is not a trait I admire in Charlie.

The water is running through a small gap between the trailer floor and the earth and only the narrowness of the entry has prevented the hole filling with water already.

'Dig at the opposite end from the water,' Charlie shouts.

'But the trailer might be sitting there.'

'Yes, and if we dig where the water is it'll flood in and we'll drown.'

I reach up and start to pull away at the earth. It comes free in clumps and Charlie squeezes in next to me and starts to claw. We hit metal and start again further along. This time my hand breaks through. The fire is all but out above, and I start to widen the space. I am kneeling and beneath me the water is up to my waist. Charlie is stronger than me. I push him forward and I take up the rear. He tears into the earth and I reach up and help with one hand.

Water cascades down the opposite wall and I wonder why would they still be pumping?

The gap is now big enough to stick a head through. The water is up to my chest and I can feel the icy cold drawing away my strength. We're losing this battle.

'Charlie, faster.' A useless thing to say. He's burrowing like a mad mole. The earth may be damp but it's still hard to shift. Each handful has to be pulled free and thrown into the rising water and this takes time. Time we don't have.

I reach over, grab at the dirt and pull. My hand yanks away a few ounces and I slam my fist in frustration. 'This isn't working. We won't get out in time.'

I wade across the hole to where the water pours in and reach up. Charlie turns to see what I am doing and shouts. 'Stop!'

I grab the edge where the water is flowing hardest and pull. The mud falls away and the water becomes a torrent.

'Jesus, Craig, don't!'

I grab another two handfuls and pull down. The water cascades into my face. I fight against the flow to grab some more and succeed. I dig deep – burying my fingers up to the third knuckle. I close them as much as I can and lean back - putting all my weight on both hands. Pressing my feet against the wall of the hole I push and a large slab of mud slides free. I fall back into the water and I'm engulfed. The surface of the water recedes and I fall to the bottom of the hole. My head is spinning. My nose fills with filthy liquid and my eyes sting. There can only be four feet of water but I can't tell up from down. I push up and my head rams the metal roof. There's no space left for air.

Charlie is behind me and I grab his hand and push him to the point where the water is coming in. He slides past me and I follow. I should have taken a deeper breath. My lungs are already burning.

I see light in the corner and Charlie seems to be climbing. I hold onto his leg. He raises it and then he's yanked from my grip. I push forward and find the edge of the hole. The mud is slippy and my mind starts to fog as the lack of air bites.

A hand grabs my wrist. I grab back and hold tight. I'm yanked up and my head breaks through the water. I suck in air and just keep sucking. Another hand takes my arm and I'm pulled out of the hole and along the ground. I emerge from under the wreck of the trailer.

Charlie is lying next to me. Two firemen are slouched beside us. Both are rubbing their upper arms. I might have lost a lot of weight but it took effort to pull me from the hole.

Charlie spits up brown water and I join him. He grasps the hand of the nearest fireman. 'Thanks.'

'Always digging you out of a hole. Always.' The fireman's accent is thick with New York.

Charlie turns to me. 'Craig meet Ryan. Ryan meet Craig.'

Ryan reaches over and shakes my hand. 'You ex-army as well?'

I nod.

'I thought you guys were supposed to be saving our skin,' he says.

'You're the ones with the dangerous job,' I say. 'They gave me a gun when the going got tough. They give you an axe and a hard hat.'

He smiles and his colleague stands up and heads for the fire engine. 'Who are the men in black?' asks Ryan.

'Bad men,' says Charlie. 'They want to talk to us and we're not in the mood for a chat. Understand?'

'Perfectly.'

He signals to the paramedic who jogs over, bag in hand. 'Both for the hospital I think.'

'The guys over there say they're in charge,' says the para. 'They want to talk to the survivors.'

'See the fire still raging in the trailer?' says Ryan. The paramedic looks at the trailer. A small line of smoke is drifting into the sky. The aluminium shell is burnt black where the fire escaped. Inside is a mass of shining black. There are no flames.

The paramedic looks back.

'Smoke,' says Ryan. 'While there's smoke I'm in charge. If they want to discuss it then fine, but in the meantime get these two to hospital.'

Three suits start to walk over and Ryan points the para to the ambulance and stands up. 'Hospital.'

He walks towards the suits and meets them as they reach the halfway point. Voices start to rise and Ryan stands like a human roadblock, hat under arm, legs slightly apart. One of the suits tries to walk round him and he reaches out and blocks him. The suit tries to free himself and a second suit intervenes. The firemen who are rolling up the hoses drop what they're doing and walk over. They take up positions either side of Ryan. Six of them in a line facing down the suits. There must be another twenty suits standing next to a clutch of black SUVs but they don't move. To be fair neither would I.

The paramedic signals for the ambulance to back up and Charlie and I are stretchered and bundled into the back. As the door shuts, Ryan turns and gives a thumbs up. Next to him Tina and Gary wave. The ambulance sets off. I lie back for a few moments as we bump over the rough ground and as we enter civilization again I turn to Charlie. 'Who the hell is Ryan?'

Charlie smiles. 'My ex-wife's first husband. Tina and Gary's father.'

'I thought you said they were your kids?'

'Kind of. When I married Susan they moved in with me but they're really Ryan's.'

'Susan?'

'My ex-wife.'

'And her ex-husband is on our side?'

'Yip,'

'Did he know what was going on?'

'Probably. He's still close with the kids.'

'And you get on with your ex-wife's ex?'

'You know what they say. The enemy of my enemy is my friend.'

This time I smile.

The paramedic steps into the cab to talk to the driver and I tap Charlie on the shoulder and whisper, 'Ryan might be our savior at a fire but ten will get you twenty that the suits will be camped out at the hospital.'

'And?'

'Time to ask this taxi to drop us off.'
'And how do we do that?'
'Next set of lights.'
'Are you up to it?'
I wasn't. 'Yes.'

The ambulance isn't on the siren. We're hardly emergency material. As we slow down I sit up. Through the gap into the cab I see an approaching set of lights as they flick to red.

'Now.'

We slip from the stretchers and I grab the handle to the back door, swing it open and jump out. Charlie follows and pushes the door shut as he hits the road. The couple in the car behind stare wide-eyed. The ambulance accelerates on the green and then slams to a halt. We jog to the sidewalk, walk into a diner and head for the washrooms. I turn as we enter the washroom and see the paramedic out on the street - scanning – trying to find us. I walk on.

The washroom is empty.

'What now?' says Charlie.

'Tropicana Field tonight. After that I don't care.'

'They'll be over the place like a rash. They know what you can do and now they know where you are it won't take long to put two and two together.'

'I'm still going.'

'It won't solve anything. In fact it'll make it worse.'

'Worse. How the hell can it be worse? My wife's dead. I've no job. No cash. I'm being hunted to be used as some sort of fucking assassin. How can it be worse?'

'You could be caught. They'd have you back on the happy juice in no time. Maybe one more gig and then a bullet in the head. Worse.'

'And what do I do instead? Run?'

'I've got some money. We skip the country and find

somewhere to let things cool.'

'Charlie, much as I like you I'm not going to retire to some tropical paradise with you. What about your kids? Are you just going to leave them? And then there's the fact that you killed my wife.'

He looks away. A low blow and I know it. Charlie no more killed my wife than he killed Sharon.

'Look,' I continue. 'Let me have one crack at this tonight. Then I'm done. Anyway nothing might happen. It took the combined expertise of Pfizer and the US government to find a way to trigger me and even then it went south in a big way. What's the odds that anything will happen?'

'I've no idea.'

'Tonight and then I'm with you. You don't even have to come to the game. I'll fly solo.'

'Sure you will. You can hardly stand as it is. You might feel a bit better than you did but you're a country mile from being right.'

'I'll make it.'

'Not without me.'

'Ok, so are you out or in?'

Charlie sits on the washroom's only sink. The door opens and man in a jogging suit walks in.

'Can you give us a minute?' The man looks me up and down as I speak to him.

'I need to use the toilet.'

I step forward. 'Can you give us a MINUTE.'

He looks at me and backs out.

'Scary,' says Charlie. 'And you think nothing is going to happen tonight?'

'We'd better move. The guy might report us.'

'We need to change out of these clothes.'

'You any friends left you haven't used up yet?'

Charlie shakes his head. 'But I know where we can get a fresh set of clothes and hang out until tonight.'

He pushes up from the sink. "I just need to lose some of the water I swallowed.'

I exit the washroom and wait until he's finished relieving himself. There's no sign of the ambulance. The man who had entered the washroom is standing talking to the waitress and pointing in my direction. Charlie walks out and we leave the diner with two pairs of eyes burning holes in our backs.

Charlie waves down a taxi. 'The Village Motel, 4100 East Hillsborough.'

The taxi driver gives us the once-over and decides we're not carrying the plague.

'Where are we going?' I ask.

Charlie closes his eyes and stretches. 'My home from home for these last few weeks. You'll love it.'

The taxi driver settles into the journey.

I don't.

Chapter 38

The Village Motel sits next to a used-car lot in a dodgier end of town. On the opposite corner sits another used-car lot and we are in sub two-grand auto land. The motel is a collection of mismatched buildings. Charlie pays off the taxi driver with a wet twenty.

'Nice,' I say.

'Don't knock it. Very reasonable. Clean, and the owner is very discreet.'

We walk to the back of the complex. As we enter the room I find myself in a spacious, well-kept bedroom. The bathroom is off to the right and a wire-meshed window looks out the back onto a small road. I look through the window and four men in hard hats are chatting as they stroll by.

'OK so I was wrong. It seems quite nice. Who has first dibs on the shower?'

Charlie doesn't answer and walks into the bathroom. Owner's privilege. I lift a newspaper from a pile on the table and place it on the chair next to the vanity table. I'm still soaked through but I'll wait until Charlie is finished before stripping off – I don't have anything to change into and hanging around in another man's bedroom in my birthday suit just feels wrong.

I hear the shower kick in and I walk over and switch on the TV. I take a minute to locate the remote and jig it around until I find the local news channel. A dark-haired stunner is giving the gossip and intelligence the once-over. A car smash on the 275, an emergency landing at Tampa International, a child abduction – all in all a normal day in wonderland.

The sports reporter is introduced and previews the upcoming game with the Red Sox. There's no mention of the senator but the Barenaked Ladies will be playing a gig after the game.

The shower stops.

The newsreader picks up on the next story. 'And now for some breaking news. Police are anxious to interview a Mr Craig McIntyre in connection with a fire near Lettuce Lake Park.'

My military snapshot sits on the newsreader's shoulder as she speaks.

'The fire relates to an illegal trailer, and in a police statement we are informed that loss of life was only avoided by the swift action of the Fire Department. If you see Craig McIntyre please call the number on the screen or contact your local station. The police are advising not to approach him. And now to the story of a dog that wanted to fly...'

I realise that the bathroom door is open and Charlie has taken in the news.

'Look on the bright side. You weren't mentioned,' I say.

Towel wrapped around his waist, Charlie nods at the statement as he crosses to sit on the bed. 'You'll never get into the stadium now the police are looking for you.'

I stand up. 'Let me take a shower and think on that.'

I close the door and wind up the hot water. Once it starts to pour I grab Charlie's shower gel and get to work on my still thin arms. Thirty seconds in I jump from the shower, grab a towel and stick my head out of the door.

'It was an old photo,' I say, dripping on the carpet. 'They used an old photo on the TV.'

Charlie is pulling on a pair of pants and looks up. 'So they did.'

'Well do you think I look like myself?'

The photo had been of me - a lean but muscled man, a hint of a five o'clock shadow, dark curly hair and bright eyes. Not the drug-ravaged skeleton with a shiny pate and eyes that had a sheen of dust over them, wrapped in a motel towel.

'Strange that,' says Charlie.

'They wouldn't have new photos of me. I don't remember them taking any. Although I was so out of it they could have put me in a movie and I wouldn't have noticed.'

'I can't see the point in using the old photo.'

I nod in agreement, drip back to the shower and try and clean out the dirt. Teeth brushed (fingers only – I draw the line at using someone else's toothbrush) and a rough shave (chin and head) and I feel a touch more human.

'What about clothes?' I say as I hang out the bathroom door again.

Charlie hands me a pile and I retire to realize that we're not the same height, width or mass. The jeans are too long and too baggy. The T-shirt is voluminous and I skip the boxers – preferring to go commando. My shoes will do once they've dried out, and Charlie's socks will suffice.

I take the belt on the jeans to the last hole and I'm a yard shy. A few minutes with a fork, and the belt holds the trousers up. The T-shirt hangs like a kaftan but the look isn't that bad. With my new baldness I have an air of rebellion about me.

'Nice.' Charlie laughs as I re-enter the room.

'Food?'

'On its way. The wonders of pizza delivery.'

The TV is still on but the sound is down.

'So to tonight.'

Charlie sighs. 'Craig, is it really worth it?'

'I'm not having a debate. I'm going. Full stop.'

He shrugs. 'I don't think it'll be hard getting close to the stadium but it will be a bitch getting in. If these guys are half as connected as we have seen so far they'll be fully loaded when it comes to tech. Face-recognition software, mobile CCTV, access to city-wide cameras, maybe even aerial recognizance.'

'Come on Charlie I'm not Ayman Al-Zawahiri.'

'Who?'

'Head of al-Qa'ida.'

'You're not that different.'

'What?'

'Get real. They tried to use you as an assassin. To kill a head of state.'

He reaches into the pile of newspapers and throws me a USA Today from the day after my escape. It details the carnage at the theatre. In the intervening weeks I hadn't been ready to view my handiwork.

Thirteen dead, fifty-two in hospital – a riot with no reason was how it was described. The two on stage had been the President-in-waiting for Nigeria and his rival for the role. Twenty years as enemies - the event at the theatre had been a symbolic burying of the hatchet. Neither had died but both were hospitalised.

I sit back. 'Hell.'

Charlie sits on the bed. 'The good news – if there is any – is that the riot overshadowed what happened on the stage. In fact if you read the detail you would be forgiven for thinking that the two politicians tried to intervene to help.'

'So I didn't kill a future world leader?'

'The suits underestimated what they had turned you into.'

I remember the feeling of electricity flowing from my fingers. Of playing it across the theatre. The feeling of hate sweeping across the building. Driven by me. 'I was drugged to the hilt.'

'And you think you have it under control now?'

'Strangely I do. Not in a way that I can explain. Hell I can't explain the half of it but there's been nothing since you rescued me. Your kids would have been prime candidates. The firemen. The suits. All were in proximity when I was in the hole with you and if it's stress that brings it on then it sure as hell should have happened then.

'So is it gone?'

'I doubt it. Not gone. Just a bit more predictable. I think. I can still feel it buried in the back of my head. Waiting. But I think it needs my permission now.'

Charlie looks doubtful. 'Are you sure?'

'I'm not sure of anything.'

'So what will you do tonight if we get in?'

'I told you. Let nature take its course.' I lie back in the chair. 'So how *do* we get in?'

The newsreader is sitting in front of a picture of me again. Only this time it's a grainy shot from a CCTV of me in my full baldness. It's a crop from the theatre. My eyes are glazed but it's clearly me.

'Shit.' We both say it at the same time.

Chapter 39

The pizza boxes lie. Fallen soldiers to our appetite. We're two large bottles of Coke down and a couple of Babe Ruths to the wind.

'I'm stuffed.' Charlie rubs his stomach to prove the point.

I stand up. 'Me too. Now to work. It's baseball night and I feel like a bleacher moment. We should get there early. Before the police and the security get into full swing.'

'Won't it be easier to lose ourselves in the crowd?' Charlie asks. 'After all they don't know you're going to the game.'

'I wouldn't bet on it. The senator, Lendl – it has to be a risk for them. I'd be betting on me being there.'

'Where the hell would we hide if we do get in?'

'Good question.'

'And we need tickets.'

'Cash only. They'll have your cards marked.'

'I'm low on cash. I need to use an ATM.'

'You can't. They'll be onto us in minutes.'

'We can't get in without money. And we sure as hell can't go on the run with loose change.'

'True. Any thoughts?'

Charlie scratches his head. 'I know where there's a wedge.'

'Where?'

'In the house in Hudson. Ten grand to be exact. Provided Sharon hasn't used it at some point.'

'That's some nest egg.' It's the first time he's mentioned Sharon since the escape. He pauses mid breath.

I'm sorry.' I say.

'It doesn't seem real. They showed me the tape but it wasn't me.'

'It wasn't. It was me.'

'Let's not go there. It won't help.'

'You can't go to Hudson. They'll be watching. Anyway, why the hell didn't you tell me you had ten grand? I wouldn't have needed the job.'

'It's the only source of cash I have and I'm not a complete charity case. Anyway, I'm betting the suits will be watching the front. Remember the house backs onto a golf course and I have the key. If I'm lucky I can be in and out before they know I'm there.'

'Charlie, they're not stupid. They'll have the house covered from all angles.'

'Have you any better ideas?'

'I'll come with you. Two heads are better and all that.'

'Will you hell. You're dead weight and anyway it's you they want. I may not have a two hundred IQ but taking you up to a house we know they're watching is dumber than a dumb thing. I'll get a cab. All being well I'll be back before five. That'll give us plenty of time to get downtown.'

Charlie stands up and heads for the door.

'Take care.' My words sound weak.

'Stay put. Don't answer the door. Don't leave the room. Watch the adult channel if you have to but stay put.'

I nod.

As the door closes on him I slump onto the bed and wait for my face to reappear on the TV.

My mind turns to the night ahead. I have no plan and no idea what will happen - but it *will* happen. How the hell do we get in? The place will be alive with cameras and, even if we go early, security won't just let us wander through.

I go back to my training. Occam's Razor. Not exactly a grunt's phrase but my platoon leader liked it.

'Occam's Razor. Keep it simple. Complexity leads to complexity. The easy way is often the best way. The more obvious the less likely they'll see it coming.'

I relax on the bed. Sometimes you just have to give your mind a chance to take a break. A little lateral thinking time and the rabbit pops from the top hat.

An hour later and I'm starting to think the worst for Charlie. He would hardly have reached Hudson by now but my mind is a dangerous thing when given nothing to do. I take to checking the windows on a rota basis. Looking for signs of suits, SUVs or police.

I switch off the TV. My face is annoying me. I also wish I'd thought about picking up some pre-paid cells. Then I remember that I haven't any cash. There's a knock on the door and I freeze. A Drain Fly flaps in front of me - its large wings in slow mo as the sound of flesh on wood settles in the room. I watch it circle the main light as a second knock breaks the silence. There's the sound of a key in the lock and I move across the room and into the bathroom. I shut the door and flip on the shower. I'm at the small window turning the latch when I hear a Spanish accent . 'Housekeeping.'

I relax a little but still flip the latch and push the window out. At a squeeze I could get through.

'Housekeeping.'

A prelude to an attack or a genuine call to scrub up the room? Hard to tell.

'I'm in the shower.'

'OK,' comes the reply.

I hear the door click shut. If they're going to come in it'll be quick. I push my head through the window. No one in sight but that means little. I check I have the room key in my pocket and clamber out. I'm better out than in.

I drop to the ground and tense for whatever it is that I am tensing for.

Nothing.

I stand up and walk to the edge of the building. I take a

breath and poke my head out. The rear of the maid catches my eye. There are no suits. No cars. No nonsense. I walk to the main road and all is clear.

Back in the room I kill the shower and settle in for the return of Charlie

* * *

When the door opens I'm half asleep. Charlie stands in the doorway like a returning hero. His face is filthy and his clothes are ripped. If he looked bad after our episode in the hole he looks worse now.

'Trouble?' I enquire.

'You might say.'

'The suits?'

'Yes.'

He flops on the bed.

'They were waiting. Two car loads. One in front of the house and a second round the corner. No SUVs this time. Old battered Cutlasses were the order of the day.' He brushes some dirt onto the floor. 'I spotted them easily enough but they had the house well covered and I didn't have the luxury of waiting for dark. I skirted the golf course and came at the house from behind. I was lucky. The car covering the back had two in it but they were more interested in chatting than watching and I got in OK. I grabbed the cash and was on my way out when the door burst open.'

'They saw you?'

'I think the house was wired.'

'What did you do?'

'I ran. Straight out the back and across the golf course. I had no time to avoid the bushes and trees and I figured it would make it easier if I took them through rather than round. I feel like I've torn half my skin off.'

'But you lost them?'

'Yes but only because I stole a golf buggy. You should have heard the owners. They were just teeing off and I grabbed the thing and put my foot down. They're faster than you think. It was all I needed to get a lead. I abandoned it a couple of blocks away and spent an hour working my way back to the main drag.

'If they had cameras inside they'll know what you were back for.'

'All the more reason to cut and run.'

'No. We're going to the game and I've had a change of mind on the plan. Clean up. I need you to run an errand for me.'

Charlie takes his second shower of the day, and once he's wearing clean clothes and fifty Band Aids I tell him what we're going to do.

'Let's not make this complicated. There will be thirty or forty thousand going tonight. So let's dress the part. Full Devil Rays kit. Baseball cap. Tops the lot. We simply merge in with the crowd. They're never going to check everyone, and with a cap pulled down, collar up and head down we just walk in.'

'We just walk in?' Charlie doesn't sound convinced.

'Yip. I need you to get two home plate tickets or as a close as you can and strip the nearest seller of a lunatic fan's-worth of Devil Rays gear. We leave at six-thirty.'

Charlie is back in less than forty minutes. He looks like the Devil Rays' best ever customer. 'I hope the hell that the suits aren't looking for odd patterns in the sale of baseball gear. The shop will stick out like a sore thumb.'

After we dress I look in the mirror. With the cap down I doubt anyone would know who I am.

I lift a knife from the table and put it in my pocket.

'What do you need that for?' asks Charlie.

'Stimulus. What's this?' I hold up a cowbell.

'Seems the fans use them. Usually on the three and two count.'

'You're kidding?'

'Nope.'

I ring the bell. 'I reckon a taxi to within a half mile of the ground. Then we walk.'

I was being optimistic. A mile out and we're down to a crawl and take to the sidewalk. We fall in behind two large families and in front of six teenagers. As we close in on the stadium the throng swells and I begin to believe this is not going to be difficult.

The Tropicana Stadium sits in St Petersburg despite being the home to the Tampa Bay Devil Rays and is a closed dome. It looks a little worn at the edges but the fans don't care. The Rays are in the hunt for a pennant and a win tonight will put them a game up on the Yankees.

We need to cross the parking lot to get to the stadium and people are threading their way through the cars - passing tailgaters who are in full beer and BBQ mode. The buzz is good, the noise one of hope.

We squeeze between two compacts and then we hit a line. I stretch to see what the hold-up is. I step out of the line to get a better look and see that a temporary fence has been set up. There are gaps every ten feet or so, each gap manned by police, security or suits.

They are asking everyone to remove baseball caps. They aren't searching bags just checking faces. As such there is only a small delay. I pull Charlie out of the line and pretend to tie my shoelace. We're next to a large van and I step behind it, out of sight of the checkers.

'Do you think they're checking everyone?" I say.

Charlie uses the front wheel of the van to boost himself up and he scans the parking lot. 'The barrier stretches as far as I can see.'

'It has to be for me.'

'Probably.'

'We wait.'

Charlie shakes his head. 'They have people working the lines. Two are on their way up this one.'

'Back, then?'

He spins to look behind us. 'More. Coming the other way. We have a minute at most.'

I turn and spot a second line snaking up on the other side of the van. 'Anyone working that one?'

'Not that I can see.'

'Come on. We'll join it.'

'But you'll be on the police in a couple of minutes.'

'Better than one minute.'

We join the new line and start the traditional line shuffle. Around us the crowd are griping at the delay.

'Checkin' for bombs.'

'Escaped prisoner I hear.'

'Police killer.'

'Terrorist.'

It never occurs to anyone that there might be something other than killers on the loose.

Charlie is eyeing me as we approach the fence. I reach into my pocket and take the knife I lifted from the motel room. We're six from the front and there are two young police officers manning our gap.

'Hats off. All hats off. We need to see faces.'

The smaller of the two officers repeats the phrase and the people in front pull off their baseball caps. I keep mine on. I place the knife, point first, into the side of my thigh.

'Hats off, sir.'

We are at the front of the line.

'Hats off, sir.' The smaller officer is speaking to me.

I shove the knife into my thigh and twist. A living pain train shoots up my leg and I drop to the ground. Charlie bends over and the policeman steps towards me. I give the knife another twist and nearly pass out.

'Sir?' The officer leans down.

One more twist and my head explodes as the kernel cracks.

I look up and remove my cap. He recognizes me in an instant and stands up. Turning to his colleague he opens his mouth. My headache rolls up and he stops, turns to me and tips his head to one side.

'Problem, Jim?' His colleague is stepping forward as he talks.

Jim's fist is already travelling when his colleague reaches him. The punch is a good one and takes the other officer by surprise. Jim follows up on the punch with a kick.

'Move,' I say to Charlie.

The world drops blue and the pain is gone. Even the wound in my thigh is a distant thing. We push through the gap as the second officer retaliates. I cut to the right and drag Charlie with me. Weaving through the crowd. The fighting police officers are lost to the rear.

'Did you just stab yourself?' Charlie asks.

I nod. When the blue world goes the wound will hurt like hell but at the moment I can move and that's all that counts.

'We need to get to our seats,' I say. 'The suits will put two and two together and be after us.'

Charlie checks the tickets and points to the main entrance. 'We're in there. At the back of home plate. Best seats I could get.'

The entrance swallows us up and we enter a concourse lined with food concessions and merchandise areas. The place is alive with people behaving like ants. Scurrying around. Charlie counts down the entrances and leads me up a set of stairs and through a tunnel.

We emerge into a filling stadium. A vast empty space sitting below the dome roof that seems to float high above. Three sides of the diamond are attended by seats and the fourth is a wall of advertising and glass. Charlie checks with the ticket girl and we are shown to our seats.

We have to squeeze by a few people to find our allocation but Charlie has done well. We are less than a dozen rows back and slightly to the left of home plate. The Red Sox pitcher is loosening up. We're a lot closer to the start than I had bargained for.

The mike is out for the National Anthem and the teams have already been introduced. I look for the senator and Lendl but there's a lot of ground to cover and a lot of people to check. 'See if you can spot the senator.'

Charlie starts to look and the blue fades. The knife wound takes this as a cue to start bitching. I feel blood on my leg and wonder why it's only starting now. I ask Charlie for the pennant he's carrying and, to the disgust of the lady next to me, I wrap it around the wound.

'Got him.' Charlie grabs my arm and points to the players' tunnel. The senator is talking to some players. There's no sign of Lendl but he can't be far away. 'You realize they'll be scanning the crowd.' I nod as Charlie says this. 'I know.'

I keep my head down.

'Keep your face out of sight,' I say. 'We'll know when the first pitch is due. Let's try and not give them anything to work with.'

The National Anthem starts up. I don't stand. The disgusted woman next to me spits at me. 'Stand up.' I ignore her. The anthem stops and everyone sits. The announcer calls for the first pitch. I look up and see the senator walking across the infield, ball in hand. The catcher is standing - ready to receive. There is no sign of Lendl. I bury my head in my lap, playing with the knife in my pocket and relax. A little.

The senator pitches and a weak cheer echoes around.

'What now?' asks Charlie.

'We wait. Where's Tampoline now?'

'Five rows down in the VIP seats.'

'Lendl?'

'Can't see him.'

The game gets underway and I keep my eyes on my lap. We hit a three and a two on the Rays' pitch and the crowd go nuts with the cowbells. I look up and a hand taps me on the shoulder. I start to turn and a familiar prick hits me in the arm.

'Just sit still, Mr McIntyre. No need to get worked up.' The voice is not one I want to hear behind me. I feel the drug take me down.

'You too Charles. Just take in the game.' Charlie slumps onto my shoulder.

'I'm afraid your bar friend may not be quite so used to our hospitality as you are.' Lendl is oozing confidence.

Treacle flows through my veins and candyfloss plays with my head. 'I'll fuckinhish, bashdard. I'll fuchsin.'

'We'll talk later. Save it for then.'

There are a hundred things I want to do and say but the drug is strong. Not the ones I'm used to. This is a new sensation. Not so much chilled as just cool. I'm cool with the world. I want to tell Lendl we're OK. He and I. Really OK. He's just doing his job. I understand.

I look at the game and I see men trying too hard. Running too fast. I want to tell them to take a drag on a Jamaican Marlboro. Inhale a little of that Caribbean slow time.

Lendl speaks softly. 'Just watch the game and we'll all have a friendly cup of coffee at the end.'

A few innings in I can feel some of the mist beginning to

clear but, on cue, another dose is administered and there are worse ways to watch baseball.

Two more shots and the Rays are Happy Larrys. Three – one. Top of the pile now. The stadium should empty but they're gearing up for the concert. Lendl leans forward. 'Time to go.'

A couple of suits are making their way down the stairs. They don't look happy. I wish I could make their day a bad one but the drugs are an anchor on my abilities. They remove Charlie from my shoulder and lift me from the chair.

'A touch too much drink I fear.' Lendl is talking to those around me. Another shot and I'm close to passing out. We wander through the maze

that makes up the innards of the stadium. I'm bundled into a cupboard. The smell suggests it was recently used to store cleaning equipment.

Lights out. Another cell.

I hear a door close nearby and wonder if Charlie has just been dumped in his own cell. I fall to the floor as the light fairies play with my eyesight. The feeling of helplessness is not quashed by the narcotics. I know I need to act. There will be no second chances. Lendl knows what I can do. The drugs running around my system are designed to keep me under control. They can't know that it will work but they are smart enough to keep me awake. I suspect, and I think they suspect, that the two incidents in Iraq were down to me – even if I was lost to the world. An afterburner of my ability.

Limbo is the best way to describe my situation. I feel for the knife but at some point in the journey it has been removed. I roll onto my front and this alone takes an unbearable amount of effort. I flop around with one hand and hear the distant beat of music and a cheer as the band start up. The floor is smooth. Masonry paint smooth. I shuffle my knees to make some headway but they slip around and I go nowhere.

Time is not a friend. The suits will be back and once I'm away from here I'm finished. I reach down to the blood-soaked pennant and work it loose. I push my finger into the hole in my trousers and find the wound. I clench my teeth and push my finger into the cut. The pain is there but still too far away. I curl up the finger and roll onto my side – forcing the digit deep into the muscle.

The pain grows nearer. My hip rises. All my effort into raising it. A few inches and then back to the ground. I ram my finger home and the pain is suddenly very real. I gasp. The kernel in my head flashes. The headache rises and falls and the blue world appears. The drugs seem to fly from my body and the stop/start blue planet engulfs me.

I stand up. My finger looks bent and might be broken. In the night vision I take in the cupboard. There's a single door and three walls of shelves. I try the door handle. I'm not surprised to find it locked. I give it a tug but it stays firm.

Then the handle turns of its own accord under my hand. I step back and flatten myself against the wall. The door opens. The corridor is dark but it makes little odds to me. A hand holding a flashlight appears and when the body follows I chop down on the wrist and the flashlight goes flying. I grab the arm and pull. Caught off guard, the man flies into the cupboard. I push him to the floor and I'm out the door. A second man is standing in the corridor beyond. I launch myself at him. No time for subtlety. My head connects with his and he starts to fall. I keep the momentum up and he crashes to the ground beneath me. I slam my fist into his face. He grabs at my head. With my new bald look his hand slides off and I bounce another fist into his face.

I stand up and leave him on the ground.

The corridor is narrow and bends in a curve. I follow it and reach a junction. It looks like a main serviceway. To my left is clear but to my right a clutch of suits are in conversation.

'Look.' The shout comes from the nearest suit and I try to break into a run but even with the blue world at my disposal I'm short on stamina. I stop, turn, place my finger into my wound and push.

'Fuck,' I shout as the pain bursts inside me.

The blue world vanishes and the headache is back. I lose the night vision. The first man is almost on me before he stops, turns and catches the man behind him in the groin with a foot. I don't wait to see how it pans out and hobble along the corridor.

The sound of a fight fills the space behind as the suits start to tear each other apart.

The corridor stretches out before me and I'm not sure I have the energy to make it far. Without the blue world my leg is screaming at me to stop – blood is running like a small river. I stop to draw breath and realize that the music is a lot louder. I pick my way along the wall and find a door. The crowd is cheering and I open it to discover a set of stairs.

Up.

So many stairs.

Up.

At the top another door, and this one swings open to reveal the stadium. I am at the extreme end of the seats – up in the gods. The band members have their backs to me and the stadium is rocking. The group are singing about having a million dollars.

I start down towards the pitch. Keeping the wall as a support as I drop. I am maybe ten rows from the outfield when a security guard spots me. I change tack and start to thread my way along a row of empty seats. A few blocks and the crowd are dotting the edges. The security guard is watching me and keeping parallel on the bottom row.

My footsteps are slowing. I want to sit down but I need to

keep going. I reach the first of the crowd and force myself up to the next passageway. Flicking my head back I catch the security guard starting up the stairs. I cut along, trying to put some distance between the guard and myself.

Shuffling along the back of a row, I'm being sucked into the crowd. The band is doing well and people are bouncing around me. I'm just a view blocker to those on the row next to me.

Head down and I'm starting to run on empty. There is no escape plan in my actions. Just movement. The exits will be sealed by now. I'm also expecting a bullet. Valuable as I am he won't risk me staying free. Maybe not a bullet. Maybe a tranquiliser dart. A man in a safari suit sitting high up. Taking a bead on me now. Waiting for the kill shot. Finger pressure light on the trigger. Tracking me. Breathing controlled. Waiting to exhale. Settle the sight. Squeeze. And like a hunted animal I'm on the floor.

I look up and there are two suits at the bottom of the next set of stairs. The passage I am on runs out and more suits are emerging from doors right across the arena. Behind me the security guard is on my level but he's on his walkie-talkie and not moving in. Under orders from the suits. Dangerous. Don't touch.

The bloodflow down my leg is increasing and my head is feeling light. I have nothing to stem the flood. My headache vanishes. A woman is waving at me to get out of her line of vision. She's waving a Devil Rays flag and I grab it from her – wrapping it around my leg as she goes off on one. I ignore her and when she steps forward I turn and look her in the eye. She stops and backs off. The man next to her doesn't even move.

I change direction and double back towards the security guard. My vision is going and my legs have the strength of fire-damaged twigs. Each step is becoming an effort. I stagger against the handrail and a woman in the row below turns round to see what I'm doing.

Lorraine?

I freeze.

Lorraine?

I mouth the words. She stares at me.

'Lorraine?' I say.

Quiet. Too quiet for the noise around me.

She shakes her head and turns away. I reach out and tap her on the shoulder. She turns round and it's no longer Lorraine but some woman wondering who I am. I start moving again. It's taking everything I have left to stay upright. I reach the stairs I climbed and, with the security guard a few yards away, I start down.

My eyes focus. Just for a second and Lendl is at the bottom of the stairs. He's on his cell. I close my eyes and open them again in case it's an illusion but unlike the woman Lendl stays as Lendl. Next to him is Tampoline. They're now both on their cell phones. Lendl is pointing at me.

A hundred stairs between me and my targets. A hundred steps that I don't have in me. And yet Lendl and Tampoline are there. Together. The reason my wife is dead. The reason my life has imploded. A man with no conscience and a man with blood on his hands.

A hundred steps.

The image of the young girl in the club floats up - blood gushing from her mouth. She morphs into Taylor and his girlfriend in Iraq. The two bodies rising from the dusty road. Both pointing at me. The air stewardess and her boss appear. Fighting each other.

My hand slips on the rail.

Then I'm back in Iraq. Only now I'm way back. My first patrol. Clegg and Johnston on point. Arguing. When they aren't having a pop at each other they're having one at me. I'm tired.

The heat and fear are eating me alive. I want to stop but we have our orders. Then there's an explosion and something hits me in the head. I go down and something opens inside me. I feel it crack wide and spill its guts. Something alive crawls around inside my skull. Exploring. Then it settles at the back. Curls up and wraps a hard shell round itself.

I scream and keep screaming.

When I awaken, Clegg and Johnston are dead.

Then I'm back in the stadium.

I tip my head to one side and I can feel the hard thing rolling around. Inside. The crowd around me go wild as the group winds up for a finish. Lendl is still at the bottom of the stairs. Tampoline is walking away and, around me, I can feel the suits closing in.

I push upright and make a decision.

Breath.

Step.

Breath.

Double step.

Breath.

Triple step.

Down.

Out of control.

Feet trying to find steps.

Feet failing.

And I'm falling.

I bounce off the handrail and I'm down. I hit the concrete stairs and tumble forward. I push with one foot and I'm out and into the arena air. I arc and come crashing back. My shoulder taking the hit. Up again. I veer to the left and clip someone. They give under my weight and I fly into someone else. My stomach crashes into the back of a man's head and we both fall forward. I can feel myself coming to a halt and I push out with my leg, catching some thigh, and I launch myself forward and over the crowd. There are no empty seats and I take to violent crowd-surfing.

Logic suggests that I should stop soon. Fall to the floor in a bundle of limbs as people shout and yell at me. But I don't. Instead I flip onto my back. I can see Lendl looking up. Tampoline has stopped and is watching me fall. Then I smash into another body and I'm thrown up. Each time I touch down I feel a lift as the people shove me back into the air. Hands, elbows, heads – it makes no odds.

I'm sliding down the seating – closing the gap to Lendl. No deviation from the path. A straight line. As if everyone in the crowd had agreed in advance that Craig McIntyre has somewhere to be and it's their job to help him get there.

I can still feel blood leaking. If I had a giant bottle of Luminol and sprayed it behind me you could track my progress through the spatter. Two old women shove my legs and a young man pushes at my head. I flip over and a large fat man, stuffing a hot dog into his mouth, reaches up and thrusts me forward.

Pain has passed me by. Left somewhere in the bleachers. The hands and the heads should hurt but they don't. The people should be complaining but they aren't. I feel my weight drop away. Ounce by ounce. Each drop of blood taking ten times its weight with it.

Halfway to Lendl and a pretty girl looks up at me. She smiles as her hand flicks me onwards. I smile back and her push lifts me twenty feet into the air. I reach the apex of the climb and look down on a thousand eyes. A spray of blood follows me like a contrail. I return to the crowd and the next heave lifts me to a new height. The stadium is spread out beneath me. The band is finishing up its set – oblivious to me. Lendl has his mouth open as I rise once more. Tampoline is edging back to Lendl. I can see the questions beginning to build on his lips.

I turn my head and see the suits lining the passageways. All eyes are on me as I return to earth. The next shove takes me in an arc that will cover the remaining distance to the stadium floor. I curl up to brace for the impact.

I land with the lightest of bumps, open my eyes and Lendl is above me. I have no energy left to stand up. I can't even lift my head from the floor. I feel the rough texture against my cheek. I dig for the kernel. For the headache. For the blue world.

In vain.

Suits begin to arrive. Lendl is shouting and I know he wants someone to pump me full as soon as possible. Tampoline is also looking down at me. His face is still registering my flight down the stadium.

A flicker. A small ember begins to burn in my head. I watch a suit unzip a bag and pull out a syringe. The ember is dull but the living thing in my head blows on it. The man breaks the seal of the small vial he is holding – piercing the rubber seal and plunging the needle into the liquid.

The breath in my head is oxygen-rich and the ember starts to glow. The man with the syringe tips the needle to the roof and shifts the plunger, pushing out a few drops. They sparkle in the stage lights. One lands on my face as the air in my head works from a breeze to a hurricane. The headache builds and I open my arms to welcome it in. I realize that my arms have responded to the mental image and the man with the needle is caught off balance and slips.

The headache arrives with the force of a diesel locomotive. I look up at Lendl but he has nothing in his face other than contempt. The man with the needle regains his balance and reaches for my arm. I try to pull away but the last of my energy is spent.

The band finishes and the music stops. The crowd go into overdrive. The roar of approval is a wave around my head. A chant goes up. They want more.

The note of the crowd changes. A subtle change. From adoration to something different. The cheer from the front of the crowd is being modulated. Adjusted. I flop my head to one side to look. The man with the needle also turns to look. Something is making its way towards us. A Mexican wave of sound and action. Screams are audible and the atmosphere phases from good to bad.

Then the wave hits us and the people nearest turn to their neighbors and lash out. One man take his index finger and plunges it into the eyeball of the person next to him. An older lady lifts her purse high and tries to drive it into the skull of a girl in the front row. Hate washes over me. A giant ball of hot revulsion spreading across the floor.

Thirty thousand people are responding to my signal. Each individual finding a vent for a long-pent-up fury. A moment of hurt, shame, selfishness, fear, recklessness - a moment of pay back.

I can't see past the front row but I know what is unwinding. This is the theater on a grand scale and there is nothing I can do to stop it. I'm no longer the conductor. A girl – hardly out of her gym slip leaps the barrier to the outfield. She is being chased by a young lad. Probably her boyfriend. He is missing an arm and a gusher of blood is running him dry. She has his arm in her hand – waving it high, taunting him with it. He slows down, stumbles. The arm is placed in her mouth and she bites – taking a chunk of forearm in her mouth and ripping at it until the flesh comes free. The boy collapses to the floor. Not understanding what is happening. Dying.

A pair of men tumble over the barrier. Locked tight. Each trying to land a blow. One lands on top and the other's grip is lost. The victor takes his enemy's head and smashes it into the ground. Behind him a girl is cheering him on.

I want to turn to look at Lendl but my muscles no longer respond. A screech rises from the direction of the stage and the band are joining in the fun. A guitar being used as a weapon.

Around me the sound is guttural – base human noise – attack and defense. Life and death. It spins around me and any individual sound is lost to the cacophony. A wet mist is dropping on me and I can recognize the smell of copper as the blood-letting creates a cloud. Plasma rains down.

Somebody kicks me in the back. Air rushes from my lungs. Then a foot in front of my face. A patent leather shoe, its shine spotted with blood. I lift my eyes and Tampoline is standing above me. His face is one of calm. He's not part of what's going on. The look of someone who considers himself superior in more ways than make sense. His hair is perfect, tie superbly knotted – double Windsor of course. The suit jacket cut low to give him the impression of height.

He bends down and is joined by Lendl – now a man in a leopard spot coat. Lendl talks but in the din the words are lost.

He has the syringe in his hand. He doesn't need it. I'm no threat. I can't move and whatever lives in my head is out on its own. He drops to the floor and places the syringe in front my face. The fluid is darker than earlier.

He leans into my ear. 'This will hurt.'

An aspirin will kill me now. My resistance is spent.

Tampoline joins him.

'What a waste,' he shouts. 'Just look at what you can do. Think what we could have done with you when it came to America's enemies.'

Lendl's face is inches from mine. I can smell the heavy scent of drink mixed with the sour smell of garlic. His eyes are red and sweat peppers his brow.

'Time to die, Mr McIntyre. Time to die.'

Chapter 40

I close my eyes. My last act of defiance. I'm not giving him the satisfaction of seeing my fear. I may not even feel the prick of the needle. Sensation is fading. The world collapsing around me. I am the calm eye at the centre of my own hurricane.

Nothing.

Not quite.

Almost nothing.

Background sound. A distant portable radio trying too hard with small speakers. A faded reproduction of what had been going on before. I force my eyes open and Lendl is still there, his head cocked to one side. The syringe is an inch from my neck – frozen in his hand.

He rises up, the needle recedes, he lets it go and it tumbles to the ground. Tampoline is walking away and, with movement that comes of training, Lendl closes the gap and wraps his arm around the senator's throat and drops to his knees. At the last moment Lendl propels himself forward and lands square on Tampoline's back. He reaches for Tampoline's head and his hands start to explore the senator's face. Searching for softness. The senator squirms but years of inaction and overindulgence weigh against his chances. Lendl knows what he's doing. This is not about killing. This is about pain.

More searching and Lendl leaps to his feet. Tampoline is holding his head and rolls over. Blood is pouring between his fingers. Lendl steps back and sidesteps once. He double steps towards Tampoline and launches a sixty yard, three seconds to go, last ditch, fourth downfield goal attempt. He takes Tampoline in the crotch and there is no way he hasn't broken a few toes. Tampoline – airless – spasms in agony. His hands fly from his face as his body concentrates on the area under attack. His eyes are gone.

Lendl limps back a little and hops on his good foot. He kneels down and picks up the syringe. He looks at me but there is no recognition. His eyes are blank. He circles Tampoline who is curled into a ball. With a flourish the needle is lifted into the night air and then it starts down. As it falls I watch it. A single drop of dark fluid flies into the air. The needle falls and then, at the very last instant, the very, very last instant – it veers away from the senator and Lendl thrusts the needle into his own leg and stabs down on the plunger. He empties it and stands up. Something goes off inside his chest and he is dead before he starts to fall.

I can no longer keep my eyes open and, as Lendl dies, my head flashes, the blue world is gone and the crowd noise takes on a new sound.

One of horror and stunned silence.

Chapter 41

Charlie speaks. 'Dead?'

He's probably right.

Another voice. 'Not yet.'

Not right. I'm dead.

Charlie responds. 'Amazing.'

My arm bristles as it's brushed.

Smell.

Bad taste in the mouth.

A beep – regular.

I open my eyes and the hospital engulfs me.

'Welcome back.' Charlie is sitting next to me. Next to him a nurse is standing.

I try speaking but I'm out of spit. The nurse reaches over and fills a cup from a jug of water. She passes it to me and I swallow enough to produce sound.

'Hi,' I squawk.

'Hi yourself,' she says.

I drift off and drift back. I note the drip feeding me nutrients and drift off again. I lose count of how many times I do this. The time between each sleep stretches and Charlie is always there.

I waken once more and it's dark outside. 'Any chance of some food?'

Charlie hits a button and the cute nurse appears. 'Your patient wants some sustenance.'

'I'll see what I can do.'

I ask Charlie to help me sit up. 'Ok, so why am I alive, what happened to Tampoline and Lendl, did they lock you up, how did you escape, what went on in the stadium, where are the suits, why are you here, do they allow JD and Coke in this place?'

'Hang on soldier. One thing at a time.'

Charlie pulls his chair a little closer and checks that the door is closed. I'm not sure why I'm in a private room. I'm fairly sure my health insurance doesn't cover this. 'And?' I want some answers.

'The stadium was a mess. Biggest story in years. One hundred and twenty dead, thousands injured and no reason found.'

'Me!'

'Oh I know that but the media don't and they're having a field day. Mass hysteria. A terrorist plot. Something in the water. Drugged hot dogs. A government experiment. No one knows. They are calling it the Tropicana Terror, or now it's the TT.'

'Yeah but the suits know it was me.'

'Maybe. Was it?'

'Yes.'

'So why are you lying here and not in some cell?'

'I've no idea.' I'm hoping Charlie has an answer. 'Lendl?'

'Dead. Tampoline is alive but in a bad way. Both victims of the TT.'

'No suits sitting outside my door?'

'I can't figure that. My best guess is that Lendl and Tampoline kept you a secret. Your trip to the theatre was a black op of the blackest type. Need to know only.'

'Need to know. There were endless suits involved.'

'Grunts I would guess.'

'And they don't talk to each other?'

'No idea. All I know is that I've been here over a week and there hasn't been a single suit.'

'Has it been that long?'

'Longer. They didn't find me for two days. No one thought to check broom cupboards while they were trying to sort out the TT. I had a few days in hospital before I was let go. It took me another few days to find out you were alive. The health system was swamped.'

'Tampoline knows I'm alive and he knows what I can do.'

'Sure but he has other things to worry about. From what I read he's blind and won't be beating off while abusing girls anytime in the near future.'

'Good. I wonder what the history was between Tampoline and Lendl?

'Do you care?'

'No.'

'I think you should get on the road as soon as you can.'

'Charlie, I killed all those people.'

'Maybe. Maybe not. There isn't a court in this land that would find you guilty.'

'They will. Whatever it is that I do is not going away. Laws are for re-writing and they'll re-write it for me.'

'Hard one to prove. At the moment it would be their word against yours.'

'All they have to do is drug me up again, video it and show the authorities what happens. I'll be dumped in the deepest hole for the rest of my life.'

'What do you want me to say? You need to move on. '

'That won't stop them looking for me.'

'I know but what else can you do.'

I say nothing.

Chapter 42

Outside, the wind is slicing through the trees. A constant keening sound as a backdrop to the backwater cabin I'm sitting in. The log fire is doing its best to fight the sub-zero temperature that wraps the building. Charlie is sitting as close as he can to the flames, reading a novel. I'm watching the fire dance.

We crossed the Canadian border a week ago and Charlie found the cabin while I was lying in my thirtieth hotel bed in as many days. It's a summer retreat for some family living in Toronto and had been shut up for the winter. As Charlie points out it's cheaper than a hotel and, if our luck holds, it may be weeks before someone spots the smoke from the chimney and decides to investigate.

Charlie flicks a page as a log spits an ember onto the hearth. I'm thinking about Lorraine and the simple fact that Tampoline is still alive. I think about that a lot. Charlie tells me I should leave well alone but a life on the run is no life. For all I know we may not even be wanted. No suits on the road looking for us. So why run?

But that feels wrong. Tampoline knows what I can do and he knows I am responsible for what happened to him. A few days ago we caught an article in USA Today about the return of the senator to the floor of the Capitol. He received a standing ovation.

Charlie sighs and I add my sigh to the night. I know I can't keep running. I stand up and walk over to him. I squat next to the fire and he looks down. He smiles and I know that somehow this has to be sorted, but for now the road will need to be my friend.

I just hope that the friendship is one with a happy future.

The End.

About the Author

Gordon Brown was born and lives in Glasgow - having spent twenty five years in the sales and marketing world working on everything from engineering to global charities and from TV to lingerie.

Gordon started out life packing shelves for Sainsbury's before moving to Canada to deliver pizzas and watch baseball. Before setting up his own marketing and creativity training business back in Scotland in 2001 he spent fifteen years swimming in the booze industry. Gordon is very bad at golf.

Gordon is married with two children and has been writing for twenty years. This is his third novel.